RING THE BELL

Ring the Bell
Copyright ©2022
Gerry Harlan Brown

ISBN: 978-1-957344-02-7

Cover concept and design by Mike Parker

Published by WordCrafts Press
Cody, Wyoming 82414

www.wordcrafts.net

RING THE BELL

a novel of everyday heroes

GERRY HARLAN BROWN

WordCrafts Press

A cry for help.
The bell rings a loud, insistent burst of tones,
summoning firefighters.

To Firefighters,
My Brothers and Sisters

Green Springs, Kentucky
Fire Department
Station 1, 2nd Platoon
May 27, 2006

A day with a crew of firefighters and those they served.

Engine 4 is a triple combination pumper with a 1,250 gallons per minute pump, carrying 1,900 feet of hose of various diameters and lengths and 500 gallons of water. It is a big toolbox with some equipment, such as axes and pike poles, little changed from what the Roman vigiles employed two millennia ago. There are a host of water-related appliances: nozzles, wyes, siameses, hydrant wrenches, clamps, adapters. Other items include breathing apparatus, medical jump kit, defibrillator, oxygen tank, ladders, pry tools, portable extinguishers, gas detection meter, rope rescue gear, chain saw, electric generator, salvage covers, smoke ejectors, foam, shovels, mops, brooms, squeegees, and a bag of small stuffed animals for upset children. An American flag is staff-mounted on the tailboard.

Captain Wayne Buckman has started saying he is getting too old for this stuff. At 56 his knees ache like thunder when he crawls around on a job. The pain comes right away and stays for a while afterward. The 70 pounds of protective gear—once no more than a summer suit—now ride heavy, sodden-like, making each step feel lumbering.

Wayne is still a bull of a man physically. He also continues to be rock solid at meeting the primary requisite of an officer: He can make a decision, no matter the storm swirling about him. No one will ever see him flinch either; not the members of his crew nor a citizen. Neither will any know when he carries a new burden away from a scene. The lives lost he will always shoulder personally, because that is how they come to him. Remembering those souls is something he expects of himself, for he sees it as exercising a solemn responsibility. And when the paperwork for a bad call is at last filed away, none will see him seek a place of solitude where he can reset his nerves, shake off what he has witnessed and done, led others to do. Those things remain hidden inside, though in the wee hours when he sometimes awakes in a sweat, he wonders if he has cried out.

Engineer David Julius (D. J.) Gibbons is a natural at maneuvering the engine. The truck is an extension of his body; another set of legs. He has an affinity for the mechanical, inherently understands how the machinery works, what the valves and gauges and levers reflect. Likewise, he has a knack for quickly grasping all the elements of a complex operation. The mathematical equations—losses from friction and elevation, hose diameters and lengths, nozzle types that figure into the delivery of water at the proper volumes and pressures—had been difficult to master at first. Now, after years of practice, he can quickly do the calculations in his head.

If D. J. were in the army, he would be a sergeant. He possesses the foremost qualities: experience, technical expertise, an understanding of the big picture, and an ever-present concern for his crew's safety. He would make a good officer. He knows his greater talents lie as an engineer, however. The job suits his personality. Unique to the positions on an engine crew, he often operates alone.

Firefighter ll/EMT Micky (Mick) McCartney, on the job 10 years, has finally decided it is time to make a move. It is a young man's business, and 40 isn't all that far off. He makes decent money at his second job, riding herd on maintenance for an apartment complex. The extra income helps, but working two places is sucking up all his time. The wife has started to complain he is never around to give a hand with the kids or take care of their house. Promotion to engineer would bring in a few bucks more, let him take an occasional day off from the second job.

He has started sliding off with a textbook when things are quiet. The others have noticed. One can't hide much, living with a group of firefighters for 24 hours at a stretch. They pick at him good-naturedly. He likes to look at the pictures, he claims. Inside, however, he knows promotion will mean leaving a special part of the fight behind. The idea makes him uneasy. He loves the nozzle in his hands, finding his way through the smoke, facing the monster, killing it.

Probationary Firefighter Ron Jacoby isn't as scared as he was his first day on shift, already a month ago—but he is still scared. It is not for himself. The personal fear of something bad happening to him has never been much. He is deathly afraid of screwing up, though. What if he does something wrong, or freezes up and someone gets hurt—or dies? The questions keep him awake at night playing scenarios in his head, trying to imagine.

It helped when he got his second structure fire under his belt a week back. Ron crawled his way through the unbelievably thick smoke—Mick on the line behind him—kept pushing as he heard things breaking, falling, located the seat of the flames by their smoke-dimmed glow when he was but a few feet away, worked the nozzle and put the fire out.

That performance was better than on his first structure. Then he had been a wild deer. Mick lit into him as soon as they were outside. "Run off and get your dumb ass in a bind, who you think has to risk his neck to save you? Me! Stay together, idiot!" It was not exactly how the instructors had stressed the all-encompassing need for teamwork, but their point was the same.

He hopes the others are gaining some faith in him. At least Mick hasn't ripped him again, nor has he recently been sent on a ridiculous new-guy task like fetching a skyhook. Being the butt of their jokes is worth it, though, for he knows he has found what he was meant to do.

Chapter 1

5:35 a.m.

Robert has been awake since four. It has been this way since she died. Sleep comes late, ends early. How long ago now? He knew the answer, of course. Six months, three days, and—

Yes, he thought, glancing at his wristwatch. *This exact minute.*

He had been there with her, seen her take her final breath. The staff was considerate, leaving them—him—in peace until he had said what he felt compelled to say one last time. He told her he loved her, of course, for he did with all his heart. He whispered it in her ear, like he had countless times down through the long years. How many years? He knew the answer: 63, if he counted only the time they were married. Add two more years for the time they had courted, waiting for him to get enough of a stake in life to support the two of them. He couldn't remember a time when another girl sparked his interest; no longer knew if he had kissed another, even held another's hand.

Of course, none of those things mattered. They had loved each other from the deepest parts of their souls from the very beginning. Of that much, he had no doubt. They had supported each other in everything, held onto each other as, one by one, family and friends fell to tragedy and disease and old age until they were the only two remaining. It had never been lonely, not so long as they were together. Then, without warning, came the attack upon her heart. Hope hung about for a few hours. He held her hand; held it as he always held it when illness came; held it as she always held his, when the turn at sickness was his. Suddenly she was gone. Suddenly the loneliness was everywhere. He could not move, it seemed, for its weight bearing down.

If there had been children—

It was a question neither one raised to the other once they knew this blessing was not to be bestowed. The sad revelation was oh, so long ago now. The pain remained however—especially for her, right until the end. Sometimes he would see it in her eyes. A child would cross their path at the market, or church, or simply go by their home, walking or riding a bicycle. Her eyes would light with joy—a mother's warm firelight—and she would smile as her gaze followed. The smile would remain for moments after the child had gone, fading slowly, the firelight dimming in measured steps, until her eyes held only a far-away look of wonder at what might have been.

It would have been easy to give in and feel sorry for himself, and sometimes, if he were honest, he did. Most of the time, though, he simply felt lost. It was the way he felt this morning as he wandered about his yard, a feeble old man in his pajamas and robe, the dew soaking through his house shoes. Not that he noticed. Not that he would have cared had he realized his feet were wet. He was moving. Why? He could not have said.

After a time, he came to a halt. For a moment he stood in place, breathing in short, patient sniffs, unconsciously turning his head, canting it slightly to one side. There was a scent upon the air, a sweet aroma softly beckoning him to find its source. He moved his feet a quarter turn, and there it was, only a few steps away—her yellow rose bush. Oh, how she had loved this bush. Once the buds had begun to form, she would monitor their progress, checking daily, counting each one, anxious as a child to see them blossom. And when the opening started, she would be there every day, several times every day, to breathe in the wonderful scent.

How could he have forgotten? He hadn't even thought to check for buds. At first, he was surprised. Then a quick feeling of shame knifed through him. Here was a place of importance—of joy—for her. How could this have slipped his mind?

Then the first bloom of this spring—a deep, buttery yellow—seemed to beckon. He moved toward it, the scent drawing him along like a silken tether, until he could at last bend over and bring his nose close. He inhaled, and she was there. How often had she called him to this very spot and bade him to smell? Every time he had been in the yard with her and there was a bloom on the bush. That was all.

His old back would not allow him to stay bent over long, not nearly long enough. When he straightened up, though, he was smiling. The memory of her finding such joy in something so simple and yet so glorious was reassuring, somehow. He didn't understand it. Didn't care to look too close trying. She was here. It was enough. It was more than enough.

Something made him glance away finally, a bird's call perhaps. The sound came from the direction of the house next door—Emily's house. Suddenly he knew he would have to show Emily this bloom. She would be by to visit this afternoon, he knew, for she came every evening. He would show her then, have her smell the sweet scent, tell her of his wife's great joy in the blooms. As always, he would tell Emily how his wife would have loved her.

Emily and her parents had moved in only a few weeks before. He had been in his rocking chair on his front porch most of that first afternoon, watching them unload their things. The process was more fascinating than he would have cared to admit. As he had grown older, seeing others work provided a certain level of entertainment. And the little girl was a show all on her own. One parent or the other, sometimes both, was calling after her every fourth or fifth breath, at least, and chasing after her the ones in between. Eventually, her parents got the U-haul unloaded. Then they, and Emily, disappeared inside.

Late in the afternoon she appeared at the foot of the porch steps just as he was awakening from his nap. "Hi. I'm Emily," the preschooler announced, her voice strong, her gaze direct, as if he had never heard her name spoken, when it was all he had heard from her parents, over and over and over, as they went about their moving tasks earlier.

"Well, hello. I'm Mr.— I'm Robert," he corrected himself, rocking forward toward her. "Bob," he corrected again.

"Would you be my grandpa, Mr. Robert Bob?"

The grandpa question threw him. He decided to get his name straight before answering.

"Bob. You can just call me Bob, Emily."

"Would you be my grandpa, Bob?"

"Well now, Miss Emily, why would you want me to be your grandpa?"

"We moved, and I've got two grandpas where we used to live, and it's way far away, and my mommy and daddy said we'd still get to see them a lot, but I haven't seen them, and it's been forever. I miss their hugs. I miss my grandpa hugs."

Robert thought it over for a few seconds before answering. Suddenly he knew she was watching and smiling. No! She was beaming. He got to his feet slowly, because time had dictated this was the way it was to be. Grasping the handrail, he moved down the steps carefully, each step measured, until he at last stood before her. Then he bent forward, bent until his eyes were even with hers.

"You understand this will have to be unofficial?"

It took a moment for her to nod yes, for the look on her face said she didn't have a clue what he meant.

He took half a step forward then, raised his hands enough to welcome her in. She stepped forward, also, suddenly wrapped her arms tight about his tired legs. His arms closed gently over her tiny shoulders.

"I love you, Grandpa Bob."

This time, he did not hesitate to reply.

"And I love you, my darling Emily."

Chapter 2

5:37 a.m.

Morning, Probie Wan," Caroline whispered as she nuzzled the back of his neck. She was always the first to open her eyes, and this had been her method of waking him the nearly two years they had been married. It was fine with him. In fact, he loved it. Ron liked to sleep on his side, feel her spooned up against his back. Stretching his legs out straight, he smiled at her use of his fire department nickname.

"Morning, Babe," he mumbled.

Ron didn't really want to get up, to lose the sensation of her skin against his, but it was a duty day. His 48 hours off were almost done. He was conflicted, as always, for he absolutely loved his job, almost—though he would never say it to her—as much as he loved her.

"It's alright," she said, as if he had given actual voice to this need to get to work. That spooked him a moment. Had he spoken aloud? Hadn't she answered as if he had asked her the question? Answered as if she understood? She stirred, slowly peeling away from his back.

The thing was, Caroline *did* understand. For the first two or three weeks after he went on shift, she didn't. She underwent bouts of genuine anger. This soon changed to jealousy. It was if he had taken a second wife, and he went to stay with her every third day. It took some getting used to, the 24-hour shift. She was not at all certain she would ever become comfortable with it. She was trying, though, and slowly, reluctantly moving toward acceptance, at least. It wasn't like there was a choice, not if she loved him.

Caroline stood and padded around to his side of the bed, sat down on the edge, her face turned toward his. He lifted a hand, cupped it behind her slender neck, gently pulled her down to him, her hair falling across his eyes. Lips parted ever so slightly, he kissed her on the mouth. The fire of 20-something passion quickly caused them both to press closer.

"Not this morning, tiger," Caroline said, pulling away after a few seconds. Her hand rose to press flat against his chest, as if to ensure he kept his distance.

Ron ran his fingers down the side of her face, her neck, began to trace the outline of her uncovered breast. She caught his hand there, held it in place.

"Work," she said, whispering.

"You are so beautiful," he whispered back.

"Tomorrow," she promised, easing his hand off her skin.

Caroline stood then and turned from him. Seeing her walk away nude left him addled. He wanted to yell out to her that she was the most beautiful woman in the world, but the words hung in his throat. At the bedroom door she stopped. After a moment she slowly turned halfway around, and he felt his breath catch. She hesitated, allowing him to stare, enjoying the look of pained longing on his face. Then she winked.

"It's alright for you to have two loves," she said, "as long as I'm your only woman."

Chapter 3

6 a.m.

R eady!" Virginia called, setting the plate on the kitchen table. "Kay," Wayne replied from somewhere down the hallway, his voice gruff, distant, as if emanating from inside a cave. He'd be there in seconds, she knew. He wasn't one to let food grow cold. It wasn't so much hunger as manners. If someone had taken the trouble to cook for him, the least he could do was eat while it was hot. He said those words to her the very first time she cooked a meal as his wife. Over the years he held true to his word, coming quickly when she called. Of course, he expected as much when he was the cook, which was often enough when he was home.

As on countless other mornings, Wayne was buttoning his uniform shirt as he strode toward the table. He pulled his chair back but remained standing while he got his shirt tail tucked in and dressed straight. Even after buckling his belt, he hesitated to sit. Virginia came around to him, reached up and fiddled with the captain's badge on his chest a second, touched the bugles on one collar tab, made a minute adjustment.

"You look good," she said, rising on her toes and giving him a quick peck on the cheek.

Virginia moved back around to her side of the table as he sat down. Placing her cup of coffee on a coaster, she took her seat across from him. *He does look good, too,* she thought, smiling to herself. Even at 56, Wayne was easy on the eyes. Seeing him in his uniform never failed to pull at something inside her. The man was born to wear it. This was always so obvious to her. It was him. Although he loved to laugh, loved to tease her, loved to mess with the kids—the grandkids, also, now—*Lord, when did that happen*—at heart he was a serious man, a man who embraced responsibility. These traits shone through most clearly when he was in uniform.

Duty days were not the same as other days. His shift started at 7 a.m., so if they were going to share any time at all together, it had to come early. To him, he was leaving for work. To her, he was going away on a journey. She had not ever been able to feel otherwise, what with his shift lasting a full day and night. A world of things could happen, did happen, in a span so long. When the kids were still home, if something took place with one of them it invariably did so when he was gone. Even now, if something broke, or started to leak, or began making a noise like it was about to blast off like a rocket ship, it happened when he was on shift. Handling the problem fell to her alone, then.

Thinking about it, she had a brief chill. Not that she didn't enjoy, even relish at times, being able to do as she pleased once she came in from her own job. Now everything was just so different. Most of her adult life she had wrestled with the here and now. There was no time to feel lonely. Now, sometimes, less than she would have liked, there was something to do with the grandchildren: a birthday party; a trip to the water park; the occasional baby-sitting stint. And sometimes, rarely, she would go out with a friend, have a bite of dinner at a restaurant, catch a movie. For the most part, though, she would be by herself in their house. A person of lesser strength might have spent time fretting, feeling lost in the odd quiet, or even worrying about what Wayne might be facing. Not Virginia. She wasn't one to cower to an empty space, and Wayne could handle himself. She was as certain of this as anything. Nevertheless, the old rhythms had changed, leaving her feeling a trifle unsettled.

She watched him eat. How many times had she fixed him the exact same breakfast? Thousands. She laughed to herself. *What a creature of habit he was!* Of course, he had his reasons for not trying something else. He claimed he didn't want to be weighed down, said his usual meal met the precise morning requirements for such a finely tuned machine as he. Therefore, it was always two pieces of toast, buttered; two eggs, fried, runny; two pieces of bacon, crisp. As she took a sip of her coffee, he bit the end from a strip of bacon.

"Just the way I like it," he winked at her. For a moment, in the slow blink of his soft blue eye, she saw him, saw a teenage boy in a man's muscled-up body, a boy taking on life head-on. Even then Wayne Buckman knew what he wanted. Here he came, brashly stepping before her and Lizbeth, her best friend, as they walked toward the school bus. They had no choice but to halt. "I'm marrying you one day," he said, the first words he ever spoke to her. Then he smiled and winked before walking away, his gait the slow, cocky ambling of a high-school ballplayer.

My word, she thought as he turned back to his food. *That was almost 40 years ago.*

"I'm glad," she smiled at his compliment on the bacon. "After all this time, it's the only way I know to fix it."

Virginia wasn't overly sentimental. At her core she was a practical person. Having to deal with issues so much on her own only reinforced this natural inclination. Sometimes, however, it would hit her about how much time, how much life, had passed, and something inside her heart would flutter. Of late, for some reason she could not put her finger on, this often occurred as they sat here of a morning at the kitchen table. Before his last shift she thought of how their little granddaughter—nearly four now—crawled up on his lap this past Easter. The memory arrived unbidden, just suddenly there, sharp as broken glass. Even now, recalling the moment nearly brought her to tears. She had mentioned it to him, how precious the thought, and he smiled the same sure, sincere smile he smiled on a long-ago day when he stepped in front of her and Lizbeth.

Susannah had put her arms around his neck and said, "I love you, Bandaddy. Now can we hunt eggs?"

Oh my, did that baby gal have him wrapped around her little finger! He loved the other grandbabies—the twin boys—and showed it, but this one had him tied up tight by the heart strings.

"Why of course we can, my Suzie Q."

She was ever his Suzie Q. Not once had he called her Susannah, not even when he first saw her in the hospital nursery. As might have been expected, her birth, too, took place while he was on duty. The whole crew showed up, scuffing along in their bunker pants and boots, thumbs hooked in their suspenders, smelling of smoke, the others loose and giggly, oohing and ahhing and pointing, slapping him on the back as if he had done something, calling him grandpa. He just stood there close to the window, smiling a smile big as Christmas, oblivious to it all, staring at the wee baby just on the other side, their first grandchild. At last, his voice so low she barely heard him, he whispered, "I love you, Suzie Q."

And he never, ever, sang. Claimed it made little animals cry when he tried. But walking out the door last Easter, his granddaughter leading him by the hand, this leather tough, grizzled bear of a man, her husband, was singing about how he loved the way his Suzie Q walked and talked.

Virginia's next recollection might well have been heralded by a clap of thunder. Painfully harsh, it shattered her reverie. It was triggered innocently enough by the most tenuous link in a daisy chain of children, the simple thought of one little girl leading to a thought of another. The memory was so fresh it ached. Only last evening the child had come to him again, as she had countless times since the first awful midnight years ago. It was a terrible, unnerving thing to witness. Sometime in the small hours Wayne's tossing awakened her. By the streetlight's faint glow, she could see him beside her, lying on his back, arm extended, hand beckoning. Without warning his features contorted. His mouth opened. His lips moved, soundlessly screaming, *No! No!*

She read about the tragedy in the paper the day after it happened. There was a house fire. A child climbed out a window onto a porch roof. The firefighters were almost to her, but something burning fell from above and knocked her tumbling to the ground. The little girl died instantly.

True to his nature, Wayne had come home from the department the next morning and not said a word about the call. Hustling, he changed out of his uniform and into a tee shirt and jeans. Such was their life in those days, when they had only moments to exchange a few words about the kids, the house, before they went hurrying out the door: she to her work; he to his second job. That night, as they lay in bed, Virginia finally brought up the article in the paper. Knowing she was violating their unspoken rule, she asked, was he there?

Virginia felt him shudder. In all their years together, she had not seen him lose his composure, not once. The thought he might alarmed her in ways she could not have given voice to. In the end, he maintained control, replied with a simple, "Yes." Heavy minutes crawled by before he added, "I don't want to talk about it."

She knew why, of course, having watched him deal with the job from the beginning. To talk was to acknowledge some weakness inside him. At least Wayne considered it a weakness. Real men didn't let a tragedy get to them, especially if responding to tragedies was their job. Knowing him she knew it was how he felt. The most she could ever get out of him regarding any bad call was he didn't want to upset her by telling the awful details.

Virginia knew better. It was he who needed protecting. Without something to blame his reticence on, the iron door might creak open, and God only knew what could come careening out. Keeping things in let him believe he was as rock hard as ever.

Thoughts of the child had been shoved far into a recess of her mind, when, as Wayne was leaving for his next shift after the fire, he stopped in the doorway and turned back to face her.

"You should know," he said, "it will not happen again." The determination in his voice frightened her beyond what she felt witnessing his dream, beyond anything she'd ever known, for she instantly, instinctively, knew he was giving his oath to do something almost unimaginable. Then he confirmed her intuition. "Next time I'll get that baby, or I won't be coming home."

Virginia glanced up, surprised to find herself in the present.

"What is it, hon?" he asked.

Wayne was on his knee beside her, his powerful arms enveloping her, pulling her close, shielding her. She hadn't realized she was crying.

"I was just thinking," she started, managing to pry a hand loose to brush away at her tears. "I was thinking about you and Suzie Q again, going to hunt Easter eggs," she filled out the lie. "It was so sweet, and, oh, I don't know. I guess it just hit me. I mean, I'm not upset. It's—they're happy tears." She wasn't about to let him go off to work thinking she was distressed. "Okay?"

Wayne pulled back a little, studying her face. After a long moment he nodded. Then he kissed her—kissed her right on the mouth. It was a soulful kiss, filled with love and longing. Virginia was shocked, especially at the last part. This was out of character for him, except when—well—well it didn't happen before he left home for the department.

He pushed himself upright, grunting at the popping complaints from his knees, and walked back around to his side of the table. He didn't sit down, however. Picking up his last bite of toast, he swirled it around in the egg goo on his plate, then popped it in his mouth. As he chewed, he gathered up his dishes and carried them to the sink.

Virginia was standing close when he turned around. She brushed a few crumbs off his shirt and made another minute adjustment to his badge. Then, rising on tiptoes once more, she gave him a quick peck on the cheek. He bent and gave her a peck on the forehead in return.

"Love you," he said.

"Love you," she replied.

Their parting ritual complete, Wayne started toward the door. To her amazement, he began to shuffle along, doing what with him passed for dance steps. Then, to top it, he burst into song.

"...walk. Baby, I love you—"

He turned in the doorway to look back at her, a huge smile across his face.

"You're crazy," Virginia laughed.

"'Bout you," Wayne laughed in return, and was gone.

Chapter 4

6:01 a.m.

Mick glanced at the clock, then went back to staring at the coffee maker, as if looking at the thing would help it run any faster. After a couple of minutes, it dawned on him the flow automatically stopped when the pot was removed. It was three-fourths of the way done brewing, so why was he waiting? He pulled the pot out, filled the cup in his hand—his Number One Dad cup the kids gave him last Christmas—and turned to lean against the countertop. His only thought was how tired he was. Of course, when you don't get home until 1:30 in the morning what can you expect? Water leaks must be stopped. Can't let an entire floor in an apartment building be flooded.

His wife's words from the other night were suddenly in his ears. Lord was she on her high horse. Of course, she was right. Margie was always right. She had a way of cutting through the bull and going straight for the logic. They couldn't go on like this, she said. Something had to give and give soon. They'd become the time-worn saying—two ships passing in the night—both so wrung out and frazzled neither one scarcely even noticed the other anymore. He was hustling two full-time jobs and then some. She was doing hair at her sister's salon at least 30 hours a week. In between, somehow, she zipped back and forth with three kids—all boys, eight, nine, and 10 years old—to school, ball games and practices, parent/teacher conferences, doctor appointments, emergency room visits—which came at least once every week—not to mention cooking meals and keeping a path open through the house. And doing it all by herself, for the most part, because Mick was never there. *Whoever said life began at 30*, she said Tuesday—no, Wednesday night—when they actually loaded up in the car as a family and went to get a shake, *was a nut!* She didn't even remember that birthday. The only way she knew she'd been having birthdays was because her driver's license said she was now 33.

Margie was so wound up, Mick didn't have the heart, or nerve, to tell her it was life begins at 40. Sometimes the only smart thing to do was stand back and let the steam vent.

Mick took a sip from his cup, then glanced at the clock again. It read 6:16. *What happened to those 15 minutes?* he thought, not really caring. The fatigue ran too deep. A shower would probably help. It generally did. Maybe he would wake up enough then to get in his uniform. "Please," he whispered. He had less than 45 minutes before he was on duty. Refilling his cup first, he reluctantly began his slow wade through molasses toward the bathroom.

As he trudged, he thought he would take a couple of hours this evening, after all the house duties were done, and buckle down on some serious studying. He'd been making real progress of late. All the hydraulics stuff, the calculations, he had down pretty good. He figured to do a few problems, just to stay sharp while the formulas were fresh in his head, then read some tactics stuff. It was his favorite subject.

He hadn't aimed to tell Margie so soon he was going for promotion, but after she blew her fuse, he figured there was no sense waiting. Knowing helped calm her. The extra money would ease the strain. The test was tough: a written exam pulled out of 5,000 pages of text; two days of proving he could drive fire trucks and operate pumps and aerial ladders. He was certain he could pass it. All it took was a bunch of hard work. Then, of course, a vacancy had to open, or it was do it all again in a year, which was why he'd been reluctant to tell her—no guarantee.

Having made it to the bathroom, he set his cup on the edge of the sink, reached for his toothbrush. From back in the house—from somewhere in the piles of clothes and shoes and books and ball bats and toys and bicycles, and probably

a motorcycle, and maybe even a Sherman tank or a buffalo—
where the boys resided, he heard Margie.

"Up and at 'em you filthy savages! Time for school! Move it!
Move it!"

Carefully, so as not to make any noise which would let them
know where he was, Mick eased the bathroom door closed.

Chapter 5

6:07 a.m.

D.J. grasped the handle, thought better, then turned to look over his shoulder. Tina stood just inside the doorway to her little house, one hand braced on her robed hip, the other resting on the door frame as she gazed back his way. She wasn't a bad-looking gal, even now, in her 40s. He liked her. He liked her enough to spend a night or two with her every week, and why not? They were both divorced and grown. They were good in bed and got along fine, otherwise, though neither expected nor wanted anything more. It was just where they were in their lives, at the point where the emotions got a little tired, a little jaded. They were content to take things one day at a time, to embrace affection without questioning its depth. And love— who knew what love was? D. J. blew her a kiss. Tina blew one toward him in return, stepped back, closed her door. He lifted the handle and pulled the pickup's door open, slid into the seat.

It was a good morning. D. J. loved this time of year, late spring, when the trees were already leafed out, but there were plenty of things yet blooming. It wasn't too hot this early, just pleasantly warm, though the humidity helped the thermometer cheat upward. You couldn't escape the juice in the air in this part of the world.

Straightening the wheel, D. J. headed down the street. He drove slowly. There was no great rush. Chances were, he would have his opportunities to do some hurried driving later. For now, he could cruise. The station was only 10 minutes away, and he was early. He was always early getting to the job. It was the way he liked it; the way he had done it for his 20 years on the department. He and Luther would spend a few moments together in easy conversation, discussing anything troublesome about the truck, one chauffeur passing the reins of the engine to his relief.

He wheeled into the lot of a convenience store. Inside he got a paper cup of thick, black, burnt-smelling gunk the sign claimed was coffee, along with a honey bun. D. J. thought about a donut. They looked fresh and smelled melt-in-your-mouth good, but he was a firefighter and in uniform. He wasn't about to be seen in public eating a donut. Donuts were for cops. The only time he ate donuts was when his cousin, the cop, and he were at family gatherings. He'd bring half a dozen and eat them in front of his favorite relative until they were gone, just to gig him.

A couple of minutes later he was stopped at a traffic light. The light blinked to green. He was about to ease ahead when a man blew through the intersection in a big German sedan. *Probably a stockbroker with a ride like that*, D. J. thought, as he raised his hand to flip the guy off. No doubt it was a wasted gesture. The sedan was probably already too far away for the driver to see his finger, if he even bothered to look in the mirror. D. J. laughed at himself. The gesture was more from reflex than anger anyway. *Job security* he thought. They'd be cutting the jerk out of a wreck one day.

At the station he rolled into a slot, took a minute to lick the taste of the honey bun from his fingers, then got out and ambled inside. Speaking or nodding to first one firefighter then another, the off-going shift mingling in among the on-coming, he made his way through the dayroom to the engine room. There he met his counterpart sitting on the front bumper of their engine.

"What's up, Knute?" D. J. asked the black engineer, the appellation a part of the department's language, meaning anything from hayseed to good buddy.

"Nothing but the rent, home boy," Luther, the other driver, answered. "Let me see those eyes."

"Bad, huh?" D. J. replied, taking a seat beside his friend.

"Mississippi road maps. You been tom-catting all night again?"

"Just watching a little TV," D. J. offered his lame excuse.

"Uh-huh. Be careful you don't get the crabs off whatever you're watching, you going to sit next to me."

"No worries. Checked when I took my shower. Didn't find but a couple."

"Surprised they're not any worse." Luther waited a couple of moments before continuing. "Changed her oil and filter, lubed the whole works yesterday. Think we finally got the latch fixed so that right-side compartment door will stay shut. Everything else looked fine."

"Good deal," D. J. answered. After a moment he added, "Quiet shift?"

"Pretty much. Overdose yesterday morning, and Mrs. Sturdivant about midnight."

"Oxy?" D. J. asked about the drug victim.

"Nah. Huffing paint. Dude been gone couple of days. Blue as Papa Smurf."

Neither man laughed. The remark wasn't meant to be funny. Luther wasn't talking about paint color.

For several more moments they sat on the bumper in silence, side by side, comfortable in their place, in their friendship, neither in a hurry to move. D. J. finally broke the spell.

"What was up with Mrs. Sturdivant? Martians again?"

"Just one," Luther answered. "Said it had three horns and a forked tail this time."

Though they both flashed faint smiles, again neither man laughed. Mrs. Sturdivant was one of their regulars, 85 if she was a day, and they both loved her like she was their own grandmother. Just because Martians hid in her walls sometimes was no reason to poke fun. Maybe if he was lucky, D. J. thought, if aliens came visiting him when he was her age, firefighters would bring their gas detection/alien locator meter and root out the little buggers.

A few more moments passed quietly between them. Then, as if they had received a signal, the two engineers rose to their feet: Luther to take his gear off the truck; D. J. to stow his on it.

Chapter 6

6:21 a.m.

The Benz purred, even at 65. It was pushing it for city streets, he knew, but who was paying attention at this hour? James Henry loved driving the big car, loved the feeling of power, of freedom, of omnipotence he experienced when he gripped the wheel. It had been a present to himself. And why not? Life was sweet. Money came easy, for he was very good at what he did. He was a natural salesman. That's all it was: selling the idea of making a killing. Imagine, he laughed to himself, getting to play with other people's money. Imagine him an investment counselor. Professional gambler would have fit just as well. Hell, he ought to dress up like the card dealers in the Old West, get some garters for his sleeves. *Ha!*

Man, it had been one wild night! Had he even been to sleep? James Henry couldn't remember. It didn't matter whether he had or not. He was wide awake now. His eyes felt like they were sticking out from their sockets on stems. He glanced down, was a little surprised to see he had his pants on. Wasn't sure for a minute there. Thought he felt a draft. Whew! Last night!

She was a beauty, no doubt, absolutely gorgeous. And she had been worth every penny. Hell, he'd even tipped her a C-note. He wasn't certain he remembered everything, but he remembered enough. He had a good time, a very good time. Ummm. Tipping her was only right.

James Henry stole a glance at himself in the rear-view mirror. Yes sir! He was one good-looking devil, no doubt about it. Handsome as all sin. She said so. "Well now, the truth's the truth, ain't it?" he laughed. He'd give her a call again. Why bother with a wife, with a girlfriend, when he could have some-one like her any time he wanted? Someone who appreciated class and looks. Someone who would keep things on a straight up and up business footing. It was the only way to go. He grinned an oily grin at his own brilliance.

There was no real pressing need to be heading to the office this time of day. The market wouldn't be open for a good while, but after she left for Nashville he figured why hang around? "The early bird catcheth the worm," he said aloud, nodding. Of course, there was always something to do, something to dig into. Got to keep after the old research, and he had a few early calls he could make. Never a bad time to work on fleecing a pilgrim.

James Henry wasn't fooling himself, though. He knew very well why he was heading to his office. His lady friend and he had taken everything at the house during the night, and he still had a taste. The remainder of his stash was beneath a false bottom in the humidor on his desk. He smiled at the idea. So obvious, such a cliché, no one would ever think to look there. He'd go see his connection today. Couldn't be running low. Bad business, that. Very bad.

Maybe he'd invite her over again tonight. Strictly a cash transaction affair. "Ha!" he laughed again. Nothing like being king.

The traffic signal ahead clicked from yellow to red. Red lights were for morons. He pressed down on the accelerator and blew through the intersection before anyone could move. Glancing in the mirror, he saw a man in a pickup truck back at the corner stick his arm out the window. An unmistakable gesture followed, finger in the air.

"Friggin' peon!" James Henry yelled in the mirror.

For a minute he thought about doing a 180 and going back to show what someone with a black belt could do to that finger. A block rolled by. No doubt he could have the guy begging in short order, he told himself, though, as another block clicked past, he had a sobering thought. In this part of the country a pickup truck often came equipped with a gun. James Henry figured he was too handsome to get shot. Acknowledging the truth of the idea, he finally dismissed his anger.

Yes sir, was his next thought. He would give her a call to join him again tonight, right after he'd seen the man.

Chapter 7

6:59 a.m.

Frank Griffin was extraordinarily careful as he sat down on the bed beside his daughter, Emily. His hand reached out, ever so slowly brushed a curly lock of hair back from her eyes. Bowing his head forward, he touched his lips to her brow. An instant later he cautiously rose back up, fearful he would awaken her. Then he simply sat there, watching her tiny chest rise and fall.

"Is she not a doll?" his wife, Darlene, asked from the doorway.

"Yes," Frank whispered. "She is perfect."

He looked up a moment, allowed his gaze to roam the cozy room. Things pink were in abundance. There were baby dolls dressed in pink. There were pink stuffed bears and giraffes and piggies and fish. The walls were trimmed around the top in a reddish stripe dotted with blond puppies and snow-white kittens chasing yellow butterflies. It was a little girl's room, for sure; a little girl who was spoiled and coddled, and oh so dearly, completely loved. His gaze returned to her.

"A perfect little doll," Frank smiled.

"She'll miss you," Darlene said.

"And I'll miss her," he nodded. A few seconds later he glanced back at his wife and added, "I'll miss you, too."

He felt his cheeks flush hot with embarrassment at the afterthought. Darlene stepped forward, laid a hand on his shoulder.

"It's okay," she said. "I know who has your heart now, and it's okay."

"You both do," he answered, reaching up to rest his hand atop hers. "Never doubt it for a second."

Darlene eased down on the bed behind her husband. She wrapped her arms around Frank's middle, leaned forward and pressed her cheek against his shoulder.

"You'll be careful on that old road?" Darlene asked.

"I'll be careful."

"Tomorrow about noon?" she said, already knowing when he expected to be home.

"Yes. As soon as I can."

For a time longer they sat on the bed, holding, touching, content to look upon the sleeping face of their child. Neither said what was on their minds. They didn't dare give it voice. All the miscarriages, all the tortured years of questioning, of wondering if, wondering why. They had both given up, to be truthful, though neither ever let their sad feelings be known to the other. Then, when Darlene was 37, surprise! And now—

"Come back to us," Darlene said.

"That's the one thing you and Emily can always count on," Frank answered, his voice suddenly strong, certain. "I'll always come home to you."

Chapter 8

0726 Hours

As was his routine after finishing the morning reports, Captain Wayne Buckman headed to the television set in the dayroom of Station 1. Time to get a weather update. He had already checked it once at the house, in accordance with his duty day routine there: bathroom, start the coffee pot, look at the forecast. He found the battalion chief standing in front of the television.

"Chief."

"Wayne." The battalion chief had a large plastic mug of coffee in his hand. He paused to take a sip. "Anything out of whack?"

"Station 3's AC is on the fritz," Captain Buckman answered. "Terry said he'd pull the panel and take a look."

The chief nodded. Nothing to worry about there. Terry, the engineer on Engine 6, would fix it, if it could be fixed. He ran a HVAC business on his off days; just one of his firefighters who possessed skills having little or nothing to do with firefighting. It was like in the old tale—a bunch of butchers, bakers, and candlestick-makers. Routine repairs on the buildings, trucks, and equipment, therefore, was most often carried out in-house, because between them all there was little the firefighters could not do.

Battalion Chief Peter Obermann—Batman to his troops behind his back—was built like a fire hydrant: short and stout, and just as unlikely to be moved, no matter what might be going to hell in a hand basket around him. He was aware of his troops' nickname for him and loved it, though he had never acknowledged this to anyone. Chief Obermann worked out of this station, driving a command car. The companies housed here included an engine, a rescue, and a 100-foot aerial ladder, each company manned with a crew of four. He also had three other stations under his charge in the district, all with a single engine company. Staffing for these totaled another 12 firefighters.

As senior company officer, Captain Buckman served as the batt chief's number two, addressing run-of-the mill matters. He also received and reviewed reports covering routine administrative requirements from the other company officers in the district. In practice, he took care of all but the most major issues. Even with these, he asked the necessary questions, made the necessary calls, garnered the information Chief Obermann would need to render a decision. There was a professional, military-like aspect to it all, an adherence to rank and a focus on task, without the snapping to attention and saluting. In reality, the two officers had worked together so many years, each having such respect for the other's competence, little in the way of true bother made it up the chain or needed to. Even then the ranking officer often simply said, "Handle it," in acknowledgment of the captain's solid judgment.

"Looks like it'll be a busy afternoon," the batt chief said, staring at the television. "Probably be up and hopping half the night, too," he added.

Bad weather had a way of making the job interesting. Wind and lightning always generated calls. Even rain alone could do the trick. There were more accidents to respond to when the streets were wet. If there was enough rain, or it came down in a quick downpour, it often resulted in flooding, which might mean rescues. This time of year, there could be some hail, possibly even a tornado thrown into the mix.

The screen was showing a vertical line of red stretching north to south along the Mississippi River. Time lapse projection showed it moving their way, tracking on a left to right—west to east—path. Other splotches of red and yellow trailed behind the squall line: dangerous islands of heavy rain floating on the surface of a roiled sea.

"Training's starting already," the captain observed, talking about the islands. He used the term in its meteorological context: storms lining up one behind the other, forming trains. The significance, other than the obvious fact a particular area could be impacted by wind and lightning again and again over a short period, was the rainfall accumulation. Such conditions could result in amounts causing flash floods, greatly increasing the possibilities for rescues.

"Look at the crawler," Greg said. He was the officer on Rescue 1. Sticks and he had just joined the group. Sticks, so named because he was thin as a stick—plus he led Ladder 1, an aerial ladder, *a stick* in department parlance—spoke up next.

"Two to four inches," Sticks read.

"Bet its closer to four," Greg opined.

"Probably right," Sticks agreed.

"What've y'all got down for this afternoon?" the batt chief asked.

"Doing a little stokes basket drill off the aerial," Greg answered for him and the other company officers.

The batt chief paused for a few seconds.

"Pass the word to the other houses," he said, speaking to the senior captain. "I want everybody back in quarters by 1430. Should give us an hour, maybe two, to get our ducks in a row before this mess hits."

Captain Buckman was already on his way back to the office.

Chapter 9

7:50 a.m.

They weren't really juvenile delinquents. Though they aspired to be tough, they were anything but. It was just how each one chose to see himself. Both were 11 and small for their age, thus much more likely to be the victims of bullies than to bully someone themselves, which was reason enough for them wanting to be tough. Then there were their names, especially their nicknames.

Timothy had been called Tiny Tim until he thought he would bust the next kid who called him that right in the mouth. So far it was just a thought. He had not swung the first silencing blow, though he never failed to give the punks serious poundings in his daydreams.

If anything, the tag hung on Marvin was worse. The first day of school somebody had called him Marvin Gay, which was bad enough. Within a day it had morphed to Marvin's Gay. This was usually delivered in a singsong manner, sometimes by an entire group of kids. Then Rusty Savage—now there was a name for a boy!—the leading jock and self-anointed wit of their sixth-grade class, who had taken to calling himself Rusty the Savage, had in turn logically dubbed him, Marvin the Gay. The tag—in concert with a limp-wristed wave in Marvin's direction—spread like wildfire through the school. Even the little kids, second and third graders, were doing it now.

Timothy's dreams of revenge moved from one boy to the next, depending on which one had insulted and/or assaulted him the worst on any given day. Marvin, however, dreamed of committing violence against only Rusty Savage. His dreams, influenced by a gruesome video game, generally involved swords and battle axes.

It was little wonder the boys took on names used only between the two of them. This was something of a defense mechanism, a retreat into a mental realm where each always prevailed over his enemies. Of course, no one else knew what their names meant. That was the point. It wouldn't be a code if everyone understood it.

"Here you go, Hammer," Marvin said to Timothy, passing him one of the two cigarettes he had stolen from his father's pack the night before. Tim had chosen Hammer because of his desire to hammer his tormentors to pulp with his fists.

"Thanks, Chopper," Hammer replied to his blade-happy friend.

Hammer stood on tiptoes and ran his hand along the edge of a shelf until he came to the little can of nails and screws. Lifting it, he grasped the book of matches beneath. In a moment he had one lit. The match burned down to his fingers just as he got the cigarette going. He dropped it to the earthen floor in sudden pain, licked his wounded fingertip.

"Gimme the book," Chopper reached out a hand.

Both boys were soon puffing away like steam engines. Chopper passed the matches back, and Hammer hid them under the can once more.

"I think Marlboros are the best brand," Chopper said. He didn't offer to add he had never tried any other.

Hammer inhaled, inspected the glowing end of the cigarette as if there was something other than burning tobacco there to see, coughed hard twice in close succession as he exhaled, steadied, nodded in agreement.

"Yeah. Smooth."

They should have already been at school. It was close enough for them to walk, and they always did, traveling together every day since third grade. The last couple of weeks, however, they had taken to stopping for a few minutes at old Mrs. Witherspoon's garage. It had been an occasional hideout of theirs for years.

The two of them were propped up on the trunk of Mrs. Witherspoon's ancient Chrysler. Dust covered, the tires half flat, it didn't appear to have been moved in years. From their seats—which they had unwittingly rubbed nearly clean of grime with their rear ends—they had a hazy view through the filthy windows of the wooden double doors. The doors had long since shifted on their outside hinges, so they no longer closed properly, leaving a gap of a few inches which served as a vent. As they smoked the boys talked.

"I'd like to bloody old snot-faced Simon's nose," Hammer said, referring to the latest addition to his enemies list.

"Asshole," Chopper answered, feeling big and manly using the profanity. He took another puff, tried to blow a smoke ring, failed, fell into a coughing fit.

"Easy, Chopper. Sshh," Hammer was alarmed. "Geez. The whole block can hear you."

"F 'em," Chopper answered, recovered, except for needing to spit, which he did twice into the pile of leaves and trash in the corner. "Catch Rusty out this summer," he spoke again, changing rows. "I'm running over his ass with Daddy's lawnmower."

"We're gonna be late," Hammer observed without concern.

"What're they gonna do to us? Ain't got but three more days of school."

"Nothing. F 'em," Hammer said.

"F 'em," Chopper agreed.

"What're you boys doing in there?!" Mrs. Witherspoon's shout nearly scared them out of their shorts. They shot up off the car. "Is that smoke? I'm calling the law!"

"Sonofabitch!" came from Hammer as he stomped his cigarette.

"Back door," Chopper ordered, giving his cigarette a quick stomp, too. "Get the hell out!"

They ran straight into each other in their haste, their feet shuffling, digging madly on the packed, oil-soaked earthen floor. Even had an observer been watching closely, it would have been practically impossible to see which cigarette butt was still issuing smoke—Hammer's or Chopper's—but an especially keen eye might have seen it propelled from the blur of flying feet into the pile of leaves and trash in the far corner.

Chapter 10

7:57 a.m.

Cody came flying into the school parking lot, his car nosing down as he mashed the brakes and slid to a hard stop in the loose gravel. Grabbing his books, he was out the door in a flash. After two paces he suddenly locked up. Something had not sounded right. He half-turned and glanced behind him. The car door was not closed all the way. He side-hopped a step and tried again, slamming the door so hard he thought for an instant he might have broken the glass. Then he was off at a quick trot for the school.

Coach Bronski came straight at him, marching like he was still a Marine drill instructor.

"Mr. Cox!"

"Morning, Coach."

"Don't *morning* me, Mr. Cox. How many times do I have to tell you to slow it down?"

"Sorry, coach," Cody replied. He paused an instant, then began to creep forward, his need to travel stronger than his will to stay planted. "I got to go. I'm late."

"Hold it right there, Mr. Cox."

The teenager stopped, sort of. His feet kept shuffling about, though he remained more or less in the same place.

"Mr. Cox, do you think I will cut you some slack because you are one of my players?"

"No, sir," the boy replied.

"Do you think, Mr. Cox, because you can, on occasion, do something halfway decent on the football field, because you actually caught a pass and scored the winning touchdown against Central last season, I should cast a blind eye toward your reckless behavior?"

"No, sir."

"I will not, Mr. Cox. That I can assure you. Not for one second."

"Coach, I'm sorry," the boy offered, trying his best to look sincere. The tempo of his shuffling feet was undergoing a dramatic increase. A thin cloud of dust began to rise about his ankles. "Can I leave? If I'm late, I'll have to go to Miss Scott's office, and she'll kill me."

"Obtaining a note from the principal, Mr. Cox, is hardly tantamount to a death sentence."

"Sir?"

"Be gone."

And the boy was off at a dead run.

"This parking lot is not a racetrack, Mr. Cox," the coach's voice followed.

"Yes sir, Coach!" Cody yelled, not bothering to look back. He was through the doorway in seconds, the homeroom bell clanging as the heavy metal door slammed closed behind him.

And there she was! Angie was standing by the end of the lockers where she always waited for him, books cradled in her arm. Her long, auburn hair rippled with fire as she turned. She spotted him and smiled, all white teeth and dimples and sparkling green eyes. He tried to swallow but found his mouth suddenly too dry.

Cody knew she was beautiful—there was not a prettier girl in the entire school—but he did not understand just how beautiful. He knew she was sweet, but he did not realize just how sweet, though he was certain he had never known a kinder person. He knew he was lucky, in a dim glow kind of way. How fortunate he was to be at this exact spot in his life, to be a part of her life, was knowledge a long way from being fully formed. He was a 17-year-old boy in love—a hazardous and often ridiculous combination hardly conducive to clear appreciation.

Cody slowed from a jog to a fast walk as he neared her, his unburdened hand rising of its own accord to touch at the pimple just beginning to sprout above his left eyebrow.

"Hi," he said as he halted before her.

"Hey you," Angie replied, if possible, smiling even wider. "Almost late again."

"Yeah," Cody grinned. "Coach busted me in the parking lot already."

She giggled, shook her head.

"Ready for the prom?" he asked.

"I can't wait," Angie exclaimed. "I tried my dress on last night. You'll love it."

He had already heard enough detail about her dress to know there was no doubt he would love it. Somehow, he managed not to drool as his imagination spun up pictures of her wearing it.

They turned together toward their homeroom then, their free hands bumping, touching, ever-so-briefly clasping. At that moment something miraculous happened. A beam of enlightenment shot through the mud puddles and briar patches of Cody's convoluted mind; found its precise mark. A lonely neuron pulsed, flashed a minute spark across to a heretofore slumbering neighbor, and for a sliver of an instant, he understood just how lucky he was.

Then he ran face first into an open locker door.

Chapter 11

7:59 a.m.

Mrs. Witherspoon saw the boys running across her back yard, one wearing a blue shirt, the other a red. She yelled again as they ducked through a gap in the wire of the rear fence, Red snagging his shirtsleeve. Her hearing was sharp, even at 82. The distinct sound of ripping fabric came back to her. Then they were gone down the alley.

Of course Mrs. Witherspoon knew them, not by name, but she knew about where they lived—one block up and one block over on Oliver somewhere. Having made her home in the neighborhood some 60 years, her knowledge was hardly surprising, for she paid attention to what was what. She had seen these two running the streets since they could stand on their own. If anything was torn up or missing, she would call the police. They could find them easy enough.

Mrs. Witherspoon shook her head. *Why did life always have aggravations? Could a body not be allowed to spend her waning days on this troublesome earth in peace?* It didn't seem much to ask. She was a good person. She always helped others, especially when the church was involved. Wasn't she there every Sunday, even when her hip hurt her so bad she could hardly put one foot in front of the other? Shouldn't those things count for something? *What were those boys up to, anyway?*

She approached the old building's side door. The boys had left it wide open in their haste to get away. How she remembered that door. Hanging it had been the last thing her husband, Herschel, had done when he built this garage. How proud he was. How proud of him she was. He put in an entire summer's afternoons sawing and hammering, tying on his nail pouch as soon as he got in from his job at the plant and picking up where he left off the day before. And when he had driven his last nail, turned his last screw, he called her out of the house. The memory was so clear. She had been breading pork chops for their supper, was still wiping the flour off her hands with her apron tail, when she came down the rear steps and saw him standing beside the door.

"Madam," he said, drawing himself up straight, sticking his chest out, as if he were about to declare something of great and solemn importance. "I, Herschel J. Witherspoon, do hereby declare this construction job done and over with. Praise God. Be honored if you were the first to set foot inside."

"Don't you dare try to carry me across the threshold," she giggled. "I've put on a bit since you did it before. You'll throw your back out of kilter."

He laughed hard at her warning; laughed that great deep-throated laugh of his. Then he took off his old work hat, held it over his heart and bowed at the waist.

"After you, my lady."

He was such a good man. Mrs. Witherspoon could see him bowing beside the open door, feel her knees bend as she curtsied in response.

"Thank you, kind sir," she answered.

The sound of her words surprised her. She had spoken aloud as she stepped across the threshold. *Oh my,* she thought. *How I miss you, Herschel.*

She found nothing amiss as she made her way beside the car, and she was looking closely. Although it had been a while since she'd been inside, she knew everything in there and its place. There were 60 years of life together in this little garage—60 years of working hard to get what they needed, and at last, just a little of what they wanted.

Oh, their car. She remembered when they purchased it as if it were only yesterday. They had scrimped so, saving every nickel, every penny. How proud he was to drive her around in style. A Chrysler! Oh, my. He taught her how to drive in this car—and her nearly 45 years old. Lord, she was scared to death, not so much of wrecking as being the one to put the first scratch on it. Neither of them ever had. And here it sat, just where he had parked it his last day on this earth. There, at the rear bumper, she had found him on the cold, packed ground, dead.

Since that fateful afternoon, she simply had not been able to drive their car again, not even to the cemetery to visit his grave, to visit the grave of their one child, Herschel Jr., in the shaded section where the soldiers lay. Had it not been for her friend, Dessie, taking her there on occasion, Mrs. Witherspoon didn't know what she would have done. *My goodness,* she thought, the loneliness all at once an anchor weight dragging at the hem of her soul. *Has it already been a year since Dessie passed?*

She saw it then, in the middle of the horrid, hallowed spot where her husband fell: a single cigarette butt on the oil-soaked floor. She could smell the smoke. Did she not remember the smell, for Herschel had smoked all those many years they were together?

So smoking was it, the reason why those boys had been in her garage. She suddenly turned away. Tears flooded her eyes as she made her passage back alongside the car. As she stepped through the doorway, she felt uncharacteristic anger. How dare those boys! How dare they desecrate the ground where the warmth stole away from her dear Herschel.

Chapter 12

Katie glanced down at her list on the countertop, pen in hand. She was a compulsive list maker, at home, at work, at ball games and summer concerts and while waiting on doctor's appointments, wherever and whenever. A pad of post-it notes was always in her purse and at least two pens in case one should run out of ink. Now, as she stared at her morning list, she felt frustrated, antsy. Something was missing, and she couldn't think what it was. Something obvious. Then it hit her—Tom's watch! How could she have forgotten it? Shaking her head, she quickly wrote it down.

It was her gift to him on their fifth anniversary. Things were tight back then. Both kids were so small—Jack just a baby. Not that there was money to throw around now, but they were doing fine.

She could remember when she first saw the watch. They were in the mall, Jack in his stroller, her pushing, simply window shopping, because they couldn't afford otherwise. Tom was carrying Clarisse on his shoulders. He, they, saw it first, Clarisse pointing at the watch, or at least something shiny, in the jewelry store's display case. Tom stopped and stared at it until, at last, Katie moved closer.

"What're you looking at?" she asked.

"There," he answered, jabbing a finger at the glass. "Now that's a real man's watch."

He moved on after a few seconds, giving in to the knowledge it was out of reach on their budget. Besides, it wasn't like him to get things, especially expensive things, for himself.

She realized as she watched him walk off, she would find a way to get it for him, somehow. The fact he had even said something, anything, was more telling than his actual words. She had squirreled away small amounts at every opportunity, keeping it all hidden in a shoe box in the broom closet. Days before their anniversary, she counted up and confirmed she had enough, barely, to make the purchase.

Tom loved the watch. He wore it everywhere. Never took it off. Then one day a few years ago it quit running. He said he'd take it to the jeweler to get fixed, but it seemed every time he would start to go something would come up—a phone call, a friend at the door, a minor emergency at work. On impulse, while at the drugstore one Saturday morning waiting for a prescription to be filled, he had spotted a cheap watch on display and bought it. That's where things had stood since. He wore his cheap replacement, and her gift lay unseen in his sock drawer.

Last month, as she studied on what to give Tom for their anniversary, it came to her. *Get his watch repaired!* And so, she had. The jeweler called her at work late yesterday and said it was ready. She would pick it up at lunchtime today. Tomorrow, their 25th anniversary, she would surprise him and give the watch as her gift, once again. Sometimes, when things worked out just right, like this had, life was particularly sweet. Katie smiled in anticipation as she dropped the list into the pocket of her purse.

Chapter 13

8:15 a.m.

Caroline Jacoby pressed the tissue to the corner of her mouth, blotting up the squiggle of lip gloss she had somehow managed to smudge out of line. A final check. She didn't use much make-up anyway, so there wasn't much else to inspect. At 23, there wasn't anything she really needed to cover up. With a jingle of silver links on the bracelet Ron had given her for graduation, she lifted a hand and hooked a stray lock of hair behind her ear.

Caroline hadn't actually graduated from college. She had one more class this summer. Ron simply hadn't been able to wait. In the meantime, she had her job as a teller at the bank. It was great experience and would look good on her resume once college was over, and she began the search for the ideal career position.

Probie Wan—Ron's department nickname just popped in her head. Caroline had to smile. It was too cute, a takeoff on Star Wars. Probationary firefighter Ron Jacoby—*Probie*, as a new firefighter was called—had been christened in honor of Obie Wan Kenobi. The similarities made it a natural choice, she supposed. Ron said they held a ceremony and everything, the members of the crews assembled in the engine room to do the honors. Greg, the officer on the rescue, called everyone to attention and read off Ron's new, official nickname, even presenting him with a certificate. Then the honoree was doused with buckets of soapy water.

Smiling at the memory of Ron telling how he had blown bubbles for an hour afterward, Caroline turned and looked into the full-length mirror on the back of the bathroom door. She twisted first one way, then the other. Everything seemed in line: no more smudges or wild hairs. Her hand suddenly lifted to cover her mouth. She couldn't believe how she had stood there in front of Ron when she first got out of bed. Of course, she was not particularly shy with him or minded him seeing her body. In fact, she appreciated his admiring looks. This morning, however, had been different. She had actually stood before him, naked to the world, and struck a pose! There was nothing lewd about it. Such was not her intention, anyway. She had simply let her body do the talking. *Look at me. I am yours.*

And she was his! They were so in love. She had meant it when she told him, *Tomorrow.* Tomorrow was a Saturday. No work. They could spend the morning in bed; maybe they would stay the whole day.

Her hand went to her tummy. She allowed it to rest there, flat against her. "Wonder how I'll look when I'm carrying?" she spoke to the mirror, turning sideways. "Will I be able to get this figure back afterward?" *Why sure*, she quickly nodded. It wouldn't be a big deal.

Her features took on a contemplative look. Maybe the day when she would be pregnant wasn't very far in the future. After all, she had gone off birth control as soon as Ron hired on with the department. The decision had been mutual. They weren't so much anxious as ready to start a family, especially with college so close to being over.

Then something inside her whispered. Her face was quickly aglow with excitement. She had to force herself to concentrate on her breathing, to slow down. Her granny said a woman knew. Caroline immediately made up her mind to find out for certain. She'd run by the drugstore at lunch and pick up a kit. Who could say? She might have a present of her own to give her husband, Mr. Probie Wan Jacoby, when he came home in the morning—the announcement he was going to become a father!

Chapter 14

8:17 a.m.

"Here we are, Emily," Darlene said, easing to a stop in the parking lot of Angels Wings Academy. "Ready for school?"

"Yes! Yes! Yes!"

Darlene laughed aloud as she unbuckled her seatbelt. Glancing in the mirror she could see Emily's hands swinging up and down, hear them slapping the tops of her legs the way she did when she was excited. Sharing in her daughter's enthusiasm was a true delight, one of the great joys of motherhood. And Emily was an enthusiastic child—about everything. Where she got the energy, though, was a mystery.

When Darlene opened Emily's door her baby was chanting, "Meer-e-um! Meer-e-um!"

"Did you miss Miriam, baby girl?"

"Yes! Yes! Yes!"

Her mother pushed the straps on the child safety seat out of the way. Emily hopped out immediately and scrambled to the ground. In half a heartbeat, she was gone, flying across the lot to the door of the day care. Darlene caught her there, snatched her by the hand before Emily could turn the knob.

"Emily Carson!"

The little girl looked up in surprise at her mother's sharp tone. *Not good.*

"How many times have I told you?" Darlene asked in her no-nonsense voice. "We always hold hands when we are away from our house. You could have been hit by a car."

"I'm sorry, Mommy, but—"

Emily's bottom lip was pooched out. Darlene saw it, of course. *So cute.*

As usual when Emily made this face, Darlene had to fight to remain focused.

"Meer-e-um."

"Miriam can wait a second," Darlene said, bending down. She cupped her daughter's chin in her hand, lifted her face up so she would have to look at her. "Put your lip back in before you step on it." Her voice was gentle now. Emily hesitated a second, then did as she was told, ever so slowly. "Now, what do we do when we are outside?"

"Hold hands."

"Right. Don't make me say it again."

"I won't, Mommy."

Her mother waited a moment before speaking.

"I mean it."

Even with her lip in, Emily was wearing the most pitiful expression she had ever seen. Well, maybe the second-most pitiful. When she got out of bed and discovered her father was already gone was the most pitiful. And, of course, tears soon followed, buckets of hot, little-girl tears. Darlene relented. She couldn't go down that path twice in one morning.

"Okay then. Let's go inside."

And together, mother's hand laid softly atop daughter's, they turned the knob.

Chapter 15

8:33 a.m.

It is a most prudent investment, sir, certain to quickly yield a profit," James Henry said into the phone.

He was speaking to Augustus Pennington in measured phrases, because that was how the aged gentleman spoke, as if everything he said was of great consequence and was being recorded for use in his memoirs. Mr. Augustus was old money and old school. He could trace his lineage—how he would say it, not ancestry, but lineage—back to the founding of Green Springs. An historical marker now stood on the spot a forefather had placed the first notched log to his cabin, not 50 paces from where the city's namesake flow bubbled to the surface.

"I am in agreement, James. The rate of return appears in line with your projections. I have given the matter careful deliberation and shall be glad to participate at the level you propose."

Mr. Augustus always called him James, an indulgence he permitted himself only because their families went back a long way together. James Henry's grandfather had been a fraternity brother of his. Through his personal old-boy network was how the man did business. None need approach without some long-standing tie.

"I shall have a courier deliver the papers to your home, sir," James Henry managed not to shout with glee.

"If you would, James," Mr. Augustus said, as if James Henry would dare do anything other than what he wished, "have the courier drop them off with Phineas. He can perform his standard perusal, then bring them to me at the club. We have a 10:48 tee time."

Phineas Moss Franklin was Mr. Augustus' attorney. He was another fraternity brother.

"I shall send those over right away, sir. How is your game holding up, if I may ask?"

"Oh, me. For some odd reason, I have developed a most dreadful slice with my driver. Perhaps I should explore acquiring another." Mr. Augustus paused a moment, remembering his son had given him the club as a gift last Christmas. "Well, we do the best we can with what we have," he started again. "At any rate, I hope to rid myself of this new aggravation today, while I relieve Phineas of some of his shekels. When I play in Boca a few days hence I must be able to keep my ball from the sea. Tends to ruin one's round, being bitten by a shark."

The old man chuckled softly at his version of a knee-slapper.

"Yes, sir, it absolutely does," James Henry played along, ready to hang up, though not about to take a chance on offending. "I envy you, sir. A golf vacation in Florida is always a delight."

"Not a vacation, young man. My granddaughter, Adeline, is having her coming out soiree weekend next. One cannot miss these signal occasions. I intend to go down the first of the week, traverse the links perhaps two or three times. Though I would like to indulge my passion to a greater degree, I do not anticipate circumstances will permit it."

"Sounds wonderful, sir. I had not realized Adeline's age. Oh my. Time has wings."

"Yes, it does. It certainly does, James," he hesitated a few seconds. "Just then I could hear your grandfather. I have heard him speak those exact words countless times. I do wish he were here to join Phineas and me."

Was that a sniffle?

"Thank you, sir. I take any comparison to my grandfather as a great compliment."

"And well you should, for such was my intention." There was a short pause, then, "Now, as you observed, time does not wait for us. I must hasten. Perhaps I can hone my putting stroke before Phineas arrives. Good day, James."

"Good day to you, sir," James Henry answered to the click of the older man hanging up.

"Destiny!" James Henry shouted. What a great name for a receptionist, he thought for the umpteenth time. Of course, with a face and figure like hers, men imagined their own destiny before they even noticed the nameplate on her desk. It was simple. Looks sell.

"Yes," she answered, appearing at his door. Her expression said, *Why didn't you just push the intercom button, genius?*

"Pennington's in on the South Third project for half a mil," James Henry said, flashing his oily smile. "Have a courier take the papers over to the Franklin and Marsh offices as soon as possible, like right now, before the old bird can fly away. Address them to Phineas Franklin."

"Okay," she answered. "Won't take but a few minutes to get them together."

"Thanks, hon," he said with a quick smile. "Oh, send a gift to Adeline Pennington in Boca Raton. Nice little gold chain or something. You know who I mean? The old man's granddaughter? Having her coming out deal next weekend. You've got the address, right?"

"I am not your *hon*," she said through gritted teeth, "and yes, I have the address. Everything's in the file." She flashed a tight smile back, said to herself, *Think I'm stupid, moron? And comb that rat's nest. Head looks like a toilet brush.*

Ever since Destiny found out James Henry had bragged to one of his Gucci-loafer-wearing buddies about taking her to bed—the sack of garbage just made it up—she had been loaded for bear. First, she corrected loafer boy's idea he should be next by slapping the taste out of his mouth, along with a cap from one of his front teeth. She may have been beautiful and Southern belle-charming, like her mom, but growing up a military brat with three older brothers left her quite capable of defending the greatest thing of value any lady possesses— her reputation.

Of course, James Henry denied saying anything, rolling the lie off his crooked tongue as easily as the original. She called him a liar and stormed for a time, promising all kinds of mayhem. As suddenly as her wind came up, it calmed. *Okay, fine,* she thought. *Won't be a little slap this time.* Like her pop had drilled into all his kids, she was primed to make certain paybacks are a mother. Looking James Henry in the eye now, her smile was broad and genuine.

Good, he thought. She was smiling. Didn't want her upset again. She had threatened to wring his neck already. *And what she did to Byron? Damn, some people couldn't take a joke.*

"Close the door," he told her. "Got a private call to make."

He dialed the number immediately.

"Yeah, it's me. Noon? Okay. No. I'm having a good morning. Double up on the usual."

James Henry air dropped the phone into its cradle, placed his hands behind his head, and leaned back in his genuine Corinthian leather chair. He had been working Pennington for a month. Now, with his cocaine order placed, he could celebrate the victory properly. In a moment he would make another call—to a certain young lady in Nashville—to ensure he wouldn't be celebrating alone.

Chapter 16

8:35 a.m.

Robert brought the cup to his lips, took a sip. *Yuk! Cold as ice. How did it get cold so fast?* Heck, he still had half a cupful. He remembered a time when a cup of hot coffee was such an indispensable part of his morning routine he would have hopped right up for a refill; checked to see if the wife needed one, too, while he was at it. He didn't move now. The urge was simply not there anymore. She was gone, so what was the point in being in a hurry for anything?

What time was it, anyway? It didn't matter, but out of habit he looked across at the old clock on the wall. 8:35. He grinned to himself in surprise. He was fairly certain, as certain as he was about anything at this stage, it had been 7:30 when he sat down. "Ha!" His little half laugh wasn't loud. In the empty house, however, it boomed like next-door thunder. Robert sat up straighter, nonplussed by the sound. *Well,* he thought, *that explains why the coffee was cold.* The fact he had sat there for an hour didn't faze him in the least. It wasn't unusual.

The chair scraped noisily across the floor as Robert pushed back from the table. He levered himself upright, using the table and chairback as props, to the familiar sounds of his joints popping. One ankle cracked sharply in rhythm as he ambled toward the coffee pot, cup in hand. As usual, it was his left ankle. It always fussed. At least it didn't hurt like so much else.

His cup refilled, Robert stood with his hands pressed flat upon the countertop, staring hopefully out the kitchen window behind the sink. At dusk yesterday he had carried a bag of trash out to the can beside the shed, and in so doing perhaps been party to the deaths of innocents. He certainly had not meant to cause any harm. The idea he may have haunted him into the night, began anew now as he peered out the window.

The door to the shed was jammed ajar, as it had been for years. A pair of Carolina wrens had taken advantage earlier in the spring. He had seen them carrying the makings for a home inside. After a few days, a quick peek through the doorway revealed their nest in an old toolbox on the workbench. Of late their number of flights in and out had increased. There was an urgency to their movements. He guessed they had babies to feed. Perhaps it was why they sang so happily: "Cheery, cheery, cheery." Such a gloriously loud voice from such a tiny bird.

Last evening Robert had carried the trash out, not because it needed to be carried out, but because he needed something to do. When he shuffled past the shed, he glanced inside and startled a young wren perched on the edge of the toolbox. With a panicked cry it darted out the door and past him. A little puff of down floated free in its wake as it struggled to fly. The bird managed to make it only the few feet to his driveway. There it huddled underneath the car's front bumper. Another wren—he imagined the mother—was beside it in an instant.

His first instinct was to rush over and pick up the chick, but a step toward it sent the mother flying. He backed off and the mother returned. There they remained, inches apart, as he kept watch through the kitchen window until the night breathed in the sun's last glimmer.

And beneath the car this morning, nothing. Even worse, not a single joyous syllable floated to him through the screen wire. Robert felt it then, the guilt of having caused loss and pain. The ache was no less sharp for lack of intention. Some nocturnal hunter—a cat, an owl—he felt certain had found hen and chick, mother and child.

He watched for a while, anyway, sipping his coffee automatically. At long last he drained the final drops and placed the empty cup in the sink. As he turned away a thought of mothers and their babies came to him—an understanding of responsibility assumed without question, of a parent's never-ending concern. There was much praiseworthy in the idea. There was also a certain indefinable sadness, such was the burden.

This was how he came to think of Emily and her mother, this second thought triggered by the first, a logical extension. Emily would come over with her mom soon after they got home, as was their pattern, and he would show her the beautiful splash of yellow on his wife's rosebush. It would be a sweet moment, he had no doubt, made sweeter by the knowledge Emily's mother didn't come simply to escort her child. She was also there in answer to a mother's inherent duty to watch over all chicks, young and old.

Robert nodded at his insight. He grasped his chairback with one hand and rested the other flat on the kitchen table, preparing to sit down, but a sudden burst of song through the screen interrupted. As fast as his stiff legs would move, he hurried to the window. It was a full chorus now, notes tumbling over one another. He leaned across the sink and looked out. From atop the shed door a wren was loudly testifying, "Cheery, cheery, cheery." From the car's roof a second wren was answering in kind. Their down-specked child stood silently frozen in place on the car's hood. Without warning it took off in ungainly flight, landing short on a windshield wiper. For a moment the tiny bird teetered, struggling to find its balance. Then it pooped on the glass.

Chapter 17

0846 Hours

Ringgggggg! Probie Wan began moving the instant the alert bell came over the speakers, leaving a just-poured cup of coffee by the pot. The unique tones for his company followed as he entered the engine room. His feet seemed about to race away from him. He tried to slow down, to appear under control, but without much success. Probie Wan found himself almost running as he reached his assigned spot.

"Attention Engine 4." The female dispatcher's voice filled the space, flat and emotionless. "Respond to a transformer fire in the alley behind 901 Market St. Repeating, Engine 4, respond to a transformer fire in the alley behind 901 Market St. Cross streets Ninth Avenue and 10th Avenue."

Probie Wan was moving quickly through the sequenced steps of donning his bunker gear: step in boots, pants up, suspenders over shoulders; head through hood, pull fringe down around neck; coat on, full zip, press velcro over zipper in quick, flat-handed swipe. He swung up into the cab, dropped into his jump seat. In the opposite jump seat, Mick was already putting his helmet on. *How did he get there so fast?* Probie Wan wondered. He reached for his helmet, reconsidered, started working his arms through the shoulder straps of his breathing apparatus, instead.

"Don't worry about your pack," Mick half-shouted to him over the roar of the diesel engine firing up. "Won't be making entry on this one."

"Oh." Probie Wan replied, feeling lost, foolish. He had never been to a transformer fire.

"Need your helmet, though."

"Yeah, right," Probie Wan said, reaching again for the heavy, yellow helmet.

"Buckle up, Probe. We're rolling."

He dropped the helmet on his head at an angle and grabbed for the seat belt, feeling the bump through his seat as the truck rolled over the lip where the engine room floor ended and the outside apron began. From the front came the captain's voice speaking into the radio.

"Engine 4, 10-6."

"Engine 4 is 10-6," the dispatcher answered, "responding to a transformer fire in the alley behind 901 Market St. Time out, 0847."

"Probably just stand by," Mick's voice managed to cut through the screaming of the siren, "until the electric boys get there. Make sure nothing else is in danger."

"Okay," Probie Wan replied, relieved. He couldn't think of any questions, which was a good sign. Maybe. His heart responded, seemed to slow down to a rate approaching normal.

"Bet it's a squirrel," Mick grinned across at him.

"What?" Probie Wan had difficulty hearing over the siren, though he had noticed before that the other crew members didn't seem bothered. Captain Buckman was increasing the racket now, blowing the air horn in short bursts.

"Squirrel. Little monkeys run the wires. Make a wrong step at the transformer, create a path. Kapow!"

"Sounds bad for the squirrel," Probie Wan offered, understanding Mick was saying the current would go through the squirrel.

"Yep," Mick nodded. "Might be making your first fatality."

The siren and air horn ceased as the engine slowed, turned, slowed even more, came almost to a stop. In the relative quiet, Probie Wan twisted around the best he could in his gear and discovered they were creeping along a narrow alleyway. They soon came to a full halt. There was a loud *pop/hiss* as D. J. set the parking brake. Captain Buckman was on the radio.

"Engine 4 to Fire Dispatch."

"Engine 4."

"Engine 4 on the scene. Transformer fire. This is Market Command."

Probie Wan could not understand the rest of the transmissions as he swung his door open and hopped down. He could hear the electrical sound, a moderate, insistent hum. As he came around to the front of the engine, he saw the metal transformer near the top of a pole, maybe 40 yards ahead. It was smoking, but not a lot, certainly not what he had expected to see. The sound surged unevenly, followed sometimes by a thin spray of sparks. He sensed movement to his right and turned his head to see the captain and Mick coming to a halt side by side a couple of paces away. They simply stood there, watching the smoking cylinder.

Boom!

The sound of the explosion was huge, with a great cascade of sparks to match flying out of the transformer. Probie Wan turned and ran. He smashed straight into D. J.

"Easy, son," the engineer grinned in his face. "Can't panic the citizens." Gently spinning him around by the shoulders, he continued, "We'll ease up here a little and see what's what."

Probie Wan found himself in a loose gathering with the other members of the crew a few yards in front of the idling truck. Embarrassed, he caught Mick's eye. Mick grinned back at him.

"Give you happy feet?" Mick asked. "No sweat. Think I had a major bowel movement," he added with a grimace. "How about you, Cap?"

"Broke a little wind," Captain Buckman deadpanned. Then he brought the mic of his portable radio close to his mouth. "Market Command to Dispatch."

"Market Command"

"E T A on the utility?"

"One moment." She was back in seconds. "Five minutes, Command."

"10-4. Inform them to enter from the 10th Avenue side."

"Affirmative, enter from the 10th Avenue side," the dispatcher answered.

"Okay, men," the captain said to his crew, "let's work our way around the perimeter of this thing, make sure nothing else is arcing or smoking, especially where the service enters a building. Watch for downed wires, Probe, and stay out from under any overhead stuff. Don't want anything hot falling on us," he added, meaning live with electricity.

Mick sidled up beside Probie Wan as they started forward.

"Not but two things you need to know about electricity. You can't see the shit, and it'll fry you like a burnt hot dog in a New York second."

Standing in the rear doorway of Secure Financial, a young woman watched the firefighters moving slowly up the alley. Destiny had made the initial call to 911. From the darkness behind her a presence approached, bumped into her backside. She swung around ready to strike.

"Easy, lady," James Henry held up his hands. "It was an accident."

"Sure," she said, thinking, "I'll accident your teeth down your throat, touch me again."

"What're these tax suckers doing? Holding a parade?" There was true anger in James Henry's voice as he stepped outside. "Need my power back on. Got deals to make."

"Why don't you go help them," Destiny's voice found him. "Maybe they'll let you plug the extension cord back in." She thought to add, *your rectum*, but didn't say it out loud.

In the alley Mick stopped, pointed.

"Told you."

On the ground by a dumpster, a good 30 feet from the pole holding the transformer, Probie Wan spotted a short piece of scorched rodent tail.

Chapter 18

8:47 a.m.

"Meer-e-um, Meer-e-um," Emily was grabbing at the girl's arm, trying to get her attention. A minute before they had been chasing one another around the playroom, first one girl in pursuit, then the other.

Miss Woods had finally called them to a halt. "No running inside, girls! Slow it down, please." They had slowed it down. In fact, they had come to a complete halt. Now, in spite of her friend's insistence, Miriam remained turned sideways, watching Grayson, who was holding Brandon by the head with both hands and doing his utmost to peer inside Brandon's ear. He kept twisting his own head around first one way then another, trying to get a better view.

"What can ooh see?" Miriam asked the explorer, her slight speech impediment making itself known.

"It's dark. Where's the wabbit?" Grayson didn't sound disappointed he hadn't spied the creature he knew must be in there. Hadn't the magician in yesterday's cartoon pulled a rabbit out of a boy's ear? He kept looking, unperturbed. Even with a bunny supposedly in his head, Brandon did not seem particularly concerned, standing quiet, compliant.

In the meantime, Emily kept pulling at Miriam's arm, still chanting, "Meer-e-um, Meer-e-um."

At last Miriam turned to face her friend.

"Em-ooh-wee!" she exclaimed, as if she hadn't seen Emily in months. She took a quick step forward, gave her friend a brief hug. After stepping back, she froze in puzzlement, staring down at Emily's midsection. A finger came slowly forward, gently poked Emily's little belly. "Pretty," she said, her fingertip tracing the outline of a rose on Emily's top.

"It's roses," Emily said, pooching her tummy out, not minding the pressure of Miriam's finger.

"I wuv woses."

"Grandpa Bob has roses in his yard."

"My grandpa's old. Daddy said he's sixee twee."

"Ummhuh," Emily replied without interest. She had started tracing a rose of her own on her tummy.

"Is ur Grandpa old?" Miriam asked.

"Ummhuh. He's a dillum hun'erd."

"Oooohhh," Miriam answered in awe.

"My mommy said we could show him my new top when I get home."

"Pretty," Miriam said again, her attention back on the rose on Emily's tummy.

"I see 'im! There's the wabbit!" Grayson exclaimed, his eye pressed flush against Brandon's ear.

"Lemme see! Lemme see! Lemme see!" Emily and Miriam were suddenly tugging at Grayson's arms, one girl on each side, trying to pull him away so they could get in to see, too. Without warning Grayson stepped back, which sent the girls swinging in between the boys. The girls' heads banged together with an audible, *pop!* In an instant they were on the floor giggling, each holding their own heads. Grayson and Brandon, not knowing or caring what the new game was, each grabbed his head and fell on the floor, too. In a flash all four were rolling and laughing and bumping into one another.

"Get up off that floor!"

Miss Woods voice was sharp, though her expression said otherwise. She was laughing, too.

Chapter 19

8:52 a.m.

Darlene closed the screen and looked up from her computer. She felt better. Everything was caught up. It was her habit each morning to run all the totals from the day before and update every account. She didn't mind the bookkeeping. Dealing with numbers came to her easily.

Her office supply store was doing great. She couldn't help but smile at her good fortune. Modern life! Enough information processing accoutrements existed in a modest office to run a fair-sized country. Many of her customers, however, were never satisfied. They must have the absolute latest version of anything electronic, or risk certain death it seemed. The near constant equipment upgrades made for good business for her. She had been in the black almost since opening the doors.

But that was the professional side of her life. Success was satisfying, but it gave her relatively little joy. What brought Darlene true joy was her family. And though she loved her husband with all her heart, the one who gave her the greatest joy within her family was Emily.

Darlene mused, was it possible she was at last a mom? She would be 42 in August! Forty-two and she felt like a young mother. Emily made her feel as if years had somehow fallen away. There was never a time in the day when a thought of her daughter might not intrude and leave her smiling, even laughing. *Wasn't it how it was supposed to be?* Darlene asked herself the question because she liked answering it. *Yes! That was how it was supposed to be.*

As had been her habit for all of her adult life, when she had a quiet moment and felt The Presence, she said a prayer. Now was such a quiet moment. She bowed her head.

"Father, I thank You for Your many blessings, especially my baby girl. I ask You to please watch over and protect her this day. Let her know joy. Help her to learn. Allow her, always, to feel loved. I ask, too, Father, for You to watch over my husband throughout his travels. Guide him home safely to us. Let Thy love ever grace his heart. Please give me the patience and the understanding to be a good mother and a good wife. These things I ask in Thy name. Amen."

She kept her head bent, her eyes closed, for a few moments more. The comfort she sought came, warmed her. Only then did she open her eyes and lift her head. She rose from her chair and moved to the front door. As she turned the lock her mind returned to thoughts of Emily.

Now what could they do as a family this weekend? Go to the water park again? Emily certainly loved every minute there last Saturday, going down the water slide at least 100 times, her dad always waiting at the bottom to catch her. She was just as crazy about the lazy river, riding down it on a float with her and Frank over and over again, splashing and laughing the whole way. In the calm pool at the end of the stream, she was even able to swim a little, just managing to keep her head above water. Swimming lessons would definitely be on the agenda this summer. She and Frank had agreed on those the instant they saw her try to dog paddle her way around.

Sure, Darlene thought. *The water park it is.* She was certain her husband would agree. He loved the water, too, and their baby girl was a water bug if there ever was one.

Chapter 20

0938 Hours

"Chowderheads."

"What's that, Greg?" Mick asked, grinning.

"Nothing but a bunch of chowderheads."

"Who is?" Mick prodded. Engine 4 and Rescue 1 were both back in quarters, the rescue having made a med call—possible heart attack—while 4 had been on the transformer run. Mick was seated on the tailboard of the engine, one foot propped up so he could rest his chin on his knee. As he watched Greg give the probie some one-on-one instructing on knots, he stirred the man enough to keep him going. It didn't take much.

"They all are," Greg glanced over at Mick. "Every stinking one." Greg turned his attention back to Probie Wan. "Very good. Shake it out and do it again. Leave more tail for your safety this time."

"Okay," Probie Wan answered. He so wanted to get it right. Knot tying was tough for him to get down. He practiced it nights in the apartment during recruit school until Caroline thought something was cracked in his head. Using a hank of clothesline, he tied each knot, checked it against the picture in the manual, worked it loose, did it over, then over and over again. Somehow, he tested out okay. Now, finally, it was getting less difficult; not smooth; not instinctive like Greg—the man flat knew his ropes—but he had some idea of what he was doing.

Probie Wan shook the last kink out. Before he started again, he reached down with one hand to tug at the right leg loop on his harness. It had worked up too high and was pinching where he didn't care to be pinched.

"Yep, get those straps situated right," Greg nodded, "or you'll bust every window in the neighborhood hitting your high notes."

Finally, comfortable in the harness, Probie Wan began to tie a figure 8 on a bight. He formed a bend. Then he crossed the free end over the standing line and brought it up through the bend. He left the knot loose on purpose, made a small loop at the bottom, and with the free end retraced the figure 8 through, doubling everything. At last, he cinched the knot tight, pulling hard on both sides. There was enough tail to add an overhand safety.

Mick was watching the probie closely. The kid was gonna be a good one. It had dawned on him that he didn't really know beans, in spite of all the initial training. There were 1,001 things you had to be able to do. It took a lot of effort to become competent in each one. The probie was pushing himself a little too hard, maybe. He still seemed a bit nervous, but he had enthusiasm and the desire to learn. Yeah, he would make a good one, Mick nodded to himself. The ass ripping he'd given the kid after his first house fire was the tempering he needed to make him slow down and pay attention.

"What do you think we ought to do with 'em?" Mick asked Greg.

"Can't do nothing with chowderheads!"

Greg seemed dumbfounded anybody would ask such a question, but Greg seemed dumbfounded about most things. The man almost always looked serious, and he was always bitching about something—had been at least since Mick was in the same company with him back in Mick's rookie days. Getting him to smile or laugh was like pulling teeth. Nevertheless, Mick thought he was one of the funniest men he'd ever met. Greg's sense of humor was dry, wicked, part of the mask he wore.

The officer was also the best rescue man in the department. It came naturally to him, how all the tools worked, how everything went together to form a system. Greg could see it all in his head, like a road map, lay it out on a scene without missing a lick. The man had ice water in his veins, too—part of what made him a good leader. You couldn't shake him with an earthquake.

"Throw 'em in the damn river," Greg continued his diatribe. "Stupid chowderheads."

"Gotta thin the herd," Mick agreed.

"Yeah," Greg nodded, his focus back on the knot the probie had just tied. He took the rope in his hands, fingertips tracing the turns, like he was reading braille. "Good. Good. Tight. Much better," he nodded. The kid allowed himself a tiny smile. "Now, why did you tie a safety?"

"Because by God you said to."

"You're a smart boy, Probie Wan. Keep listening to me, you'll make something worth shooting yet."

The kid's grin got bigger.

"Now hook in your harness," Greg continued.

Probie Wan thumbed the carabiner open, dropped the loop in, then released the spring-loaded bar and spun the lock closed around it. Greg grasped the rope a couple of steps from Probie Wan and drew it across his hips. Holding it with a hand on each side, he widened his stance to brace himself.

"Lean back," Greg nodded. "Let the rope take your weight."

Probie Wan did as he was told, trusting the knot wouldn't slip and Greg would keep him from falling.

"Everything okay?" Greg asked. "Don't feel like you're getting neutered or nothing?"

"I'm good."

Greg took a step back, pulling Probie Wan upright.

"Now break it down and do it again, while you're seeing it," Greg said. "Then we'll work some on tying off to anchor points." He turned to face Mick. "What's for lunch, fart breath?"

"Kraut and roadkill. Just like grandma used to make."

"Ring the bell! My favorite. What kind of flattened jaywalker you cremating this time?"

"Not sure. Couldn't make out which way the stripes ran, longways or crossways," Mick replied, pushing himself up from the tailboard. Raising his arms above his head, he stretched for the stars, his face all but swallowed in a massive yawn. Dropping his hands, he shook all over, bones jiggling back in alignment, and went ambling off toward the kitchen.

Chapter 21

1049 Hours

Probie Wan made his way to the kitchen. Lunch should be anytime now. It had been an interesting morning. He had to laugh at himself over the transformer. Man, when that thing blew it was time to make tracks. Thank goodness the rest of the crew didn't pick on him about his aborted sprint to safety. No wonder. Obviously, it had scared them, too. Now he got it why they hadn't spent much time on transformer fires in recruit school. Carbon dioxide was the preferred method of extinguishing electrical fires, but who was going to climb a pole with a barrel-sized gadget shorting out right over his head and spray the thing with a portable extinguisher? Nobody. Good way to get fried, Mick had said. So, the power company cut the juice and the fire went out. Easy breezy, as long as the transformer didn't go blooey!

Greg had worked with him on ropes for the better part of an hour. He had just finished stowing the gear away moments ago. The impromptu training session had resulted from a simple question to the officer about anchor points. Next thing Probie Wan knew he was wearing a harness and tying knots. The one-on-one instruction had been great. Greg made it real, giving examples of where he had employed certain knots and haul systems, and why, in carrying out rescues.

All the guys were open to helping him, willing to go over anything he wanted to know about. They might aggravate the snot out of him otherwise, playing jokes and teasing, but if he had a question concerning firefighting, they would do their best to answer it. And Lord, did he have questions. But the guys were patient. As a result, he was getting more comfortable with each passing shift. Perhaps more importantly, thanks primarily to Mick's willingness to chew on him when he fell short, he was beginning to understand the vested interest the others had in him being good at the job.

Probie Wan poured himself half a cup of coffee and took a quick sip. Then, instead of finding a seat, he set his cup on the counter and went ambling over to where Mick was working at the stove. Here was something else to learn—something he hardly had a clue about—cooking; and for three companies. That was a dozen men. No, 13. Couldn't forget Batman.

Mick pulled a long roasting pan from the oven and placed it on top of the industrial-size stove just as he walked up.

"Hey, Probe. Grab a big spoon out of the drawer there."

"One with holes in it?"

"Naw. Regular." The young firefighter dug one out and offered it to him. Mick didn't take it, however. "Work it loose there on the far end." Mick nodded, talking about the sheet of aluminum foil covering whatever was in the pan. "Careful. Don't get steamed. Grab a mitt, Goober," Mick ordered, shaking his head. "Okay. Crap should be about ready. Go on. Check it."

Catching an edge, Probie Wan moved the foil back further. The pan was crammed with meat, potatoes, carrots, and onions.

"What do you want me to do?" he asked, looking up.

"See if it's done, knothead. Cut stuff with the edge of your spoon. Slices easy, it's done."

Probie Wan tried the spoon. It sliced through the potatoes and carrots like they were nothing. The massive roast fell apart at his touch.

"Looks ready," Mick said. "Let's give her the old taste test."

He grabbed a fork and speared a bit of meat. Bringing it to his mouth, he blew on it a couple of times, then stuck it in. After chewing a moment, he said, "Mmmm, mmmm. This heifer is ready." A second later he elbowed Probie Wan to the side. "Gotta take a look at my cornbread," Mick said, pulling an oven door open. "Golden!" he declared, using a mitt to grab a skillet handle. He placed the iron skillet atop a burner. "Feast your eyes on that, son. Hunk of butter and a piece of ole Mick's blue-ribbon cornbread, don't need anything else. Tongue'll slap your brains out. Help me get the rest of this on top," Mick added as he began flipping a row of burner knobs to the off positions.

Probie Wan slid out two other huge pans of meat and potatoes. Then he fetched a butcher knife and some big ladle spoons, as Mick ordered. He watched with interest as his crewmate carved eight slices in each skillet of cornbread. Done, Mick turned to face him.

"Holler signal 13. Time to slop these hogs."

Probie Wan crossed the room and picked up the intercom transmitter. He glanced back at Mick making his way along the stove, plate in hand, as he keyed the mike. "Signal 13! Signal 13! Luncheon is served in the main dining area," he said in a loud voice, mimicking how he had heard others announce a meal was ready.

In an instant, firefighters were striding into the room from every entryway. Probie Wan dropped in on the rear of the quickly formed serving line, where protocol dictated a rookie belonged. He had just filled his plate and turned to find a seat, when—*Ringggggg!*

Individual company tones followed, continuing until every company in the station had been knocked out. They went on, notifying an additional company from another station.

"Attention," the dispatcher began, "Battalion 1, Engine 4, Rescue 1, Ladder 1, Engine 7, respond to a structure fire at 1142 South Sunrise."

The dispatcher repeated her initial transmission as firefighters hustled out of the room, heading toward their trucks. Behind, plates of steaming food rested unattended on the tables, on the counter, by the stove, as if every firefighter had been suddenly abducted.

Chapter 22

1058 Hours

Probie Wan twisted his head around to see as they rolled up. Orange and yellow flames were boiling out the front of a detached garage and curling up over the eaves. Thick, black smoke belched out with them in mad waves which swept low across the ground before rolling skyward. For a split second the smoke lifted enough to reveal the rear window of a car inside the garage. Engine 4 came to a stop.

His air pack bounced on his back as Probie Wan hopped down from the jump seat. He paused, bent forward, gave the shoulder straps a quick tug, cinching them tighter. It was noisy—sirens and air horns, things popping, cracking, break-ing, falling. There was a house to the side of the garage, with a drive made of two narrow strips of concrete running straight up to the fire. An elderly lady was standing in the grass between the strips of concrete, her hands to her face. Something in the garage exploded with a dull bang. The lady disappeared in a wave of smoke.

"Inch and three quarters," Captain Buckman said over his shoulder as he started to stride up the drive, ordering a precon-nected line of that diameter. His voice was as controlled and matter of fact as if he had said, "Pass the ketchup." Then he was gone in the smoke.

The order settled Probie Wan's nerves. Pulling a preconnect was a standard two-man evolution. He had practiced it dozens of times, training by rote until the moves were hammered in. Turning to the hose trays just behind the cab, he reached up to a layered stack of hose, worked his stiff-gloved fingers between the ends of the accordion-like folds midway down the stack. He gave a sharp tug to get started, then pivoted to face the fire as he pulled. At the same time, he twisted the ends of the folds, so they flipped and draped over his shoulder upside down to how they had laid in the bed. His opposite hand kept the pile in place, the nozzle a weight on his chest as he stepped away. Once his part was clear of the truck, he stopped and waited for Mick to pull the second half of the load. His breathing sounded labored and heavy, alien-like, inside the mask. Strange. He didn't remember turning the air pack on.

Mick pulled his part in one smooth motion, and they began moving. Probie Wan went up the driveway, angling off to the left, away from the house; Mick headed into the front yard as successive folds played off his shoulder. The captain passed them coming back, his arm wrapped around the shoulders of the lady as he guided her over the line. Probie Wan made out, "Jesus God, help me."

Halfway up the drive, Probie Wan allowed hose to start playing off his shoulder, too. He stopped 20 feet from the garage and dropped his last folds. Heat washed through his turnouts suddenly, rocking him back. He steadied. A wave of disorienting smoke rolled over. Nozzle in one hand, he caught the hose with the other and flung it about into a zig-zag pattern, leaving about 40 feet of line up close for maneuvering. Down the drive, Mick jerked a kink out, came toward him at a fast march.

Without warning the line charged violently. It snapped and slid about for a few seconds until the new weight of water forced it to yield to gravity and settle. Probie Wan cracked the nozzle. Compressed air whistled out. Mick snatched the line behind him and pushed up against his back. Less than a minute had passed since they stepped off the engine.

"Give the house a shot," Mick said, his voice muffled and distant through the mask. "Then kick this bastard's ass."

They leaned forward as one to absorb the coming back pressure. Probie Wan opened the nozzle on narrow fog, swept the wedge of water across the side of the house, bricks and boards steaming, then turned it on the garage.

The two men took the fire head-on. Probie Wan switched the nozzle pattern back and forth as the pair advanced—wide angle to shield when the heat pushed hard their way; narrow when he needed some reach. Mick ran a constant commentary, his voice sometimes calm, sometimes angry, and inexplicably, sometimes happy? Probie Wan caught a glimpse of movement off to the right. Captain Buckman stepped past. He spoke in a conversational tone. "Knocking it down."

The building wasn't quite fully involved. Most of the fire was in the front half and had vented out the big folding doors, which pulled the flames away from the rear of the garage. The fact the top half of each door was burned away allowed them to reach the main body without entering. The team quickly had the worst of the flames beaten into submission. Firefighters—truckies from Ladder 1—pulled open what remained of the bay doors. Someone opened a door on the house side of the building. Cross ventilated, the smoke started to clear, except for what was coming from a tire on the old car. It stubbornly spewed out oily, black globs. Probie Wan and Mick moved in close and finally drowned it when D. J. dialed down the pressure, which allowed them to bend the line enough to shoot water up under the wheelwell.

The laddermen swarmed in, poking and pulling with pike poles and chopping with axes, doing the hard work of overhauling, opening up areas bleeding smoke where hidden embers might generate a rekindle. Probie Wan and Mick gave them room as they worked the line about as necessary to lob water on each hot spot. Soon there were no more places to wet down.

"Let 'er breathe, men," the captain said. "And watch the back of the car there on the way out. Might be some evidence."

Mick and Probie Wan pulled their masks off and stopped to linger with the captain near the rear of the car.

"Owner ran some boys out this morning. In here smoking," the captain said.

"Figured it was suspicious," Mick nodded, sweat dripping

from his chin. "No electric lines. Grass growing through cracks in the concrete. Old Chrysler probably hasn't been moved in years. Shame. Bet it was cherry."

Probie Wan bit his lip. Even after the transformer fire earlier, he hadn't thought to check for power lines. The instructors had only hammered on the dangers of electrocution about 900 times in recruit school. After a minute Captain Buckman and Mick moved outside. Probie Wan followed.

He shucked his pack and turnout coat and dropped them in a pile in the middle of the driveway beside Mick's. D. J. came up carrying an air bottle in each hand. Together the three of them quickly replaced the partially depleted bottles in the breathing apparatus. Part of getting ready for the next call.

"How'd weiner-head do?" the engineer asked Mick in a voice loud enough for the whole block to hear.

"Dragon-slaying sonofabitch," Mick barked. "Tried to hold him back. He jerked the car up with one hand and went to ripping a burning tire off with the other. Scared me, and I ain't scared of nothing."

D. J. grinned and turned toward the engine, taking the depleted air bottles with him.

Probie Wan was grinning a little, also, proud of Mick's praise, though trying not to show it. He was soaked with perspiration, dirty as a pig, and as satisfied with life right that moment as he had ever been. He wanted to tell somebody how sweet this feeling was, but only firefighters were nearby, and he imagined they already knew. His gaze began to wander. It stopped in a corner of the front yard where the elderly lady was seated in an old metal lawn chair, head back, legs splayed out before her. An oxygen mask covered her mouth and nose. A firefighter from Rescue 1 was bending over beside her, checking her blood pressure. On her other side, Greg was down on one knee holding her hand.

Chapter 23

10:59 a.m.

Letha Ledbetter was a shy thing as far as her physical dimensions—half an inch under five feet tall, and a pound or two short of 100. There wasn't a corpuscle in her being, however, capable of backing away from anything. She was a force of nature, wound tight as a tornado and just as fierce, primed to take on man or beast at the snap of a finger. Her husband, Odell, swore to his friends she'd sandpaper a wildcat's hind end, just to get limbered up before she set in on him. He was careful not to whisper anything along those lines in Letha's presence.

Odell had been a tall man once—something in the neighborhood of six foot three—and stout as an ox as well. There had been a time in those days, he was fairly certain, when he could think things through and reason them out on his own. The best he could remember, it had been the case right up until he said, "I do." That was his first big mistake. He put his foot down 47 years later and made another decision—he retired. This had turned out worse than the *I do* train wreck. He soon found out how hard it was to find a place to hide in their little shotgun house. All day, every day, was spent trying to dodge the verbal paper cuts and eardrum piercings and general bashings about his head and shoulders so liberally bestowed by his dearly beloved.

He didn't have much luck.

Lord, he thought this morning—for the millionth time—as he heard her come fast stepping through the house, *did the woman have a tongue.* When she started fussing, rocks split and the woods caught fire. She didn't need anything else. Just her bullwhip of a mouth sassing and ripping would cripple anybody. This past year, since he hung up his brushes, he had ducked so much he had developed a permanent forward lean. Now when she lit in on him hard, he automatically stooped over a few extra degrees, with his shoulders all hunched in toward one another and his arms drawn up like frozen chicken wings.

"If you'd done like daddy said, and took a job at the bat'ree plant back when they were hiring, I wouldn't have to scrimp like a pauper," Letha fired in his direction the instant she entered the room, as if testing to see if her pilot light was lit.

"That was in '69," Odell mumbled. "They shut down years ago."

"Guess I'll have to get Lurie to buy me lunch again," she said, not acknowledging his muted reply. "It's so embarrassing being the poor sister," she went on, glancing in the hall mirror and fooling with her hair. "Could have been working at the bat'ree plant, but I reckon making big money was too good for my man. Rather paint houses. Guess if I want a new dress, I'll have to borrow the money for it from Lurie, too," Letha added, cutting him a hard look.

"Not that poor," Odell mouthed to her back when she swung about to grab her purse.

"Got beans on the stove. Don't let 'em cook dry. Hear me?" Letha demanded, her index finger pointing straight at him.

She didn't wait for an answer, turning about and stepping back to the mirror. With the flat of her free hand, she fretted with the bottom edge of her hair where it flipped up in a loose curl, trying to get it to stay to suit her. Her hair kept falling back, threatening, it seemed, to unroll all the way to her collar. "I swan," she moaned, disgusted. "Reckon I'll have to get a new curling iron while I'm out. My old one's done bit the dust. Won't stay hot two seconds." Giving up, she took a step toward the screen door. "There's Lurie now. Be dark before we get in. Gonna see that new Tom Hanks movie after we're done shopping."

And she was out the door and gone. In one minute and seven seconds—just long enough for Odell to dig his old, paint-speckled work boot out of the closet and grab some cash from under the insole—he was gone, too. Three minutes later he slid onto a stool at the nearby Hideaway Pub and Cafe.

"Give me a cold draft, Joe," he said to the man behind the bar. "Been working up a thirst all morning."

Chapter 24

An ambulance quietly pulled up in the street. Two paramedics soon relieved Greg's crew from tending to Mrs. Witherspoon.

At the rear of Rescue 1, firefighters were taking up the five-inch supply line, reloading the bulky sections in the hose bed. Sticks walked off to the side of the slowly backing truck, guiding the engineer with hand signals, keeping him centered. Two other men were working ahead of the loaders, dragging a twin-roller along succeeding 100-foot lengths, wringing the water out.

Probie Wan turned around to a view across the backyard. Engine 7 was in the alley. Behind it, firefighters were draining sections of a preconnect, paying line over their shoulders as they walked. He hadn't realized the engine was there, or another handline had been stretched. Mick noticed him staring.

"Exposure protection," Mick said.

"Huh?"

"Tactical progression," Mick answered.

Probie Wan thought for a moment. Then a light came on, dimly.

"You mean like with RECEO?" he asked.

"You're not as dumb as you look," Mick deadpanned. "Explain how we followed it here."

Probie Wan concentrated a long moment. Finally, he tentatively offered, "Exposures. You told me to hit the house first. Wanted me to cool it down because it was exposed to the fire."

"Hope you didn't tear a ligament in your brain coming up with that." Mick shook his head. "Okay. It's also why 7 pulled a line, to protect this house and the other house."

"What other house?"

"Far side of the hedge," Mick answered, his eyebrows rising in frustration.

Probie Wan looked at the overgrown hedge running alongside the drive, for the first time noticed a roof rising above it only a few feet away on the opposite side. "Oh," he said.

"But it wasn't the first thing we did," Mick kept at it.

"Huh?"

"You *huh* me again, and I will hit you with an ax," Mick snarled. "What's always the first priority?"

"Rescue," Probie Wan answered confidently.

"And?"

Probie Wan thought for a moment. "I don't get what you're asking," he finally said.

Mick didn't say anything in return for several seconds. When he spoke at last there was a sadness, a tone of resignation, in his voice.

"No way I can crack a head like yours with just an ax. Gonna need a sledgehammer, too. We had a rescue here, right off the bat. Did you not notice?"

Probie Wan's empty gaze said, "Help me."

"Captain Buckman?" Mick leaned in. "The elderly lady?"

"Oh yeah," Probie Wan finally nodded. After a moment he added, "That qualifies?"

"I imagine. She was in danger, right? All rescues are not packing somebody out of a burning building or swinging off ladders and snatching up babies, Tarzan. Lord amercy. I'm afraid to ask you about the rest."

"What's up there, Mickaroni?" a tall man in department coveralls interrupted as he came walking up the driveway toward them.

"Nothing but the rent, old man," Mick replied, taking a step forward and extending his hand. Their handshake quickly turned into a hug. Stepping back, neither seemed embarrassed by their show of affection.

"Met Probie Wan here?" Mick asked.

"Yeah, had his bunch a day in training," the tall man replied. "May the force be with you," he said to Probie Wan, grinning broadly as they shook hands. "Need it with this guy."

"Bull," Mick snorted. "I watch over him like he's my own grandma. Now you and I were the ones who needed some force, back in the day." Turning toward Probie Wan, he explained, "Me and old Rich—alias Cinder Dick—came on the job together."

Rich noticed Probie Wan's confused expression and cut Mick off.

"Great uncle was a railroad detective, a cinder dick. Cinder for the coal slag from steam locomotives; dick is old-time slang for detective. Let it slip to motor mouth here, and he can't get it out of his head. People with good sense just call me Cinders."

"Yeah, yeah," Mick started up again. "A Rich by any name. You're still an investigator. Anyhow," he switched tracks, turning to Probie Wan, "we rode the same truck for two years. Somehow the town didn't burn to the ground, and we personally rescued Tiny Tim."

"Oooh, Tiny," Cinders shivered. "Had to bring him up, didn't you? All 991 pounds? When he went to sliding off the bed toward me, thought sure I'd die a pancake. Why I went into cause and origin."

"He was a nice un, alright," Mick laughed. "Your eyes were big as his mouth."

"We should have got medals," Cinders shook his head. After a moment he added, "C'mon, let's do the grand tour before you stir up more old crap. I'll wind up back in counseling."

As they inspected the damage to the building, Mick told how things looked on arrival, then briefly explained their actions fighting the fire. Winding down, he pointed at the car's trunk.

"Yep. It's a handprint," the fire investigator nodded, studying the trunk. "Juvenile."

"Where?" Probie Wan asked, speaking sharper than he meant. The investigator did not take umbrage, gathering his thoughts first, then patiently explaining. Firefighters who could discover what he was looking for made his job easier.

"Thumb's a little smudged," he pointed, "but the fingers look good. And over here, paint's a little shiny underneath. All around is grimy looking. See?"

"No." Probie Wan hesitated. "Oh wait, yeah. Even through the soot it's different."

"Looks like a butt rub to me," Mick grinned.

"Yep. Sure does." The investigator paused a couple of moments. "These boys been coming here awhile," he said at last, casting his eyes over the floor.

"How do you know?" Probie Wan was fast becoming enthralled by the detective work.

"Well, there's one, two, three—" Cinders was eyeing different spots on the dirt floor as he counted, "six cigarette butts. And in this corner," he squatted down, "is number seven. What's left. See? Doubt two boys would smoke seven cigarettes on the way to school."

Probie Wan squatted beside him and stared. Suddenly he saw number seven. Though burned black and shriveled, there was no doubt he was looking at a cigarette butt.

"People don't realize things survive," the investigator said. "Now, if I was a kid," he continued, talking softly to himself as he rose to his feet, "where would I hide my matches?" He glanced toward the firefighters. "Kids don't generally carry matches or lighters. Mama finds 'em in the wash just one time, there's hell to pay."

He began looking under cans on a head-high shelf. Moving an empty quart mason jar out of the way, he came to a can of nails. He tilted it and peeked under. Flashing a grin toward the pair, he pulled a plastic baggie from his pocket. Holding the bag open next to the edge, he scratched around on the shelf with his pen until he suddenly flipped a matchbook inside.

Mick gave a quick chuckle. "Guess you'll be going back to school."

"Yeah, soon as I take some photos and stretch a little caution tape," came the reply.

Chapter 25

11:58 a.m.

B e back in a few," Katie said to Sylvia, thumbing her purse strap over her shoulder.

Sylvia looked up from her Subway sandwich, managed to mumble around a mouthful of lettuce and grilled chicken, "Take your time."

A minute later, Katie started her car. She waited a bit for the air conditioning to get a leg up on the noonday heat, then pulled out of her space and into the lunchtime congestion on the boulevard. The only problem with her business was where it was located. It was a catch-22. Traffic meant people, and people meant more business. She was accustomed to fighting her way through it, though. No big deal. Her little car was easy to maneuver, and she had Tom Petty on, playing "Running Down a Dream." No problems. She would be at the jeweler's in no time. The town square was only 10 minutes away, even in the midday mayhem.

She smiled to herself, anticipating the look on Tom's face when she gave him his anniversary gift. He would love it, she was certain, and he would tell her how much he loved her for thinking of him. Those words from him were just as certain. Her smile widened. She was as completely head over heels for him as ever. How often had she told their children to care for someone with all your heart was the only important thing in life? With love everything else would take care of itself.

Before she knew it, she was there. She zipped into a parking spot and hurried inside, propelled by anticipation.

"Hi, Katie," Mr. Hendershott said, glancing up at the tinkling of the doorbell. He slid the glass closed on the back of a display case, his rearranging of the rings inside completed.

Straightening, he smiled at her. "Come in out of this heat, little flower, before you wilt."

Katie laughed at his name for her as she stepped toward him. It was what he had called her all those years ago when they first met, when she and Tom had come shopping for wedding bands. He had seemed an old man then. Now he appeared, well, ancient. He reached a mottled hand across the glass top—the skin paper thin, translucent—took her hand in his and squeezed ever so gently.

"How are you today, my child?"

She smiled at his words. Here she was, charging hard at 50, and this sweet, old dear always made her feel youthful. No wonder she and Tom had been loyal customers all these years, though, in truth, they had not purchased much. What they had in the way of nice jewelry however, they had always acquired at Hendershott's. It was simple. They trusted him.

"I am fine, thank you. And how are you?"

"Wonderful. I continue to be blessed." He paused a moment, an impish grin appearing, before adding, "Are you ready to see?"

"Yes," she replied quickly, unable to hide her anxiousness.

"I shall get Tom's watch then," he said.

She shook her head in wonder as Mr. Hendershott padded noiselessly to the rear of the little shop. His knack for remembering names was simply amazing, the mark of a good businessman. He hadn't seen Tom for a long time, and she didn't think she had said his name when she brought the watch in for repair. In a moment he came padding back. With a little flourish he placed a small box atop the glass, then slowly lifted the lid.

It was beautiful—more beautiful, she thought, than when she bought it all those years ago.

"My, how it shines! Gorgeous, just gorgeous."

"It is an exquisite piece," he said, lifting it from the box and passing it to her. "Wonderful craftsmanship. Keeps perfect time."

After a moment she turned it so she could see the back.

"And the engraving. How did you do that?" she asked. "The new matches perfectly with the old." Not hearing, or even expecting an answer, she continued, "I am so glad we added the last word. 'With all my heart,'" Katie read, "'still.'" She suddenly glanced up at Mr. Hendershott, her eyes glistening.

The ancient gentleman leaned forward, whispered conspiratorially, "I suspect he already knows."

"He better!" Katie snapped, laughing. "Oh, he will be so happy."

"Then I, too, am pleased," Mr. Hendershott said, a smile creasing his lips.

Chapter 26

12:09 p.m.

James Henry allowed the Benz to coast forward. Up ahead he spotted his connection's car, a sporty silver Audi, parked on the far side of the picnic shelter. Then he spotted the man, literally, the man, seated atop one of the picnic tables inside. As James Henry eased into a parking space close by, his connection didn't so much as turn his way. James Henry waited, casting glances to the sides, checking his mirrors, trying not to move his head too much when he did, afraid that alone would attract attention. On the picnic table beside the dealer was a soda can set on a paper napkin. James Henry's eyes kept coming back to it.

After a minute the man turned slightly his direction, one hand pressed against his thigh, and gave a discreet thumbs up. *Don't get anxious, now,* James Henry thought. He did one last 360, consciously trying to slow his breathing, satisfying himself that no one in the park was close, no one was watching. He opened the door to the Benz.

The dealer slid off the table and took a step toward him, his hand extended. They greeted each other with a handshake, their free hands both clapping the other on the shoulder, for all the world like two friends who hadn't seen each other in ages. James Henry passed him the folded cash in the handshake. They talked but a moment, then the man moved on to the Audi.

James Henry started to sit down at a table as the Audi backed out. Suddenly he shook his head, acting like he had just noticed the soda can, and instead of sitting, sidestepped a pace and picked it up. A pouch of white powder was beneath the napkin. As he ambled over to the trash can he palmed the bag, then slipped it into his pants pocket. The Audi was rolling away at an easy pace atop another rise, passing a city parks pickup in the grass alongside the tennis courts. *Tax eaters hiding out,* James Henry thought with disgust.

He was back inside the Benz in two minutes. That was the really hard part, doing everything like there was no reason to hurry once he had his stuff. He had looked up high into a nearby oak for an instant, shading his eyes from the noon-time sun as if he were watching a squirrel or something. Then he had stood another moment beside his car, hands on hips, apparently taking in the view from the hillside, before finally pulling the door handle.

Never again, he thought. This light of day crap was for the birds, and he had done it two days in a row. *Enough!* Of course, both times were because his special lady friend was coming to visit, which took some edge off the risk worries. Nevertheless, meeting on a quiet, dark street, making the exchange through the drivers' windows, that was the best way. But today's deal was done now. He was safely inside. James Henry did a slow look around. Nothing had changed. Satisfied, he pulled out his wallet, laid a credit card and a $100 bill on the dash. Using a slick-covered prospectus on the South Third project, he sprinkled out a little powder, gave the mound a quick chop, formed a line. In an instant he had the bill rolled tight. He bent forward, snorted.

"Yeah," he sang aloud.

"Yeah," Kurt Leachman, the narcotics officer behind the wheel of the parks truck said, snapping away with the camera. "These are gonna look real good in court."

"Asshole couldn't wait," his partner, Bryan Congreaves, noted as he lowered his binoculars. After a few seconds, the Benz backed out of the parking spot and turned away from them. Congreaves raised the radio mic to his lips. In a couple of crisp sentences, he communicated the need to stop the Benz to a uniformed officer. The patrolman was parked in his black and white on a side street near the park's west gate for just such contingencies—stopping drivers who might be in possession or under the influence of narcotics.

Three minutes later patrol officer Dusty Williams keyed his mic as the Benz rolled past the intersection with his side street.

"Suspect in sight. Initiating pursuit," he said as he swung out of his hiding place in a line of parked cars. At the corner he spotted the Benz, already almost a block away. He glanced at his warning lights switch, thumbed it on, and started to pull out onto the main street.

"Where did they come from!" He yelled to himself as he suddenly stomped the brake pedal. No more than 15 feet in front of him, a young woman with a small boy in tow was strolling along the crosswalk in the direction of the park. She turned her head and smiled at him, mistakenly believing the flashing blue lights were meant to protect them. It took only seconds for the pair to clear the way. That was enough. By the time Officer Williams was able to go racing down the street in pursuit, the Benz was nowhere in sight.

Chapter 27

1215 Hours

See you, Mick," Cinders said, stepping around the firefighter rolling a section of hose. At the sidewalk he met Captain Buckman and Mrs. Witherspoon. The captain was scribbling on a clipboard. She had been dizzy, the lady said, what with all the excitement, but she felt okay now. The investigator took a moment to explain what he had found and to promise her he would be in touch. She suddenly reached up, grabbed him around the neck, and kissed his cheek.

I got one, too, Captain Buckman mouthed to him, beaming. Then he and Mrs. Witherspoon started walking toward the house.

What a shame, Cinders thought. Someone, some kids, he was certain, had just destroyed part of this sweet old granny's life. It was how he thought of it. People who caused fires didn't only destroy property, they burned holes in lives. Well, he couldn't fix what the flames had taken, but he could durn sure let the ones who had started them know they had stepped in it.

A few minutes later he pulled into a visitor's slot in front of West End Elementary. Before he could get out of his department vehicle, a white sedan glided into the spot next to him. The two police detectives inside turned his way. After a second, the one in the passenger seat nonchalantly flipped him off. He returned the gesture. Yeah, these two were okay, for cops.

"What's up there, Cinders?" the flipper asked Rich once everyone was standing outside their cars. "Thought you fire boys had your remedial reading classes this time of day."

"Got a tip some hoodlums here were aiming to torch the Krispy Kreme," the investigator answered. "Figured you might want to come over and bust them up some."

"Shoot, they won't let us do stuff like that anymore," the second detective said. "Besides, I love kids."

"Yeah," the flipper chimed in. "Especially if you dip their little heads in icing and top 'em with sprinkles."

The inane conversation went on for only a moment longer. Then the fire investigator gave them a serious briefing. As they made their way to the front door of the school, each man was thinking the same thing. Fathers, all three, they were hoping they never had to make a similar trip because of something their kid had done. Inside, the school resource officer led them to the principal's office. The voices of hundreds of elementary students eating lunch, in full uprising it seemed, floated into the room. The resource officer turned and closed the door, somewhat muting the roar from the riot.

"And to what do we owe the pleasure of this visit?" the principal asked without cringing, knowing full well it could not be good to have these men in his office. He had been at the job long enough, however, for little to surprise him.

"Had a garage burn over on South Sunrise a little while ago," the fire investigator began. "Think a couple of boys smoking caused it. Might have been students here."

"Got any smokers among your kids?" the detective who loved kids with sprinkles asked.

"Only about half," the principal replied with a straight face.

"Most of them don't do it in class," the resource officer added.

"These boys were probably a few minutes late for school," the second detective said.

"Victim believes they live in the 1,000 block of Oliver," Rich added.

"Now you're narrowing it down to things I can work with," the principal nodded, smiling a stern professional administrator smile; the kind which does not portray mirth, only a twinge of disappointment.

Chapter 28

12:27 p.m.

Katie took the box out of the bag, opened it, and took one more look at Tom's watch. Mr. Hendershott was right. It was an exquisite piece. *Oh, to see the look on Tom's face!* After a moment she started to put it back in the bag, but something made Katie hesitate. *Maybe,* she thought, *there will be an opportunity to look at it again on the way back to the shop.* A stoplight or two was bound to catch her, which would give all the chance needed. It was childish, but why not? She placed the box on the passenger seat, its lid open. Canting her head to the side the least bit brought Tom's watch into view. "That's better," Katie laughed aloud, turning the key.

The noontime traffic was heavy on Porter Pike, as usual. People who worked downtown traveled it in droves on the way to lunch, for there were dozens of restaurants in the district. Katie glanced at the clock in the dash. There was enough time to grab a sandwich if she went to a drive-thru window. There was an Arby's half a block on the right at the next light. She'd get something there and take it back to eat at her desk. The traffic signal up ahead turned red. Katie came to a stop a few cars from the intersection in a line of traffic and flipped her signal for a righthand turn onto Broadway.

James Henry was laughing, too, though not at himself. He felt like a million bucks. No! He felt like $10 million. Maybe a $100 million. *Yessirree. Nothing like being on top of the world.* It was all so easy, the money—how his clients bought what he said, especially the old geezers—and the women. The women sought him out. Who could blame them? After all, he was good looking as original sin, and a success in business. Plus, he knew where to get all the cocaine anyone could ever want. What was not to like?

Man, the view from up here is great. James Henry nodded. *Nothing like a little noontime pick me up to get the old blood racing.* Sure, he was flying, but wasn't that the point? He giggled, then giggled at how silly he sounded giggling, then giggled again. "Wonder how the poor people are doing today?" he said aloud, then lost it, laughing his head off. "Tax-suckers," he added a moment later, feeling a flash of fire. He pressed the gas pedal down, felt the big engine sling the Benz forward.

Suddenly it hit James Henry. He had an appointment with the Montague's at 1 p.m. sharp. Audie was not one to be tri-fled with. Twice already he had told James Henry he would gladly take his business somewhere else if he didn't think he and his wife, McKenzie, were being treated like they were at the top of his list. And they were list toppers! The Montague's were loaded to the gills: old money. Audie hadn't touched the handle of a shovel or a hammer in his life. He didn't know either from a boomerang. Taking the time to learn what they were for, even had he been so inclined, would have interfered with the counting of his coins. And McKenzie? She came from old money, too. Truth be known, her family had a greater fortune than Audie's. No, James Henry couldn't afford to risk alienating the couple. He glanced at his Rolex. *Not a problem.* He could make it back to the office with an easy five minutes to spare. His foot pressed down harder. Seven or eight minutes would be better.

The light just ahead turned red—something which momen-tarily escaped James Henry's attention. He finally saw it, though, when he was only yards from the intersection. Spurred by pangs of panic at the fear of being late for his meeting with the money bags, James Henry floorboarded it. He was focused on the far side of the intersection when the first car crossed in front of him—a near miss, made nearer by his lack of reaction.

His laugh at the close call hadn't passed his lips when a second car appeared mere feet beyond his hood ornament. He cut the wheel hard to the right, every muscle drawing tight for the coming impact. Nothing. Somehow, miraculously, he had avoided a collision.

James Henry's eyes followed the bumper of the second car a split second as he shot past. He still had not touched the brake. His hands held the steering wheel in a hard-right turn, so now he was nearly 70 degrees off his original line of travel. Finally, returning his attention to the front, he saw a car filling the span of his windshield. The sound was like a bomb exploding.

Chapter 29

1228 Hours

Probie Wan was content. He had done alright, pulled the line according to the book, worked the nozzle with accuracy and efficiency, even got a little feel for the hunt. Now the low growl of the engine—without the accompaniment of sirens and horns—was actually soothing. He and Mick were in their jump seats. Engine 4 was on its way back to the station. Probie Wan allowed his bent knee to rest up against the diesel's cowling. It was hot, but not so hot he couldn't leave it there. The vibrations coursing through the metal sent warm waves through his leg. He glanced over at Mick.

Mick smiled back at him. Yeah, this kid had the look. He could see himself 10 years back in the probie. The boy didn't know what he had walked into, but he knew he liked it. Mick remembered the feeling. Hell, he still had it! He was anything but sentimental, but suddenly he hoped Probie Wan would feel this way, also, after he had been on the job 10 years. Yeah, the kid had done okay. Just the same, it was a good time for a lesson.

"Ass kicker, ain't ya?" Mick asked, nodding at Probie Wan.

Probie Wan grinned back, a wide toothy grin. He didn't say anything. His face said it all.

"You did good," Mick said.

"Thanks," Probie Wan nodded slightly, keeping his response low key, in accordance with custom.

"One thing you need to keep in mind, though."

"What?" Probie Wan felt a sudden knot in his stomach.

"You've got a right to be proud, maybe even happy about what you did, but our little old lady just lost something special to her. Doubt it's the worst day of her life. Probably not even close. It's a bad day just the same, though, so she's not seeing things the way you are. Okay?"

Probie Wan had been warned back in recruit school about being careful with his expressions, with how he acted on a scene. For the first time he understood, because of Mick's words making it personal, something of what the instructor meant.

"Hold off until we're back in the station?" he asked, nodding in response to his own question.

"Yeah," Mick agreed. "At least until you're back on the truck. Now, we were talking about the RECEO sequence before we were rudely interrupted. Remember? Gimme the CEO part."

"Confine, extinguish, overhaul," Probie Wan answered with confidence. He had to grin to himself about Mick. The man had been studying so hard for the promotional exam he couldn't hold everything in. Without realizing it, he was compelled to share his knowledge, to teach.

"Well, I'll be hanged with a new rope," Mick grinned. "You got it. Anything else?"

"The ladder guys ventilated. Ventilation and salvage come in wherever they're needed."

"Give that man some bugles," Mick grinned, easing back in his seat. "We got us a chief."

Ringgggggg!

Tones followed hard after the bell, sounding through the speakers. The dispatcher began her litany.

"Rescue 1, Engine 4, respond to an injury accident with entrapment, intersection of Broadway and Porter Pike. Repeating, Rescue 1, Engine 4, respond to an injury accident with entrapment, intersection of Broadway and Porter Pike."

"We're close." Captain Buckman had twisted part of the way around to speak directly to the pair. "Probably beat EMS, maybe the cops, too. Rescue 1's right behind us," the captain added, then turned back. The siren and the air horn blared their usual insistent racket as Mick and Probie Wan worked in the cramped cabin to get their bunker coats and helmets back on.

Chapter 30

12:31 p.m.

The door swung open, the little bell above it announcing someone was entering the shop. From behind the glass display cases of wedding and engagement rings, Mr. Hendershott looked up. A smile, warm and welcoming, spread across his face. Another smile of a somewhat different kind of happiness warmed him inside. Anniversaries were so important to his business.

"Hello, Tom," the old jeweler said. "It has been such a long time."

"Hello to you, sir," Tom answered, smiling in return. "Looks like the years have treated you well."

"I have been blessed," Mr. Hendershott answered, nodding slightly. "In so many ways."

Their period of small talk was necessarily short lived. Though they had transacted business between them several times over the years, their relationship did not extend further. After a few moments Mr. Hendershott asked the question successful merchants inevitably ask of those who cross their thresholds.

"How may I be of service, Tom?"

Tom nodded at the question, the thought the jeweler had not inquired about Katie flitting through his mind. A bit odd. He always made over her so.

"Looking to get something for Katie. I was thinking maybe a new watch. Can you show me what you have?"

"Certainly," The old man said, smiling inside once more. This time it was in recognition of the unexpected vagaries with which life turns.

Chapter 31

1231 Hours

A re you okay? Lady, are you okay?"
It was a child's voice. She was confused. Why was a child, an excited boy-child, talking to her? She knew she had been in a wreck. The noise had been deafening. Now, other than this child's voice, it was so quiet, so peaceful, so eerily peaceful. She opened her eyes. There were shiny little granules on the dash. She could see them through the haze. Why was it so foggy?

The fog was slowly dissipating, however. As things began to come into sharper focus, she could see it wasn't fog. The sun seemed to highlight every grain in a cloud of fine dust as it floated over her. She hurt—her neck especially, and her ribs. Oh, it hurt to breathe. She managed to bow her head slightly. *God Almighty! That was painful.* What was it about her leg? It didn't look right. She couldn't make out most of it. She dared not bend her neck any further, but there, just above her left knee, just where the door pressed up against the flesh of her thigh, her leg was turned at an angle to the left. It was almost as if another knee joint, one which worked sideways instead of forward and backward, had somehow been inserted there.

"You'll be all right, lady," the boy-child said. "They're coming. Hear the sirens? They're coming."

D. J. slowed the engine as he neared the intersection. He had been to a ton of wrecks and knew what he was looking for. The first thing was to make certain he didn't park downhill of the accident. That's how you could get yourself and your truck incinerated if a flow of gasoline came tracking down the slope to you. He had other considerations popping through his mind—shielding the site from any vehicles that might come rolling in, threatening both victims and rescuers; leaving enough space for a line to be pulled, should the captain call for it; parking far enough ahead for Rescue 1 to be properly positioned. It would have the lead here, would need to be closest, for this was obviously an extrication job—the little car had really taken a lick—and every step saved lugging the heavy Jaws-of-Life equipment was important. Not incidentally, driving past the scene gave the officer an opportunity to survey more of the full picture before anyone exited the cabin. D. J. stole a second glance at the little car, saw long hair.

A few yards beyond the conglomeration of wrecked vehicles, the outbound lanes canted slightly uphill. D. J. steered for a spot on this slope.

"Engine 4 to Dispatch," Captain Buckman said into the radio mic.

"Engine 4."

"Engine 4 and Rescue 1 on the scene. Two-vehicle accident with injury. This is Broadway Command," he added, establishing he was in charge of operations and all further radio transmissions from Dispatch were to go through him.

"Engine 4 and Rescue 1 are on the scene," the dispatcher answered. "Engine 4 is Broadway Command."

D. J. brought the truck to a stop, setting the parking brake with a loud whoosh of air.

"Give me a preconnect with foam," Captain Buckman ordered in a voice strong enough to be heard over the dying siren.

The four doors to the crew compartment swung open, as if operated by one lever, and the crew spilled out.

"What's with these crazy sons of bitches?" James Henry said aloud as a second fire truck made its way around the Benz.

He was still in his vehicle. Blame air bags scared the crap out of him. Why had they gone off, anyway? Then he remembered the physical shock, the blast of sound. He even remembered the merry-go-round swirl of sight as the Benz spun out. Now he was stopped in the opposite lanes, the car headed back the way he had come. There was a small car turned sideways just a few yards in front of him, its passenger side smashed against a utility pole. He gazed through the windshield. It was not unlike watching a movie. After a minute he realized there was someone in the car, a woman. He could see her hair.

"Ignorant bitch!" James Henry shouted. "Pulled out in front of me!"

Then James Henry noticed the hood of the Benz had waves in it. The hoods of Benz's were not supposed to have waves. At this point he got really mouthy.

"I'll kick your ass!" he screamed, trying to find the door handle in the mass of deflated air bags.

Glancing up, he saw a white-helmeted firefighter striding his way.

Chapter 32

1233 Hours

The scene was becoming noisier by the second, with sirens from approaching emergency vehicles reverberating off the surrounding buildings. Donnie, a firefighter/EMT on Rescue 1, worked his eyes back and forth over the pavement before him, looking for fuel or motor oil or anything else which could be of concern, before he set the medical jump kit on the pavement beside Katie's car. A teenage boy stood close-by, fidgeting from one foot to the other. When Donnie made eye contact the boy mouthed, *Her leg,* as if fearful Katie would hear if he spoke aloud. Donnie nodded, and the kid quickly disappeared. Both front and rear driver's-side doors were smashed inward, their window glasses shattered. Donnie stepped forward, raked some glass granules off the windowsill of the driver's door with his sleeve, and leaned his head inside to talk to the driver. From close behind he heard Greg call for the spreaders.

"Ma'am. Can you hear me, ma'am?" he asked, performing a quick scan of what he could see of her body. No obvious severe bleeding. The door was caved in against her, but he could make out her left thigh, the odd angle inches above the knee. *Broken femur. Worrisome. Lose a lot of blood quickly with a torn femoral artery.* Katie started to slowly turn her head toward him but stopped short and groaned.

"Need some help with C spine," Donnie barked over his shoulder. "My name is Donnie," he said, switching immediately back to a conversational tone. "I'm an EMT. I'm going to hold your head still. Okay?" he asked, carefully placing his latex-gloved hands to cup her head firmly on each side. He noticed a swelling distorting her left eyebrow. She had taken a blow to the head. *Possible concussion, brain injury.* Nothing he could do if that were the case. *Move on. ABCs—airway, breathing, circulation—first.* "This is just a precaution, ma'am. We don't want you to move your head. Okay?"

"I'll get the C spine" Greg said, appearing at his shoulder.

"Thanks, Cap."

"Give me a second."

Greg quickly stepped around the rear of the car to see if he could get in from the passenger side. A glance revealed it was out of the question. The car was crushed up against a utility pole. Hustling back to the driver's side, he tried the rear door handle, but the door was stuck, too damaged to move. Next, he attempted to swing a foot up through the broken window, but quickly determined he wasn't limber enough in his bulky gear to make the move. Deciding on the only reasonable choice left, Greg leaned through the window opening and bellied his way into the back seat. Moments later he slid his hands along Katie's jawline from behind, moving them in place just below Donnie's.

"Got it," Greg said.

"Okay," Donnie answered, moving his hands away from her head and returning to his assessment. "What's your name, ma'am?"

"Katie. Katie Johnson."

Airway seemed okay. Next, he watched her chest for a moment, glancing a couple of times at his watch to get her respirations rate. Breathing was labored and shallow, as if she were consciously trying to control it. He reached for her wrist, laid two fingers on the inside below her thumb, looked at his watch again for a few seconds. *Rapid, thready.*

He pulled back and dug a hand into the jump kit, came out with a blood pressure cuff and a stethoscope.

"I'm going to take your blood pressure. Going to put the cuff on your arm, okay?"

"Ummm."

Donnie wrapped the cuff quickly, pumped it up. He placed the stethoscope disk on the inside of her arm at the elbow, listened as he bled off the compressed air: *88 over 46. Not great.* He left the cuff on her arm so he could check her pressure again in a minute. Any drop would be a sign that things were going the wrong way.

"Where does it hurt the worst? Can you tell me exactly?"

"Ummm. Neck."

"Alright. In a moment we'll put a collar on to help stabilize your spine. Can you move your fingers?"

Katie slowly wiggled the fingers of her right hand, then her left.

"Very good."

"Can you wiggle your toes?" Donnie asked, glancing down to watch. He could only see a little bit of her left foot—there was too much of the crumpled door protruding inside—but he could make out the toe-tip of her right shoe moving a bit, as well as her leg. "Good," he said.

"Where else does it hurt?" he asked, moving on.

"Side. Hurts to breathe."

"Is there anything else?" Donnie prodded.

"Leg—left leg—not bad as my side," Katie exhaled.

"Alright, Miss Johnson, we'll have you out of here in a few moments," he said.

"Katie," she breathed. "No one calls me, Miss Johnson." Somehow, getting her name right seemed important. She tried to focus, needing something to hang onto. Of course, she knew she'd been hurt in a wreck. Where had she been? *Lunch? No.* Where she was going when the wreck happened. Then it came to her. "Watch. Tom's watch."

"Ma'am?" Donnie didn't understand the reference.

Katie tried to twist around to face him. "Oh, God! My side!"

Probably some broken ribs, Donnie thought. *And with her hit hard enough to break ribs, no telling what else was messed up inside.*

"This side, Katie?" Donnie caught himself. *Accuracy!* "Your left side?"

"Like a knife," Katie moaned.

"Okay. That's what I needed to know. Don't try to move." Donnie answered, trying to sound reassuring. He was momentarily ticked at himself for not nailing down which side was hurting at her first complaint. You never knew. Out of the corner of his eye he saw an ambulance pulling up beside the rescue. A few feet away, the other two members of his crew were hooking up the hydraulic lines to the Jaws spreader.

"Can I take a quick look at your eyes?" Donnie asked, leaning in until their faces were only inches apart. He looked at her left eye first, then the other, shining a tiny pin light into each for a couple of seconds, watching the pupil for reaction. Both pupils were equal and reactive. Good. "Can you see okay?"

"Yes."

"Any dizziness, nausea, anything else?'

"No."

All good. He'd make certain to note the bump above her left eye when he briefed the paramedics. As he moved back, Katie spoke.

"My leg is broken, isn't it?"

Donnie hesitated. It was her leg. She had a right to an answer. He leaned back in.

"Yes, ma'am," he said, much of the detached, professional tone gone from his voice. It was a moment for empathy.

"Thought so," Katie replied weakly. A few seconds passed before she asked, "Bad, isn't it?"

Again Donnie hesitated. This time he sensed she wasn't talking only about her leg. True, she could be bleeding seriously, blood pouring into the large muscles of her thigh. No apparent swelling was hardly definitive. There were other things to take into account, such as she almost certainly had broken ribs. Internal organs were possibly injured also, and her spine might be compromised.

"You have some significant injuries, Katie." Donnie leaned in a little further and rested his arm along the window opening before he added, "But we are going to have you out of here in no time. You are going to be okay," he added, instantly regretting the words of optimism, though hoping he was right.

"Thank you," Katie answered, slowly reaching across to pat his arm. "Thank you, Donnie."

Donnie took her hand in his and squeezed it gently. He continued to hold it as he stood up straight and took a look around.

The paramedics were rolling their stretcher toward them.

From inside he heard Greg explaining to her it would get loud in a few minutes when they started removing the door.

Chapter 33

1233 Hours

James Henry found the handle and was just swinging the door open when the firefighter in the white helmet came to a halt beside his car.

"You okay, sir?" Captain Buckman asked.

"Yeah, I think so," James Henry answered.

"Not hurting anywhere?"

"No, uh, just a little turned around."

"I'll have someone check back with you in a moment. Okay?"

"Whatever," James Henry replied.

Captain Buckman was already striding away. His two firefighters were almost done stretching the handline. As he passed by the pair, he grabbed Mick by the shoulder. "Soon as you're set up, break away and check on the Benz driver. Says he's all right, but make sure." Mick nodded in confirmation as the captain went marching off again.

The captain made a quick circuit of the scene, completing his size-up, then finally settled on a spot at the rear of Rescue 1 where he could watch the operation as it unfolded. He hadn't seen any smoke or any indication of a fuel leak, nothing sparking. In fact, he hadn't found anything of particular concern, other than the passenger side of the lady's vehicle was pinned against a utility pole. The pole appeared stable and the wires hanging from it looked to be holding securely in place, but the electrical crews would confirm everything. A radio transmission from the captain to Dispatch initiated the notification process to the utility.

Now he started making mental notes of the positions of each first responder. Greg was in the back seat of the wrecked vehicle, performing C spine immobilization. Donnie, one of the firefighter/EMTs from Rescue 1, was leaning through the driver's door window of the wrecked car, assessing or treating the driver's injuries. The engineer and the second firefighter/EMT from Greg's crew were just completing the hydraulic line connections between the power unit and the jaws spreaders. A police officer had arrived while the captain was making his circuit and was now directing traffic around the wreck. An ambulance had rolled to a stop on the other side of the rescue. Though he couldn't see D. J., he could plainly hear the diesel revving up on Engine 4, so his engineer must be at the pump panel. He glanced toward his two firefighters, confirming the handline was stretched and charged. As he looked, he saw Mick lean toward Probie Wan.

"Remember, open the nozzle all the way so the foam will work right, okay?" Mick said to Probie Wan. "I got to check on this other driver. Anything happens, I'll be right back." Mick stepped over to the jump seat door on their truck and climbed up on the running board. In a moment he hopped down with the medical kit. Probie Wan turned his attention back to the wreck.

He had been handling his nerves fine, so long as Mick was there. Now it hit him just what his role was. If there was a fire it would probably happen in a flash, especially if it involved gasoline. All it took was a little leak, a spark, and a ball of flames could engulf the car. Extinguishing the car wasn't what had him concerned. It was all the people, the lady driver, the crew of Rescue 1, the paramedics who were just now rolling their gurney up close to the wrecked vehicle, who would likely be in the fire. Suddenly his gaze was so locked on the wrecked vehicle he was scarcely aware of anything else around him.

D. J. heard the second police car arrive on scene, its siren working intermittently, but he did not see it. He was looking, instead, at the Benz. There was something familiar about this car. He had seen it before. Suddenly the memory was there. This was the fruitcake who blew through the red light in front of him this morning. *Well*, well, he thought, *didn't take long for the idiot's number to come up.*

Turning back to his pump panel, D. J. checked the gauges and control handles to make certain all Probie Wan had to do was open the nozzle if he needed foam. He swept his hand under the small stream of water running out of an uncapped outlet to make sure it wasn't hot. It was a habit of his, flowing a few gallons a minute to keep fresh, cool water coming into the pump. A loud voice interrupted just as he completed his inspection.

"Not putting that damned thing on my arm!" D. J. glanced around to see the Benz' driver waving his finger in Mick's face. Not that Mick needed any help looking after himself, but in the manner of sergeants everywhere, D. J. wouldn't tolerate someone messing with one of his crew. Mick and the Benz' driver weren't 20 feet away. The sergeant/engineer covered the space in a heartbeat.

"Put your finger down or you'll be doing your own prostate exam," D. J. ordered as he came to a halt a step away from James Henry.

James Henry looked puzzled, but he slowly lowered his hand.

"Now what seems to be the problem?" D. J. asked, the heat gone out of his voice.

"I know my rights! You can't touch me," James Henry answered, his voice lilting up and down as he worked to hold in his anger.

"Huh," D. J. scratched his chin. "New one to me. Course, we're firefighters, so we don't know all that rights stuff." Finished scratching, he turned to the other firefighter. "Alright, Mick. What's going on here?"

"He said he was feeling a little dizzy, so I told him I'd check his blood pressure. A second later he goes into a full-blown rant about I can't touch him. Heck, I never even got close."

"Did you hit your head in the wreck?" D. J. asked, turning back to James Henry.

"No, I didn't hit my head!" he answered, the sarcasm practically dripping from his lips. "Only thing hit was my car by that bitch."

D. J. and Mick rolled their eyes at each other.

"I'm telling you right now, nobody better lay a hand on me. I've got friends in City Hall. I'll sue your asses," James Henry barked, leaning toward the firefighters. "Nothing but another bunch of tax-sucking bastards!"

Suddenly D. J.'s face was inches from James Henry's. He wasn't looking him in the eyes, however. His attention was focused a bit lower. Then he raised his face enough to where he was looking at James Henry, eye to eye.

"Those your real teeth?" D. J. stage whispered.

James Henry leaned back in confusion. D. J. followed, leaning in further, patiently waiting. At last, James Henry answered.

"Yeah. Why do you—"

"Wanna keep 'em?" D. J. cut him off. When James Henry didn't reply, D. J. turned toward Mick. "Hey, I just remembered, isn't one of those rights something about keeping silent?"

"I believe you're correct, sir." Mick answered, happy to be part of the act. D. J. caught a glimpse of movement a few feet behind Mick. He canted over to the side to see better.

"Well, would you look who's coming. It's my old cousin, the po-lice-man. What's happening, cuz?" D. J. asked as the officer came walking up. "Want a powdered doughnut?"

"Don't start—" The officer stopped short to stare at D. J., not understanding why he was touching his upper lip with his fingertip. Then he noticed his cousin was cutting his eyes toward James Henry, so he turned to face the Benz driver. It took a moment, then he suddenly caught sight of the cocaine mustache on James Henry's upper lip. "I guess Aunt Nell didn't drop you on your head as many times as we thought," the officer said, flashing D. J. a quick smile. Then he returned his attention to James Henry. "Turn around and put your hands behind your back." The sounds of handcuffs being snapped into place quickly followed.

As D. J. and Mick walked back toward Engine 4, they heard the officer say, "You have the right to remain silent."

"Didn't I say that already?" D. J. asked Mick.

Probie Wan was beginning to relax. He had watched closely as the crew of the rescue used the jaws to tear apart the hinges on the driver's door. When the door came loose, one firefighter grabbed it at the top of the window frame and carried it toward the front of the car, where he left it leaning against the fender well. With room to access the victim, a group of paramedics and firefighters carefully immobilized the lady's broken leg, then moved her the minimum amount necessary to secure her on a spine board. Next, they lifted the spine board out and placed her on the gurney. In moments, she was loaded in the back of the ambulance with the two paramedics. Donnie spoke quickly to Greg as he shut the unit's rear door, then hustled around to the driver's compartment and got in behind the wheel. Probie Wan was not surprised. He had been told firefighters were sometimes called on to drive an ambulance. It was an indication the victim had serious injuries, for both paramedics were needed to provide treatment. The siren came on as the unit pulled away.

Chapter 34

12:58 p.m.

S he'll love it!" Tom said, looking up from the watch to smile at Mr. Hendershott.

Tom returned his gaze to the watch. Silver, with a ring of small diamonds encircling the face, a simple slender bracelet for a band, it was beautiful without being pretentious—her kind of jewelry. He was pleased with his choice, but also relieved. Uncharacteristically, it had taken him forever to make up his mind.

"Elegant, classic," Mr. Hendershott nodded. "I am certain she will be pleased. Had you thought to have something engraved on it? People often do, especially for anniversary pieces."

Tom hesitated a moment, thrown off by the anniversary comment. Had he mentioned he wanted the watch for their anniversary? He couldn't remember. Surely he must have, he finally concluded. Even Mr. Hendershott couldn't be expected to have that good a memory.

Mr. Hendershott, meanwhile, was pretending to look closely at the watch's back, having realized the instant he spoke he had let something of importance slip.

"Yeah," Tom got around to answering. "I believe I would. How long will it take?"

"I should think it would be ready by tomorrow afternoon, provided what you wish to say is not too lengthy," Mr. Hendershott smiled. "The lady who does our engraving will be here in the morning. I would do it, but my eyes are not what they used to be."

"I understand," Tom replied. "Tomorrow afternoon will be fine."

"And what would you like to say? Take a while to decide, if you wish."

Tom thought for only a few seconds.

"A heart," he began, "with an arrow through it. And inside the heart, the number 25."

"Excellent," Mr. Hendershott nodded. It actually wasn't bad, he thought, but then again, it did not matter to him. He was but the provider.

Tom extracted his wallet and dug out a credit card. A minute later he was ready to go, having already folded the receipt and placed it behind Katie's picture, before returning the wallet to his pants pocket.

"My pleasure to be of service," Mr. Hendershott said, extending his hand.

"Thank you, sir," Tom replied as they shook. "I'll see you tomorrow afternoon."

As he slid in behind the steering wheel, he noticed his cell phone in the little cubby hole just beneath the radio. It was where he kept it while he was driving—he hated it in his back pocket when he was seated—but he always took it with him whenever he got out. Oh, well, so he forgot this one time. He turned the key and was just about to back out of the slot but caught himself. Better check, he figured. He had a 1:30 with the construction manager on the school job. Best to be certain nothing had come up before he drove to the site. He retrieved the phone, looked at the screen. There was a message from his daughter.

Where are you? Mom in accident. ER, Memorial.

Chapter 35

1304 Hours

I'll touch base with you after the holiday," Cinders said as he closed the door of the unmarked car. "Get our paperwork lined out."

"Sure thing," the detective answered, taking a glance at the two watery-eyed kids in the back seat. "Sucks, don't it?"

"Yeah," the fire investigator nodded. "No fun. Never is with kids."

"Poor Tim," the detective shook his head. "Your thing about the brand they were smoking broke it loose. Ha," he added mirthlessly. "*Where'd you get the Marlboros?* Melted him right down in his socks."

Cinders gave a weak half smile.

"Wish they were all this easy," he said.

"Don't we?" the detective answered, pulling his door open. "Sure you don't want to ride downtown with us? Say hello to the proud parents?"

"Would, but I gotta see a man about a dog."

From inside the unmarked car the other detective called out to him.

"Later, Cinders."

"Later, Sprinkles."

Chapter 36

1:07 p.m.

Katie hurt all over. Her neck and side were killing her. So was her left leg. Even before she asked Donnie about it, she knew it was broken. There was a picture in her mind of what the break looked like with that strange turn of her thigh. It was a horrible sight in a distant, detached kind of way, like the picture was something she had seen on television. The child had been at her window, reassuring her, when she glanced down and saw the crazy turn. She hadn't screamed or called out in pain. She simply looked down and said to herself, *My leg is broken*, as if she were talking about a fingernail. Now, though, the pain was there. Katie tried to scream, but all she could voice was a low, moaning whimper which in itself was painful to hear.

As they wheeled her through the ER, Katie caught only glimpses of people. Some were talking, others appeared briefly alongside, touched her, were gone. All of them seemed so serious, in such a hurry. Then she was in a big room with an overhead light so bright she had to squint her eyes. She felt her clothes being cut away and tried to cover herself with her hands, but her movements caused her to cry out in greater pain. Things were being stuck to her skin. A hand cradled her arm as something sharp pressed into it. Another needle? Strangely, she barely noticed. It was but one more straw on the pile. A worrying thought intruded.

"Shaneesha," she whispered the name of the paramedic who had tended to her during the ambulance ride.

"Ma'am?" a woman in a mask asked, bending over Katie so their faces were only inches apart.

"Shaneesha? Need to tell her—" Katie said, her voice dropping in volume with each new syllable.

"Mrs. Johnson, my name is Katie, like yours. I'm one of your nurses. What do you want to tell Shaneesha?"

"Tell her—my husband's watch—"

"I'll tell her, Mrs. Johnson."

Then there was a man's face close above her, also covered in a mask. A surgery cap hid his hair. Dark eyes met hers.

"Katie, I'm Dr. Phillips."

How could eyes smile so? she mused.

"You've been seriously injured. We need to operate. Do you understand?"

"Yes," she managed to say. Then a black wave of unconsciousness washed over her.

Chapter 37

1:13 p.m.

Audie rose to his feet and made his way across to Destiny's desk as if he were carrying a king's crown in a coronation ceremony. He was so stiff and straight, so obviously full of himself, it was all Destiny could do to keep from laughing. The Montagues were always this way, pompous to the point of absurdity. Their attitude, like their money, was inherited, having made its way down through generations. James Henry claimed most of their cash remained in pounds and shillings.

Mrs. Montague, 70, painted up like she was half her age, had not lifted an eyelash when her husband stood. No words passed between them. She simply continued to flip through the pages of her magazine in slow rhythm, as if showing true interest in what lay inside was beneath her. Audie stopped before Destiny's desk. He took a moment, visibly composing himself, before speaking.

"Have you heard from James Henry?" he asked, knowing full well she had not. He and his wife had been seated in the small waiting area for 20 minutes. If the phone had made a noise they would have noticed.

"No, sir, I have not. This is not at all like him. He is always so punctual," she lied. The piece of whale shit had been late for half of his appointments during the last six weeks. She was no idiot. He wasn't the first user she had known. Probably laid up with some skank, both of them stuffing their noses. "I'm certain whatever has detained him must have been unavoidable."

Audie tilted his head back slowly, moving it in tiny, evenly spaced increments. After a moment, Destiny imagined she could hear the clicking of gears inside his neck. Audie didn't stop until he was looking straight down his nose at her.

"I am not a man to be trifled with, young lady."

"Oh no, sir. You have my utmost respect."

Audie continued to stare, though he did not speak again for several seconds.

"I am correct our appointment was for 1 p.m., am I not?"

"Yes, sir. It was."

"Time is money, and I waste neither. Would you please so inform James Henry?"

"Absolutely, sir."

"Very well," he said, as if Destiny had just confirmed he was no ordinary mortal. "McKenzie, dear, let us leave this place."

As McKenzie Montague crossed the floor to her waiting husband, he held his hand toward her at a ridiculous level, nearly shoulder high. She reached up and lightly grasped his fingers. Together they moved toward the door, each step seemingly choreographed, the prance of the high born. At the threshold they paused. Audie spoke to Destiny, not bothering to turn and face her.

"Our solicitor shall be in touch. We shall transfer our funds to a firm where the proprietor can decipher the positions of the hands upon a clock."

Chapter 38

The haul chain was securely attached, the smashed car was out of gear, the fire trucks had just pulled away. The winch made a low electrical sound as Chuck laid a gloved hand upon a lever and started pulling the car up on his rollback wrecker. All the cops were waiting on was for him to get loaded and out of the travel lanes. He would make a quick sweep with the push-broom after he had the vehicle tied down to clean up the broken glass and strips of chrome from the pavement, and he would be out of here. Then the cops could finally thin out the lines of backed-up traffic.

The car's rear wheels were hardly clear of the pavement when something told him to take one more look inside. A watch was missing. Everyone had searched for it—firefighters, cops, him—and no one had found anything but the jewelry store bag laying on the front floorboard. They said she was begging them to keep searching as they rolled her to the ambulance. He had arrived too late to see her, but they said she was hurt bad. *Maybe,* he thought, *that's what's scratching at my conscience. Maybe I can relieve her of a worry.* Chuck had been doing this work a long time. He knew how important seemingly little things could be for the victim, for the family: a pocketknife; a picture of a child in a wallet; a watch. Shaking his head, he moved away from the controls and stepped the few paces over to the car.

Chuck inched up on the slanted deck and leaned in the driver's side the best he could, which wasn't far because the firefighters had placed the detached door there. Scanning everything one last time with care, he saw nothing resembling a watch. Then he made his way around to the passenger side, braced himself on the metal deck and pushed his face up to the door glass. He cupped his eyes with his open hands to cut down the glare and looked. Nothing. As he carefully stepped toward the ground, Chuck paused by the rear door long enough to glance into the back seat. Something shiny caught his eye. He tried to wrench the door open, but it was jammed. He hurried around to the rear door on the driver's side. This door was jammed, also, but the glass had been broken out. He leaned in, stretched until only the tiptoes of one foot remained on the deck, reached down and moved a corner of a floormat out of the way. A watch box tumbled out from beneath the seat, and a man's watch was suddenly visible beside where the mat had been. How they found their way back there was anyone's guess. Maybe when he started hoisting the car up on his rollback, changing the angle, they had tumbled loose from whatever had held them.

After Chuck had wiggled his way out, he gave the watch a close look. The lens wasn't cracked or scuffed. He couldn't find a mark anywhere. The second-hand was ticking. Even the time seemed right. Satisfied all was as it should be, he carefully placed the watch in its box.

Maybe this will make her feel better, he nodded to himself. Without closing his eyes, he said a quick prayer it would. Chuck hadn't been in a church since he was a kid, but it didn't mean a man couldn't pray, he figured; and this job would make you say a prayer every now and then.

As if he were carrying the most delicate, precious object imaginable in his hand, he made his way over to the cop directing traffic closest to him.

"Here," Chuck said, his hand extended. "They said the lady was asking for this."

Chapter 39

1:15 p.m.

Odell stood on the sidewalk, staring at his front door, trying to decide if he should go in or maybe just sit down on the hot concrete. He was having some major difficulties with his cognitive functions. His downing of nine beers in two hours at the Hideaway were to blame. The total was exactly nine times his usual daily intake of alcohol, although, on rare occasions like today, when Letha was absent, he slipped down to the bar and had one or two. This day, however, the beer was ice cold, just the way he liked it, and went down smooth as branch water. He kept ordering one after another, and Joe, the bartender, kept bringing him one after another, until he leaned back to drain the last drops of number nine and fell off the barstool. At that point, Joe cut him off.

He seemed to remember bits and pieces afterward, although about the only thing the old, hen-pecked soul was certain of was going to the bathroom at the Hideaway before he left. Odell recalled with clarity his relief at finding the urinal. Some of the hazier bits and pieces consisted of lines scrawled all over the wall behind it. These were mostly names and phone numbers of ladies to call for a good time. A few of the good times were described in explicit detail. Though he had no memory of specific names or numbers, he had stood there reading those scribblings over and over until somebody pounded on the door and yelled, "Hurry up, buddy! My eyeballs are floating!"

Apparently, he had gotten out to the street without incident, though things were pretty shaky, literally. The walk home had been like watching an old movie when the sprockets on the projector are all out of whack, everything jumping and jerking and stuttering and going blurry, then suddenly snapping back into focus for a second or two. It was enough to wear a fella out. The way he felt now, standing on his walk, tired and sweaty and very much in need of a long nap, remained very shaky. He decided taking a nap was exactly what he'd do, just as soon as the steps made up their mind to quit their dancing and land in one place. A moment later they slowed down enough for him to charge forward. He made it up to the porch fine, though he did smash his shoulder hard against the doorframe when he went to high step over the threshold.

The couch beckoned to him like he figured one of the ladies listed above the urinal at the bar might. He made his way over to it, was about to sit down, when a jolt of electricity snapped him straight up, stiff as a fencepost. *Beans! Son of a—* Letha would kill him if he burned the beans. The idea he might be too late momentarily took enough of the edge away from his drunkenness to allow him to head straight to the kitchen. He jerked the lid off the pot.

"Yow!" he screamed, dropping the lid to rattle on the floor. He managed to skip-hop around it and thrust his hand under the faucet. The cool water soon eased his pain. It was a minor burn, anyway. He left the water running and moved back to the stove. *Thank the Lord! The beans look okay.* He picked up the wooden spoon Letha had left on the counter and stirred them around a few swirls, to make certain. Then he poured in a couple of big glasses of water, bringing the brown, soupy concoction almost to the top of the pot. A chunk of fatback bobbed around in a tight circle for a moment before casting out a sea anchor and slowing down.

"That ought to hold ya," Odell nodded toward the pot. He found a potholder on the counter near the stove and used it to lift the lid off the floor. Then he dropped the lid in the sink under the flowing water. After rinsing it off, sort of, mostly, he touched it quickly with a fingertip to make sure the mean thing had cooled down. It felt cool enough. Having been once bitten, however he still used the potholder to pick it up again. Without bothering to dry off the lid, he placed it back on the pot.

It was a lot of concerted focus and effort to throw on a man not accustomed to drinking nine beers in a row. His drunkenness immediately returned. Hand walking along the hallway walls, he set sail for the living room. A wobbling minute later, Odell finally made it back to the couch. He plopped down and reached for the TV remote. Somehow, he managed to remain only 10 or 12 degrees off plumb until he found a baseball game. Cards and Cubs? Didn't really matter to him who was playing, he just wanted some noise. He flopped over on the couch, stretched his legs out and wadded up one of Letha's embroidered pillows under his head. She wouldn't like him mistreating the pillow. He smiled to himself. She wouldn't like for him to be sprawled out on the couch with his shoes on, either.

"Go ahead and fuss all you want to," he said aloud, closing his eyes. Dutch courage fueled one last line. "My house and I'll do as I please." Odell was snoring a second later.

Chapter 40

1315 Hours

The officers had gone inside to start their reports as soon as the companies rolled into the station. Mick had headed toward the kitchen to see what he could do to get lunch ready once more. Since when the next call might come in could not be determined, the primary goal on returning to quarters was always getting everything ready for that next call as quickly as possible. Now in the engine room, the engineers and firefighters from Engine 4 and Rescue 1 worked with their counterparts from Ladder 1 to get the two apparatus back in order. It was mostly routine grunt work—firefighting 101—wrestling hose. One group coupled 400 feet of inch and three quarters into two equal lines and reloaded it on Engine 4, reconstituting its preconnects. Eight sections—another 400 feet—of wet and dirty hose was unrolled, rinsed, scrubbed, rinsed again, rerolled, and carried to the hose dryer in the rear of the engine room. The water in Engine 4's booster tank was topped off, as well as the fuel in the jaws power unit on Rescue 1. Air masks and hand tools were inspected and cleaned. Compartments were opened and checked to see if the proper equipment was in the proper place.

As the work wound down, individuals began to gather in a loose knot near the hose dryer. Ladder 1 hadn't been on the extrication run, so its crew members wanted to know the details. It fell to Paul, the engineer from Rescue 1, to begin.

"Right on top of it when we got the call. Little woman, mid-40s, in a little Nissan, older model. Big Mercedes T-boned her right in the driver's door; knocked her into a telephone pole. Looked like he was really trucking it, too. Mashed everything in. Donnie did her assessment."

"She's in pretty rough shape," Donnie picked up the story.

"Neck pain. Cap immobilized her C spine while I got her vitals. Wild-looking compound femur: right-angle turn. Said her side was really hurting, too. I'd guess some broken ribs. Took a bump on the head, but she seemed herself mentally. No telling what she's got messed up inside. Pressure was low. Pulse wasn't great, either."

Donnie paused a minute, allowing the information to sink in. Probie Wan noticed how the others briefly looked down or glanced away and saw it for what it was. The lady might not make it, and they knew.

"Straightforward door removal," Paul began speaking again after a few moments. "Me and Biceptual here," he said, nodding to a tall firefighter with huge arms and a chest like a linebacker, "popped the hinges. Then B-boy picked the door up with his pinkie and chucked it to the side."

Biceptual—whose given name was Maurice—yawned like he hadn't noticed Paul was talking about him, then gave it away by placing both hands behind his head and stretching, putting the fabric of his shirt at grave risk.

"Took all of us and the paramedics to get her on the spine board and out of there," Donnie began once more. "Tough to keep both her C spine and her leg immobilized while we moved her. Poor lady, she kept telling us to get her husband's watch out of the car right up until we put her in the ambulance. Never did find it."

He fell silent then. For a few moments the rest of the group remained quiet, also. Then Paul turned to D. J.

"Saw you and Mick up there with the other driver. He okay?"

"Why, of course," D. J. answered. "Not a scratch. Bona fide prick if there ever was one."

"Oh yeah?" Paul pressed.

"One of them $1,000 suit types," D. J. replied. "Mouthy fart. Blamed her. It's just like you said, of course. He knocked her into a light pole. 'Course, I wouldn't have even been up there if he hadn't jumped on Mick."

"What?" Willy, the engineer on Ladder 1, asked, his tone serious. "That's dangerous."

"Damn skippy," D. J. agreed. "Old Mick'll fight a circle saw. When golden boy went to shaking his finger in Mick's face, I knew the crap was about to hit the fan. Didn't have no choice but to get involved. You two would have done the same," D. J. asserted, glancing at first Paul, then Willy, the other two sergeant-engineers.

"Gotta take care of your boys," Willy agreed.

"Yep," Paul seconded. "Even if they're as big a moron as Mick," he went on with a straight face.

"Sure enough," D. J. nodded. "Shoot, I'd even take up for Probie Wan here," he added, patting the rookie's shoulder, "and we have to bring him inside every time it starts raining."

"Sad what they send us these days," Willy shook his head.

"Yes," Paul shook his head, also. After a moment he asked, "So, what set golden boy off?"

"Mick said he was just going to check the guy's vitals, and the next thing he knew the man went banana cakes and started shaking his finger in Mick's face. That's when I got involved. I wanted to tell him I'd break his finger off and stick it up his tooty hole, but it wouldn't have been professional."

"No," Paul agreed, shaking his head. "Got to be politically correct," he went on, then hesitated a few seconds before asking, "What did you say to him?"

"Said I would help him use that finger to examine his own prostate."

It took a moment or two for the thought to settle in and start all the firefighters laughing. None of the engineers, however, even cracked a smile.

"Well played," Willy acknowledged, maintaining a straight face once the laughter eased up. "Prostate problems being so common, I commend you for your concern about the gentleman's health."

"'Preciate it," D. J. replied. "Of course, it wasn't two seconds before he set in bitching about his rights and saying he was going to sue us."

"Don't you just love it when they start threatening?" Paul asked.

"Yeah," D. J. nodded. "Like I'm gonna whiz down both pant-legs. Hell, I go in burning buildings for a living. If you're scared, jump in my pocket," he added, rolling his shoulders. "Anyway, you know me. I had to get up close and tell him he had the right to remain silent. That's when I noticed something unusual."

"Oh?" Willy's eyebrows lifted.

"Then I looked over and here comes my cousin, the cop. You all know Donuts?"

Most of the group's members nodded they did.

"Well, I kind of hinted he ought to take a good look at the fella. Next thing I know he's slapping cuffs on him and telling him he has the right to remain silent."

"What did he see?" Biceptual broke in, unable to wait any longer.

"Hold your horses there, muscle head," D. J replied, exasperation in his tone. "I'm coming to it. You see, between his upper lip and his nose there was this kind of dusting of white powder. Even had it in his nostrils."

There was no laughter at this revelation, but after a moment smiles began to spread across the group. Willy finally spoke.

"There is a God."

"Attention!" Mick's voice boomed over the intercom. "Attention you heathen savages. Boot leather and rubber veggies are now being served in the crystal dining room. Proper attire is requested."

Chapter 41

1:16 p.m.

Tom glanced back at his vehicle. It was parked at an angle in the ER lot, the wheels on the passenger side over the dividing line for the adjacent space. *It will have to do*, he thought. Somehow, he kept from breaking into a wild run; somehow, he managed to think clearly enough that this was a time he needed to compose himself. Thinking the thought was easier than putting it into action. He was moving at a fast trot when he got to the sliding doors. After pausing an instant for them to open enough, he barged through. The young woman in Reception met his eyes as he rushed up to her desk.

"I'm Tom Johnson. Katie—my wife, Katie—she was in an accident. Can I see her?" He practically shouted his question at the last.

"Mr. Johnson, I think she's—"

"Daddy!"

Whatever bit of control he had been holding onto was swept away by the sight of his distressed daughter. In an instant they were in one another's arms, the tears beginning for both. Clarisse quickly regained her composure, though just barely. Seeing her father's display of emotion, however, tore at her. It was something she had witnessed only one other time—when her grandmother died.

His daughter's reaction steadied Tom. At 23, Clarisse was Katie made over, only a few inches over five feet, dark haired and dark eyed, and most importantly for this day, able to function in a crisis. Tom caught something of her self-control and held on tight.

"She's in surgery, Daddy."

He felt himself tilting, but a hand caught at his elbow before his knees buckled.

"Mr. Johnson."

A security guard was beside him. Tom felt the weight of an arm across his shoulders, the support of a hand beneath his elbow. The guard was a large man, a few pounds past prime and several inches taller than Tom. He had a great round face, flushed red as if he had been laboring under a terrible strain. Tom looked up into that face and saw concern. "We have our Prayer Room over here," the guard said, his quiet, easy manner in contrast to his appearance. He dropped his arm from Tom's shoulders, kept a hand on his elbow.

"Perhaps you and your daughter would like to go in for a few moments."

"Yes. Yes, thank you."

Clarisse grasping his free hand, Tom began to follow the guard's easy prompting. Suddenly he stopped.

"My son," he said, looking first at the guard, then at the receptionist, and finally to Clarisse.

"He's on the way, Daddy," Clarisse explained. "I got in touch with him. He was over in Glasgow, so it'll be a while."

"We'll bring him to you the minute he gets here," the guard said, shifting his hand to the small of Tom's back.

"Good, good," was all Tom could say as he began walking toward the room again. It seemed so important to have all their family together.

"Stay here as long as you want," the guard smiled as they reached the door. He shoved it open with his free hand and waited for Clarisse to enter, then gently ushered Tom in behind her.

"Thank you," Tom replied, pausing a minute in the doorway to look into the man's eyes. "We appreciate your kindness," he added, receiving a nod in return before the door clicked shut.

The room had a softness, an inherent warmth enhanced by the deep carpet covering the floor. A small stained-glass window let in light from high on the front wall. A Gideons' Bible rested on a polished wooden table beneath the window. Two short, padded pews guarded the walls along the sides. Above each a pair of sconces flickered pale yellow fans of light. It was as if Tom and Clarisse were in the sanctuary of a tiny church which, of course, was exactly the effect intended. Father and daughter stood together in the room's center for a moment, then suddenly fell into each other's arms. This time they cried unabashedly, cried until the knots of wrought emotions began to loosen and uncoil inside them. At last, they reluctantly untangled. "How serious?" Tom asked the question, not knowing if he wanted to know. He had tried to find out on the way to the hospital, but Clarisse hadn't answered his repeated attempts to reach her. "I kept calling, but—"

"They're afraid she's hurt really bad inside. Took her straight to surgery," Clarisse replied. "Sorry I couldn't answer the phone, Daddy," she continued, her voice suddenly quavering, "but I was talking to the paramedics, and the ER staff had so many questions, then there you were at the reception desk before I knew it. She paused for a moment, fighting back the urge to fall to pieces, managing not to say how scared she had been to be there all alone. Now the feeling she had let her father down was almost overwhelming. She pushed back just a little and from somewhere inside came a tightening of will. When she began speaking again it was with a detached tone, as if she were reading off a list. "They're worried about her neck. She has a broken leg. No doubt, some broken ribs, too." Clarisse stopped for a few seconds. "Her blood pressure's dropping. Bleeding internally, but they don't know where it's coming from."

It was more than Tom could wrap his mind around. Any one of those things could be too much.

"What happened?" Tom asked after a long breath, his voice wooden.

"A guy ran a red light on Broadway, at Porter Pike, I think. Hit her in the driver's side. It's all I know."

Tom simply stood there, lost somewhere in a place where everything was draped in a stifling fog. Clarisse was somewhere close by. That much he knew. He also knew he was in a prayer room, and he should pray, he needed to pray right now, but he wasn't sure how to go about it, at least not in these circumstances. Katie was the one who was religious. She had taken the kids to church every Sunday, to Vacation Bible School, to church camp. Tom believed. He simply chose not to participate in the public functions and displays of organized religion. He found it all tiring and pretentious.

On Sunday mornings, while the others in his family were at church services, he could be found at home with his feet propped up in his recliner, newspaper pages scattered about him, the television tuned to one of the talking heads shows.

Now he must do something. He must reach out for help. His Katie might be dying this very instant. For a long, empty, terrible moment he continued to stand there. Then he reached out without looking and caught Clarisse by her hand. He slowly dropped to his knees. Clarisse dropped down with him, her hand squeezing his.

"Our father, who art in heaven," Tom began, speaking slowly, reverently.

Clarisse listened in mild surprise. She had heard Tom say a blessing over a meal many times, but those prayers of thankfulness were about it. Now there was something new and deeply humble in his voice.

"Thy will be done," she said softly after a few moments, reciting the Lord's Prayer in unison with her father.

Chapter 42

1:33 p.m.

Attorney Stephen Grimes hung up the phone. He had friends in useful places. One of them had just informed him that a mutual acquaintance—James Henry—had really done it this time. It wasn't enough for James Henry to be coked up when they arrested him. It wasn't enough the police had observed him buying drugs, and they'd later found those drugs in his car. Those things alone could keep him locked up for a while. No, the greater problem was while he was high, he caused a wreck and injured someone. Hadn't he warned the man his life was spiraling out of control? Hadn't he told him he was going to have to slow down, that he was running too close to the edge? Those pearls of wisdom had been shared a month back at the benefit concert when he ran into James Henry, all glassy-eyed and spacey. Obviously, he hadn't listened. Then, 20 minutes ago, it had been Stephen's turn to listen when he took James Henry's pleading call for help.

Now that he had a better picture of the problem, it was time to get busy. He picked up the phone and rang a contact who worked in the Emergency Room at Memorial. It didn't take long to get the troubling report. Katie Johnson was in bad shape. She was in surgery. They'd taken her straight in.

He thought the name over for a moment. It was familiar. Then it came to him. Of course! They met at the benefit—the same one where he had stumbled into James Henry. Her husband was there with her. *Tom. Yes!* Stephen smiled to himself. Remembering people's names was something he was good at and took pride in. One other tidbit came to mind. It was Mayor Cashman who introduced them, a self-important blowhard if there ever was one.

Stephen focused, recalling everything he could about the Johnsons. They were businesspeople, he quickly remembered; late 40s—early 50s, and at least somewhat successful, or they wouldn't have been at the shindig; and, of course, they personally knew at least one local politician. None of this was good. The prosecutor's office was hardly disposed to deal when upstanding members of the community were the victims. It was human nature.

Okay, nothing to be done about any of those things. What else did he need to do right now? *Ah, yes. She should be alerted to the possibility of the police showing up. Besides, any excuse to speak to her was welcome. Who knew where the conversation might lead?* He pulled up the number for Secure Financial, punched the button. James Henry's secretary answered.

"Destiny, this is Stephen Grimes."

"Hello, Mr. Grimes."

In spite of their having met several times, and especially because he had hit on her—to no avail—during a few of those meetings, the attorney was disappointed to hear Destiny's reply sound all business.

Of course, he couldn't know it was exactly how Destiny intended to sound. The instant she heard his voice it flitted through her mind that the last thing she cared to do was talk to this pretty-boy lawyer again. How many times did she have to say no? Shoving the idea aside, she continued, "I'm sorry, sir. James Henry is not in. He should be back any time. Shall I have him return your call?"

"James Henry will not be back today."

He waited a moment to let the message sink in, imagining her breasts. She was built like the proverbial brick outhouse. James Henry said she was pure centerfold. James Henry was right. The thoughts spurred his intention, once he had addressed the business end of things, to ask her out again.

"I don't understand, Mr. Grimes." Concern softened Destiny's voice. Stephen found it attractive and sexy. She had a sultry lilt to her southern accent that made his palms sweat.

"He has been in an accident."

Is the sonofabitch dead? was the first thing Destiny thought to ask. *Probably not. Couldn't be so lucky.* Then another question popped in her head. *Did he get anything cut off?* She gleefully imagined the idea for a second, then said, "Goodness me! Is he all right?"

"Physically, I think he's okay. He's in jail, though."

"What?" she practically shouted. She immediately put her hand over her mouth, afraid she was about to burst into laughter.

"His vehicle collided with another."

Hope it was a concrete truck, Destiny thought, but she simply said, "Oh, my."

"The other driver was seriously injured."

Destiny felt a tinge of guilt about her earlier thoughts as she spoke. "I am so sorry," she said sincerely, and meant it, for the other person. A moment passed in silence before she added, "What can I do?"

It was time for him to think before answering. Later he would admit to himself that he had indeed thought, but not about the right things. What suddenly found its way into his mind was the idea of sharing a confidence. Perhaps this would result in a chance, an opportunity to expand the borders of their, uh, relationship. As soon as he opened his mouth, he knew he was taking a step onto treacherous ground, an area he normally avoided like the plague. *It will be okay*, he assured himself as men on the prowl have since their days in the caverns. Any risk was minimal, practically nonexistent. Besides, James Henry was a friend—sort of—and after all, she had asked how she could help.

"Well—now this is very important—I need you to check on something."

"Okay," she hesitated, biting her tongue at his suddenly condescending tone.

"You see," Stephen paused a moment, seeking the appropriate phrase. In the end, there was simply nothing to do but say it.

"James Henry was on cocaine when the accident occurred. An officer at the scene also found it in his car. That much I know. It is enough to make me believe the police may seek a warrant to search the premises. What I need you to do is carefully look through everything in his office for drugs. If you find anything, flush it down the toilet. Alright?"

Destiny waited a few seconds before answering. Apparently, this legal version of a rocket scientist didn't know she was taking law classes at night.

"Now, Mr. Grimes," she started, her voice smooth as melted butter. "I want to make certain just exactly what it is you want me to do."

"Sure, Destiny." Why did he feel the urge to crawl?

"You want me to search my employer's private office for illegal drugs—drugs which may be material to charges regarding serious bodily harm caused to another individual—and upon finding any such drugs to destroy them, and thus eliminate the possibility of their being discovered by the police and entered into evidence against my employer?"

She stopped there and waited. *So, this is what it's like to fall off a cliff,* Stephen thought. Half a minute passed before he tried to ease his way back onto solid ground.

"Well, now," he uncharacteristically stumbled. "I didn't intend to imply—"

"I must say," Destiny cut him off. "How shall I put this? Your suggestion has the feel of a solicitation to conspire in illegal activity. Why, I would think such a thing could cause one to lose their license."

"Now, Destiny, I—"

"Please do not interrupt me," she cut him off again.

Stephen knew he was lost and tumbling through black space, but her voice! With an effort, he managed to quickly control himself. It was a well-practiced reflex to her punch in his stomach. Such responses went with the job.

"I apologize," he said, hoping.

"I'll tell you what, Mr. Grimes," she started again, her voice as sweet as the proverbial pie, "should I discover any drugs in James Henry's office, I will give you a call to come over. Then you can flush both them and your own conniving ass down the toilet. That would save me the trouble of filing a complaint. Those can be such a bother. Have I made myself clear, sir?"

"Yes," Stephen answered through gritted teeth.

"Excellent. And when you see James Henry, please tell him I do so pray they put him under the jail, because that is where a brain-dead bastard like him belongs."

She gave him a moment to stew before she spoke again.

"Now, you will please excuse me, I'm sure," she cooed, her southern belle, *shuure*, the final nail in their conversation. "So nice to speak to you again, Mr. Grimes."

She hung up without waiting for an answer and immediately punched in another number.

"Hi, sweetums. I'm certain you've heard about poor James," she said, then paused to listen for a few seconds. "Why I'd just be tickled pink if they dropped by. You might let them know the humidor on his desk has a false bottom. Of course, you didn't hear that from me." She paused again. "Eight is perfect. I'll be waiting with bells on. Don't you let them keep you at that ole po-lice department too late and mess up our evening, okay? Bye now. Smoochy smooch."

Chapter 43

1:38 p.m.

Sweetums. Oooh, give us a kiss, sweetums," undercover cop, Kurt Leachman, said. The officer was seated behind the steering wheel of the parks truck. He leaned in close to his partner. "Smoochy smooch," the officer added through puckered lips.

"I got your smooches right here," Bryan 'Sweetums' Congreaves answered as he punched keys on his cell phone. "Might as well have the damn thing on speaker," he snapped, raising the receiver to his ear again. "Like trying to work with a pet monkey. Always sticking your nose in my business.

"Oh hey, boss," Bryan quickly switched to speaking into the phone. "Yeah, uh, on the James Henry thing. I just picked up some interesting info."

He listened for a minute, occasionally nodding his head. When he finally had a chance to speak, he ran off a full string.

"Sure do. Dead to rights on the buy, and you can see him snorting 30 seconds after he got in the car. Moron couldn't wait. Got good shots of it all."

Bryan listened again for a couple of moments.

"Unhuh. We wondered. Here 'bout every day." Bryan paused. "Uh, Loo, what I called you about. Probably find something in his office." He paused again. "Great. Tell them to check his desk good, especially the humidor. Got a double bottom." He stopped to listen one last time. "Now lieutenant, you know a good narc never gives up his sources," he said with a quick laugh and hung up.

"Doing a search warrant for his office, I take it?" Kurt asked.

"Heading to the judge right now. Loo thinks he might also be selling."

"Like we been saying. Friggin' idiot. Hope they find enough crap to bury him."

They were quiet for a moment, watching a Lexus cruise slowly by the picnic shelter.

"Loo say how the lady was?" Kurt inquired as the Lexus rolled out of sight.

"Rough shape. Sounds like 50-50," Bryan replied.

"Damn." Bad news was part of the business. Just the same, one didn't have to like it, especially when it involved a total innocent.

Several minutes passed without a word between them. Kurt finally broke the silence.

"Feel for Dusty."

"Yeah. Me, too."

Both officers fell quiet again, each thinking of the patrolman interrupted in his pursuit of James Henry, knowing the ensuing accident would haunt the man, though it was no fault of his own. A heavy minute dragged by. Once more, it was Kurt who spoke first.

"What's a humidor?"

"A fancy box where rich people keep their cigars," Bryan answered, glad to have his train of thought broken.

"Oh."

"Or in your case, suppositories."

"Hee hee. You know, I kept listening for her to say it."

"Say what?"

"The same thing all the other ladies you've dated said. You know? Something about a magnifying glass."

Bryan didn't answer. He was looking through binoculars at the Lexus, which was circling back again. Finally, he lowered the glasses, then pitched them in his partner's lap.

"What the hell?" Kurt shouted. He snatched up the binoculars and brandished them as if he meant to whack the other cop.

"Thought you said a while ago you had to take a leak," Bryan explained.

"I did. I'm 'bout to pop," his partner answered, reaching for the door handle.

"Take them with you. Keep from straining your eyes," Bryan added, reaching for the camera on the dashboard. Time to get a few shots of the Lexus.

Chapter 44

1402 Hours

Mick hung up the phone. Steph, an ER nurse and Margie's best friend, had been guarded with her assessment of the lady's condition. He glanced around the dayroom and kitchen. Scattered about, most of those who had been on the extrication call were watching him. Even Probie Wan, seeing the others stop what they were doing, had paused in his sweeping.

"Still in surgery," Mick announced. "Go either way."

No one made a comment, though a couple of firefighters shook their heads as they returned to what they had been doing. Probie Wan went back to his sweeping. Donnie finished cleaning the stove. Biceptual gave the last pan one more brush with a sponge, then dropped it in the rinse water. D. J. reached in and fished it out. He shook it over the sink for a few seconds, then dried it with a towel. Finally done, he took a step to the side and shoved the pan in a cabinet with a bunch of other pots and pans. Meanwhile Biceptual had drained and rinsed out the big double sinks. Together the two men quickly wiped down the countertop in the area, then started to walk away.

"I got 'em," Biceptual said. D. J. tossed him his towel. Biceptual walked on toward the laundry room to drop the wet washcloths and towels in a hamper.

The way at last clear, Probie Wan went to work around the sink, his one remaining area to sweep. Then he carried the broom down the hallway to a utility closet. He returned in a couple of minutes, pushing a wheeled mop bucket. A mop rode in the bucket, soaking in the sudsy water. It took him five minutes to swab the kitchen. He was careful to do a good job, like he was with all the household chores, not wishing to get his hind end ripped. It hadn't taken him long to get the idea anything less than a job done right brought the wrath of the other firefighters and the sergeants down on one's head. The officers seldom said anything or needed to.

Probie Wan returned the bucket to the closet, dumped the dirty water, and after rinsing mop and bucket both clean, hung the mop up to dry. Then he wandered back down the hallway to the dayroom, taking a position a few feet behind where the officers stood watching the television. The weather radar was on. A line extending almost straight north to south was off maybe 70 or 80 miles to their west. Behind the line individual storm cells trailed in long columns. Time lapse showed it all moving their direction. The crawler at the bottom of the picture was reporting potential large hail and wind gusts to 65 m.p.h.

"Rocking and rolling," Greg said. "Nasty looking."

"Intensifying," Captain Buckman noted.

"Gonna be an interesting afternoon," Sticks chimed in. "Wide line. Take a spell to blow through."

The battalion chief was standing a bit off to one side, hands on hips, his gray eyebrows canted inward in concentration. Though he was also staring at the screen, Batman waited a little while before commenting.

"Just got off the phone with Dispatch," he finally began. "They've got damage reports coming in from all over the area around Land Between the Lakes. Trees and wires down. Couple of mobile homes rolled over. That kind of thing. Had a little tornado spin-up, they think, outside of Cadiz. Too early to say. I told them to give me a call if they hear of anything major."

Batman turned then to face his company commanders. "You're right, Sticks. This thing is going to take some time to get through here. The way those storms are training behind the main line worries me as much as anything. Probably going to drop an ocean of rain on us. We all know the places where flooding usually blocks the roads. Running around those slows everything down, takes longer to get help if you need it. Not telling you anything you don't know.

"Still aiming to work with the stokes some?" Batman asked, looking at Greg.

"Yeah. Just a little refresher on rigging haul systems. Quick walk through in the engine room is all."

"Very well," Batman replied. He felt like there was more to say, but his officers knew their business. There was nothing of consequence to add. He returned his gaze to the weather radar on the TV. "I'd say we nailed it on the head this morning. Be hollering *Auntie Em* before you know it."

Chapter 45

2:05 p.m.

Robert opened his eyes to the sounds of babbling voices coming from the TV. He stared at the picture until it finally came into focus. *Good grief,* he thought. *Not another talk show. Where do they find stuff to talk about? They don't,* he answered himself. *At least nothing new. All they do was rehash what somebody else had already discussed.* He glanced about for the remote. It took him a minute to realize it was on his lap and another minute to find the on/off button. He didn't pay attention to the crawler line at the bottom of the screen warning about a Severe Storm Watch. There was always something running across the picture. Then the screen went black.

Grasping the recliner's handle, Robert pushed and slowly brought the chair up to a sitting position. Okay. Now he was upright, so what was he going to do? He didn't have any idea. He just knew he had to get up and move or he would sit and molder in his doggone chair until he was mummified.

That was the good thing about when he was working—he always had something to do. Then came retirement and Jean to fill his every void. What a joy he had found those days to be. Finally, the two of them had all the time a couple could possibly want to share. They never sat around in the middle of the day watching talk shows. There was always something to make them get up and go, be it a yard sale, a game of bridge with friends, a new exhibit at the museum, or a play. She loved school plays, especially those put on by the littlest ones. How she would laugh and clap at their performances, whispering in asides to him, "Isn't she the cutest thing ever?" or "I've never seen a smiling Scrooge, but he's adorable." No one ever seemed to notice how no particular child came running up to greet them afterwards. They could have been anyone's grandparents. Were a person to have paid close attention to Jean, however, they would have seen how she sought out the child who flubbed his lines or burst into tears when faced with her terrible stage fright. Those children inevitably found themselves in her embrace; heard her say how wonderful they were.

On warm afternoons they would often walk the two blocks to the ice-cream shop at the corner of Rosewood and have a cone. Butter pecan was Jean's favorite. He was a strawberry man, himself. No matter how careful he tried to be, he always managed to dribble some on his shirt. She always laughed when he did; always fussed a little about how she couldn't take him anywhere; always smiled her I'm-happy-just-being-with-you smile as she dabbed at the mess.

In the evenings they would sit in their porch swing, often for hours, simply talking. What a joy it was to discuss things with her. Politics, science, whatever was blooming, anything, everything, it didn't matter. She soaked up all she heard, all she read, could offer a considered opinion on practically any topic. It was what first attracted him those many years ago, her intellect. Of all the things he missed about her, simply sharing a conversation was the greatest.

Robert tried to figure out how long he had been sitting there. He didn't have an idea, not that it mattered. There was no place he had to be, no one he had to see. It was okay, regardless of how long the chair held him captive. At least he had been able to spend some time with her in his dreams.

With an effort, he scooted to the edge of his seat, then, with a greater effort, pushed to his feet. The mere act of getting up was getting harder every day. He guessed he would have to cheat, put a thick cushion there in the recliner's seat, like he already had on his kitchen chair, so he could start from a higher point. Yes, he would have to cheat. The fear of the time soon coming when he couldn't get up at all was ever present, nearly as frightening as his constant concern he might fall.

Robert took a slow step forward. Everything on the right side seemed to be in working order. He ventured a second step and found his left side functioned properly, too. Increasing his pace incrementally, he made his way to the refrigerator. He got the orange juice out, fished a small glass from the dish drainer, poured himself a couple of swallows. Done, he left the glass sitting there on the countertop, untouched. He ambled over to the side window and looked out at the yard, toward his adopted granddaughter's house—little Emily's house. There, almost midway between the homes, was his wife's yellow rose-bush. What a wonderful splash of pure color! Suddenly he felt a yearning for Emily to pay him her usual afternoon visit, the same yearning he had felt early in the morning, but more intense. How she would love the bloom.

As he gazed through the window, Robert realized he was smiling. Yes, he did have something to do today after all. Soon he would be showing a sweet, precocious child a gift of nature, a gift from his wife.

He lifted his gaze a bit, noticed the sky was somewhat darker to the west. Rain? Robert hoped it wouldn't arrive until after he—Grandpa Bob—had shown his grandbaby the beautiful flower.

Chapter 46

2:13 p.m.

Hammer and Chopper were scared to death. Every new part of the unnerving experience seemed to worsen their situation. First, there had been the ride to juvie. Neither one had ever been in a police car, never mind an unmarked one. There was something sinister about the idea. Being in a cell now did nothing to ease their worries. Maybe the blank-faced detectives who had arrested them would come back and haul them down to some dank and smelly dungeon and do something God-awful horrible, like hang them from chains and beat them with clubs; or maybe they would drive them way out in the empty country somewhere and dump them, leave them miles from home in the dark woods, where fanged monsters ate kids who started fires.

At least Chopper had those wild imaginings bouncing around in his head. Hammer, however, was close to being beyond imagining. Every noise made him jump, especially the sad, lonely sound of the jail's big metal doors slamming closed. He was ready to cry. He wanted to cry. Only his suspicion he would soon be locked away with a bunch of crazed maniacs kept him from boohooing. Something told him crying in jail was not a good thing to do.

"You idiot," Chopper said, glaring at Hammer. "If you hadn't ratted us out, we never would've been busted."

"They know it's us," Hammer whined. "They got our DNA off the butts. That fireman said so."

"He just made it up."

"How do you know?" Hammer snapped. Anger, even if it was directed at his partner, helped settle his nerves. "You know what it looks like?"

Chopper hesitated a few seconds before admitting, "No."

They wanted to believe what the fireman had said was a bluff. Both had watched enough cop shows on TV, however, to be convinced DNA evidence was something no crook could dodge. The science had them cold then. They were also young enough to believe lying was not allowed for adults in positions of authority.

Their parents, though, were exceptions. Thoughts of them slipped in and out of the boys' jostled minds. Chopper's father was a boozer. Like his mother, Chopper was so worn out from dealing with the old man's lying crap he didn't know what to believe. Hammer was in a situation every bit as warped. His mother was so looped on her meds most of the time she didn't know right from wrong, light from dark. No wonder his old man had split. Without spending a second talking it over, both boys reached the only conclusion either could. Help was not coming from the home front.

"That fireman said we burned the garage down." Hammer spoke, ending their reverie.

"I don't know how it could have started." Chopper answered, the puzzlement and worry in his voice sincere.

"He said we almost gave the old lady a heart attack. She was crying."

Chopper started to reply, but whatever he was going to say got all jumbled together and hung up in his throat. He had enough good clinging to his soul for the idea of the elderly woman being upset to tear at him. Thoughts of his grandmother, always so kind and loving, flitted through his consciousness. For a moment he imagined her hugging him, saying everything would be all right. Now he was the one on the verge of crying.

"My old man is gonna beat me to death," Chopper finally got out, his voice sounding weak and small, simply uttering what he expected to happen.

The door to their little room opened.

"Let's go, boys," the corrections officer said. He was a big man, his voice gruff. His eyes, however, pale blue and soft, seemed kind. Both boys looked into those eyes, found a thin strand of hope to cling to as they moved through the doorway.

Across the hallway the door connecting to the main jail swung open, and a second guard stepped out. He looked up and down the hallway, holding the door open wide.

"Seen Billy?" the man asked their escort.

"Last I saw, he was up front."

"Okay." The man hesitated, taking another look up the hallway, then down, as if Billy might suddenly appear, be beamed in somehow from up front. In the area behind him a racket broke out.

"You sons-of-bitches will pay for this! I'm James Henry! When I get out of here—"

"Oh, give it a rest, honey buns," a third man, unseen, said. His tone was tired and unsympathetic. "Only place you're going is the big house."

"Yeah, some greasy ape's going to make you his sweetheart," the jailer who was looking for Billy added, turning toward the open doorway behind him. "Call you sugar."

"Powdered sugar!" the unseen man corrected.

The laughter of both jailers filled the hallway. Then the second jailer stepped back through his door. It slammed shut with a loud *clang*.

Chopper's and Hammer's eyes met as their officer herded them down the long corridor. Looking back, Hammer managed to ask the question they both wanted answered.

"Where're you taking us?"

"See the judge."

Neither said another word. They didn't need to. Their eyes said, *Oh shit!* plainly enough.

Chapter 47

Meer-e-um, Meer-e-um, Meer-e-um," Emily chanted over and over, her arms held straight out from her sides, as she turned in slow circles near the spot of bare earth at the bottom of the slide. Miriam was climbing the slide's ladder.

"Em-ooh-wee, wook out," Miriam called from the top.

"What is it?" Emily asked, finally stopping her spinning. She wobbled in place a moment before she spotted Miriam. "I'm dizzy, Meer-e-um. Stay still?"

"Ready or not," Miriam announced. Down she started. She didn't pick up much speed. The slide wasn't very long, and she kept her hands on its sides, braking. Just the same, when she scooted off the end she bumped hard into a dizzy Emily. Both girls went down in a heap of flailing arms.

"You knocked me down!" Emily exclaimed.

"You knocked me down!" Miriam exclaimed in return as the girls struggled to stand.

"Do me! Do me!" Brandon exclaimed as he came running up.

"Me, too! Me, too!" Grayson pleaded as he joined the group.

"First you have to spin round and round and round," Emily said, "till your head gets all dizzy."

The other three were spinning in an instant.

"And stand here by the sliding board." She put her hands on each spinning child, in turn, and guided him or her to the proper location in line at the bottom of the slide. Then, wobbly still, Emily zig-zagged around to the ladder.

The three others were in danger of crashing on their own, when Emily called to them from the top of the board.

"Ready or not, here I come!" And she was off.

Like with her friend, Emily's downhill speed was not great

when she bumped into Miriam. Miriam bumped into bunny-head Brandon, who bounced off and bumped into Grayson. All three slow-motion crashed on the bare dirt at the foot of the slide. Emily, having managed to stay on her feet until then, purposely stumbled about a couple of seconds, then fell over on top of the pile of friends.

Ms. Woods and Ms. Gina, her assistant, didn't see the pileup. They were busy studying the screen on Ms. Woods cell phone. It showed the same line of bad weather approaching that the officers at the fire station had been watching a few minutes earlier. As they looked, the phone beeped loudly, then flashed SEVERE THUNDERSTORM WATCH across the screen.

Both teachers glanced toward the west. The sky was darkening ominously there.

"We'll get everybody inside in just a minute," Ms. Woods said, "soon as they burn off a little more energy. Okay?"

"Okay," Ms. Gina answered, not turning toward the older lady. Her focus remained on the sky.

Wild screams and laughter from the pile of kids at the foot of the slide made them both jerk their heads around. None of the original dizzy four had managed, or even tried, to get to their feet. Now other children, in ones and twos and threes, were flopping and falling onto the stack.

"Enough!" Ms. Woods ordered, clapping her hands as she strode toward the heap of kids. "Everybody up!" A rumble of distant thunder rolled through. She paused a moment to look over her shoulder at Ms. Gina. "That does it. Let's bring them in now."

Ms. Gina nodded and began moving to the far corner of the yard to round up the strays wandering there.

"On your feet boys and girls! Everybody inside," Ms. Woods demanded, reaching into the mass and grabbing a girl's arm with one hand, a boy's shirt collar with the other. "Oh, my goodness," she fussed, hoisting the pair of kids upright. She brushed her hand across the seat of the boy's pants. A cloud of dust arose, was instantly carried away in the breeze. "Look at you! Filthy. Just filthy. Your parents will wring my neck."

Chapter 48

2:15 p.m.

G et you another cup, Dad?" Jack leaned in close to ask.
Tom looked up at his son. *Dad, is it?* he thought. Jack had taken to calling him Pops since he started college this last year. He was a good one, his son, a little hardheaded, a little cocky and too sure of himself sometimes, but nonetheless a good person. Looking at him, it came to Tom his son was a man now. He was tall and straight, the teenage growth spurts of ever greater height had faded in the past, yet he had not stopped growing. No longer a skinny rail, his body was filling out. His thighs stretched the worn, dirty denim of his work jeans. The muscles in his arms and shoulders were tight and defined. All the growth came from working construction part-time this last semester. He and Katie had worried when Jack announced he was cutting back on his classes, but when Jack explained it was so he could work and keep his debt paid down they saw it as a welcome sign of maturity. If calling him *Pops* went with Jack's growing maturity, Tom figured, it was okay by him.

Now, though, when it was time to hang together as family, apparently Pops had gone by the wayside.

"No thank you, son. I'm fine," Tom answered Jack's question, offering a weak smile.

He was anything but fine. None of them were fine. Tom could see it in the faces of his children, knew their world must seem to be spinning backwards like his own. It didn't help restore any sense of stability being in the waiting area for the ER, where they held their own small corner against the incursion of a veritable Noah's ark of distressed humanity. Clarisse was seated on his left. Jack sat on his right, perched on the edge of his seat, bent slightly forward as if he might be called upon to spring into action, to rush at an instant to do something vital.

It felt strange, Tom thought, this clear return to the role of parent he had filled for 20-some years. Perhaps it shouldn't have. Their children had been gone from home barely long enough for him and Katie to realize the nest was truly empty. He stole a quick look at Clarisse first, then Jack. He liked to think he had been a good father to them as they grew, believe he had played a hand in shaping them. So much of their early lives, however, he was absent, consumed by his work. He was determined back then to provide well for his family, and he had, but there was so much he missed out on. Katie had been there, of course, somehow managing to fill all those gaps while she worked, too. Remembering, there was a sudden stabbing pang in his heart. It was not because of what he had missed. It was over how Katie had always been the one who held them all together.

Moments drifted past, Tom's mind drifting along with them. His thoughts eventually returned to Jack. So now he was Dad again to his son, Tom mused. Would miracles never cease? There was a time during Jack's teenage years when Tom had all but given up and come to assume his son was determined to bang his head into every wall in sight. There were a few instances when Tom would have gladly helped him with the banging. They had clashed often, a couple of times very angrily. Tom liked to tell himself now that challenging authority was just part of any boy's growing up, though down deep he reluctantly acknowledged Jack had pushed him right to the end of his rope. Tom shook his head. The biggest miracle of all might be they survived those days with their love for each other intact. *Dad?* He would gladly take the title if Jack wished to bestow it again, though he suspected it was transitory, applicable only in times of crisis now.

Clarisse, however, had never ceased called him *Daddy,*

though in contrast to her younger brother, she had seemed to be an adult most of her life. She was so like her mother— sweet, kind, understanding, straightforward in all her dealings, and when things were rocky, decisive. Three months ago, she had become engaged. How many times since then had Katie remarked what a wonderful mother Clarisse would be? Katie always spoke those words as a certainty.

Tom glanced over at his daughter once more. Without surprise he found he was looking not at a mature young woman, but at his little girl. She still held his hand. She had not turned loose since they recited the Lord's Prayer. This was the way she had been when she was a small child, and they went on a tour of Mammoth Cave. How old was she then? Five? Six? It did not matter. What mattered was she had been frightened. His daughter had been afraid of that great, dark, empty space, and she had reached out to him. She had grabbed his hand as they walked into the cavern's mouth and held on; held on until they at last emerged into the sunlight.

"Clarisse will be a wonderful mother," he recalled Katie's words again.

Tom looked down at his and his daughter's clasped hands. Realization struck him like a bolt. Their roles had reversed.

"I'm going to get another cup, Dad," Jack said, his hand on Tom's knee. "Could I get you something?"

"Yeah," Tom replied, relieved to have his chain of thought interrupted. "I'll take a cup. Black."

"Be back in a second," Jack promised as he vaulted from his seat, glad to have something to do.

Chapter 49

All right, Probie Wan, why do we need a tag line on the stokes during a hoist?"

"Uh, so we can maintain stability; keep it from spinning like a top."

"Did y'all hear him?" Greg asked, smiling for the first time during the drill. "Our little rookie got it. Ain't it amazing what you can do when you put your brain back in right after you're done playing with it? Let's show him our appreciation."

The comments from the rest of the group were all jumbled together.

"Smart ass!"

"Know it all."

Someone gagged. The three chauffeurs posed as a group and flipped him off. Biceptual farted loudly, somehow managing to change pitch twice.

"Damn it, you're rotten," Mick exclaimed, waving his hand in front of his face. "Muscle-bound freak. Need an air pack."

"Hey, don't blame me. You're the cook," Biceptual replied, sounding offended. He was grinning with pride, however.

"All right, men," Greg barked. "Let's break it down. Enough for today."

Greg wandered over to where Captain Buckman stood outside on the rear apron, feet braced wide apart, arms folded.

"Some things never change," the captain said, flashing a smile.

"No," Greg replied, assuming an identical stance. "Remember when you said the same thing to me, about putting my brain back in right?"

For a long moment, the captain simply stood there in place, though the smile had returned.

"Just yesterday," he said at last, almost whispering.

"Yeah, just yesterday," Greg agreed.

For a while they didn't say anything, simply watched as the men replaced the Stokes basket—a stretcher made of hard plastic and cupped to hold the patient—on Rescue 1 and removed the rope haul system paraphernalia from the tip of the aerial ladder. Probie Wan shucked out of his harness and dropped it into the rope gear bag. As the firefighters finished stowing the equipment and went wandering away through the station, the two officers turned their attention to the western sky.

"There's our leading edge," Greg finally said, staring at the dark mass growing across the horizon.

"Looks ugly," Captain Buckman commented.

"Be rolling soon," Greg opined.

"Yeah. Like you said, some things never change."

The look on each officer's face appeared to signal a decided indifference to the approaching menace, but such was hardly the case. Members of sports teams would have instantly recognized the true meaning, for they know such expressions well. The time for practicing has passed. Let the game begin.

Chapter 50

2:35 p. m.

Thank you, Your Honor," Detective Wilson said as he slipped the search warrant into the inside pocket of his jacket.

"My pleasure," Judge Snodgrass replied. The reply set the detective back, for the old, crabby judge would have usually said, at the most, "You're welcome." Even those mild words would have been delivered in a voice like a bear growling. Of course, the detective didn't know James Henry, that slimy little eel, had practically bankrupted his honor's favorite aunt. "Good hunting," the judge added to Wilson's further surprise, a quick smile lighting his stern features.

Less than 10 minutes later, Wilson and his partner stepped through the doorway to James Henry's business to the accompaniment of a loud roll of thunder. He walked straight to Destiny's desk, reached inside his jacket, and produced the official document giving him permission to prod and poke anywhere within the specified confines.

"I'm Detective Wilson," he said, laying the warrant in front of her. Outside the storm suddenly hit with a roar of wind-driven rain. Water pounded the roof and windowpanes. Wilson was forced to wait to be heard. "And this is Detective Boards," he finally added as things eased up a bit, pointing with a thumb over his shoulder at his partner.

"Ma'am," Detective Boards responded drily.

"I'm Destiny," she smiled coyly, offering her hand without rising.

Both detectives, in turn, briefly shook hands with her before Wilson began speaking once more.

"This is a search warrant, uh, Destiny," he said, trying to keep his focus on business. Given her looks, he was finding it difficult. "We are going to search these premises."

"Whatever you must do, gentlemen," she nodded, not offering to so much as glance at the warrant. "May I be of service in any way?"

Her voice sounded like a warm caress. Wilson didn't stop breathing for all that long. In the interim, Detective Boards spoke up.

"Mr. Henry's office in here?" he asked, gesturing toward the inner door.

"Yes, it is," Destiny cooed.

Boards opened the door and stepped inside.

"Thank you, Destiny," Wilson flashed a smile. He picked the warrant up from her desk and fumbled a few seconds before finally managing to get it situated back in his jacket pocket. "We will let you know if we need anything."

"Got a key for this desk?" Boards bellowed from James Henry's office.

"Why yes, I believe I do." She opened her top drawer, found the key in an instant, and handed it to Wilson. Their fingers briefly touched.

"Thank you again," Wilson said, his smile beginning to morph into a teenager's goofy you-sure-are-purty grin as he reluctantly moved toward the inner office. He was out of sight when his voice came back to her. "Sweetums says hi."

Chapter 51

2:48 p.m.

Lemme have your books," Cody Cox said, extending his free arm.

"I'm okay. I don't have but a couple," Angie replied.

In spite of her words, she let him take them from her arms when he made a move to scoop them away. His attempt was awkward, as it had to be, for he had his own books in one hand, plus a gym bag over his shoulder. He managed to balance her texts for a minute, but the covers were worn slick with use. The history book slid off the top. He dropped her trig book trying to catch it.

"Shit," he exclaimed loudly.

"Mind your mouth, Mr. Cox," Coach Bronski admonished him in a voice equally loud. The coach stood watching from the other side of the drive bordering the student parking lot. A sudden gust of hard wind scoured the gravel and sent a dust devil spinning off from directly behind the man.

"What the..." Cody wondered for the briefest moment if the coach had somehow conjured the little whirlwind on his own. Then he thought how stupid the idea was. As the dust devil hop-scotched across the school's lawn, it suddenly dissipated. Cody's mind wandered back to Angie. He immediately felt his face burning. It was bad enough to drop her books, but to have Coach bark at him again, and in front of her. Was the man stalking him?

"It's okay, Cody," she said, kneeling beside him. "You've got your hands full already."

Angie liked it when he did nice things for her, such as carry her books. She also liked how he was a bit clumsy at times. Cody could catch a football one-handed, running, jumping, doing cartwheels, yet around her he was often a bumbling, stumbling fool. She really liked when he did goofy stuff, for she knew she was the reason. It was part of what made her love him. She picked up her trig book. Reluctantly, he handed her the history text.

"Don't know why we even have to come back next week," Cody fumed. "Three more days and we're out. And who gives homework on prom weekend, anyway? Plus, there's a holiday Monday."

"I'm just taking these home so I can study for finals a little," Angie said as she began to stand up.

As he rose beside her, another sharp breeze whipped through. For an instant, her hair brushed ever so lightly across his face. Oh God! The way it smelled did things to him.

"Yeah, I aim to do some studying, too," Cody lied, struggling to stay focused on the subject. He had just grabbed some books because the teachers said they didn't want to see him, the jock, leaving school empty-handed anymore. The teachers seemed to be everywhere of late, always with their eyes cocked his way. It had started when his grades began to slip, which coincided with when he had first fallen in love with Angie. Coach had said Cody was putting his scholarship at risk. Colleges didn't want dummies, even ones who could catch a football any which way it could be thrown.

They got to her car. She unlocked the door, leaned inside, and laid her books on the passenger seat. "Have mercy!" he thought, unable to look away from her. She moved quicker than he anticipated, standing up and turning so fast she caught him staring at her all goggle-eyed.

"Cody, are you okay?"

"Uh, yeah," he grinned suddenly, acknowledging he had been caught checking her out. He might as well fess up, he figured. Her knowing he liked to look at her was fine as far as he was concerned. Besides, the hint of mischief in her eyes revealed she was toying with him. He was fine with that, too.

"Good," she said, and smiled "See you tonight." She bent and slid into her seat.

"Can't wait," he said. "Six-fifteen? Right?"

"Yes, hon, 6:15," she agreed, pulling her door to.

It was the *hon* that did it. Cody didn't even notice when Angie's car began to roll forward or realize Coach Bronski was now standing directly behind him. Fortunately for the starstruck teenager, the coach was paying attention. He jerked Cody back a split second before Angie drove over his toes.

Chapter 52

1449 Hours

Batman was the first to hear it coming. He was seated on the hood of his command car in the engine room, staring out the open bay door, watching how the wind was stirring things. For the last five minutes it had been picking up, gusting at only a few miles per hour at first, falling to a steady breeze, then gusting again, faster than before. The wind continued in these cycles, constantly gathering strength until the gusts came in angry bursts and sent hordes of leaves and trash fleeing down the street. The breezes in between were suddenly gone, replaced by a hard, steady blow which carried dead branches from the trees across the way and set the utility wires to vibrating with a high, eerie keening. What Batman heard above the wind, above the skittering sounds of leaves and scraps of paper rushing past, were rumbling rolls of thunder trampling so close on the tails of numerous other rolls that the rumbling never died. The cacophony only momentarily rose or dropped a decibel or two.

Half expecting to see a funnel twisting toward him, Batman slid off the hood and slowly walked the few feet to the open bay door. He leaned his head forward and peeked around the corner toward the west. The sky was evil-looking. Though he saw no tornado, a long wall of black cloud stretched across the horizon. Along its face, towering waves broke to stumble and tumble over one another in mad confusion. Lightning sparked and flashed within the mass, across it, to the ground beneath in crazed, strobing lasers and searing muzzle flashes, as if fired from some great alien warship sent to scorch the earth down to bedrock. Batman glanced at his wristwatch and made a bet with himself about when the first call would come in.

"What did you pick?"

Batman turned to see Captain Buckman easing up beside him. "Two minutes and 10 seconds."

The captain studied the storm front for a few moments, then glanced at his wristwatch. Like Batman's, it was an inexpensive, throwaway piece. It didn't make sense to wear anything pricey in hot, wet, smoke-filled environments.

"If I had to put money on it," the captain began, glancing at Batman, then back at the towering storm wave. "I'd say you're being optimistic."

Ringgggggg!

"Attention all companies. Watkins County is now under a tornado watch. Attention all companies. Watkins County is now under a severe thunderstorm warning. Damaging winds, quarter-size hail, and heavy rains may be expected. Repeating—"

As the dispatcher broadcast the information once more, Batman turned to the captain and said, "At least the tornado stuff is only a watch."

"Things can always be worse," Captain Buckman replied.

"Quarter-size—Standby—"

Ringgggggg!

The individual company tones began going off, kept going off, as firefighters came hustling into the engine room. At last they stopped. Then: "Attention, Battalion 1, Engine 4, Engine 7, Rescue 1, Ladder 1, respond to a structure fire at 1131 Meadowlawn Drive. Cross streets Oakwood Way and Birch Tree Court. Repeating, Battalion 1—"

Batman was already in his command car and rolling out the door by the time the dispatcher finished repeating the knock-out information. *Buckman was right,* he thought. He had been optimistic. Stuff, things, were splattering and thumping against his vehicle as it rocked with the wind. Even on the fastest setting, the windshield wipers were only barely keeping up. His next idea was, *This might be interesting.* He voiced it in the understated way people in the disaster business often talk, even sometimes to themselves. A structure fire was bad enough on its own. Coupled with high winds it could be a sure-enough monster, doing its utmost to reach out and devour anything and everything downwind. He reached over, flipped the switch for the warning lights, clicked the siren on at the hi/lo setting. In the rearview mirror he saw the companies rolling out of their bays, forming into a convoy behind him. He keyed his radio mic.

"Battalion 1, 10-6."

Chapter 53

1453 Hours

Limb in the road. Let's go," Captain Buckman yelled over his shoulder to his firefighters in the jump seats.

Both lanes were blocked. Cars were backed up in lines four or five deep on each side. At the jagged, broken end, the limb was as thick as a man's thigh. A mass of leafed branches fluffed up at the other end, some 30 feet away. As Probie Wan joined up with Captain Buckman and Mick, he was shocked to hear a constant stream of profanity emanating from Mick.

"Sonofabitch! Dirty, rotten-ass sonofabitch! Bastard had to fall right here!" With each new verse, Mick repeated his original curses, sprinkling new, ever hotter ones in among them as if the previous blast wasn't ugly enough.

The roaring wind tore at Probie Wan's turnouts, splattering wet clumps of leaves—and who only knew what else—to stick against the stiff fabric. Heavy raindrops drum-rolled against his helmet; stung his skin when he turned a cheek into the wind. A trash can appeared out of nowhere, sailing through the air, passing closely over the pick-up truck at the head of traffic on the opposite side of the street. He saw the driver duck in response. The can smashed against a tree 100 feet beyond. Only a dull, metallic thud made its way back to them. It was so noisy he could barely hear the captain's directions. At least Batman and the engineers had cut off their sirens. From so close, their high-pitched wails were painful and deafening.

The three firefighters bent down as one alongside the limb at its broken end and curled their arms underneath it.

"On three!" Captain Buckman shouted above the racket. "Three!"

They lifted their end and duck-walked forward in the

direction of the pickup, swinging the last few splintered feet of timber over the truck's hood. The three firefighters kept pivoting the limb around until they had traveled a quarter circle. Parallel to the street then, they rolled it off into a ditch. Batman carefully eased past the stopped cars on his side as soon as the way was clear, then swung back into his lane and took off, his siren's screams quickly lost in the wind. Now Captain Buckman took a position at the front corner of the pickup, holding traffic on both sides with raised hands. Rescue 1 and Ladder 1 responded to the captain's signals and came looping around Engine 4 and the stopped cars to follow Batman. Once they were clear, the captain released oncoming traffic, pointing and waving to the lead vehicle, and hustled back to join his crew on the engine.

In his jump seat, finally, Probie Wan settled back and snapped his seat belt closed. He was just about to ask Mick what set off his cursing spree when Mick spoke.

"Believe this monkey crap?" he asked, turning toward Probie Wan. "I'd bet Margie's drawers, 7's done beat us there!"

So that was it. The rookie grinned to himself. First-in was everything to his smoke-eating partner because the first-in crew always pulled an attack line.

1502 Hours

It was a mattress. Even after being soaked by Engine 7, it kept rolling out gobs of smoke into the room like only a smoldering sack of cotton wadding could do. Two truckies from Ladder 1 slid it onto a reinforced salvage cover they carried on their rig just for this purpose, then folded the cover over the top the best they could. Picking the package up enough to slide, they hustled it out into the front yard where Mick and Probie Wan stood waiting with a red-rubber line that looked like an obese garden hose. As soon as the truckies took the cover off, the wind fed the hot spots down deep in the bedding of the mattress, puffing them up into flames again. Probie Wan immediately began spraying water, beating the blazes into submission. Holding the booster line loosely, Mick provided commentary from a couple of feet behind.

"Stinking-ass thing," Mick said, loud enough for Probie Wan to hear over the wind and rain. At least the wind had let up some from the storm's opening blast. "Pissy. Smell it? Hate mattress fires."

"Shoo," Probie Wan agreed. He and Mick had shed their masks and packs while they waited for the truckies to drag the mattress out, foregoing the protection provided by the breathing apparatuses. "Nasty."

Under the roof of a little side porch, two firefighters from Rescue 1 were giving oxygen to a male victim who was sitting on a plastic milk crate. The man was in an undershirt and boxers. Fortunately, the firefighters didn't seem to be treating any burns, but smoke inhalation was plenty bad enough. It was the real killer. The screen door off to the victim's side swung open. A firefighter's arm appeared, handed the man a pair of sweatpants.

Captain Buckman came ambling over, watching Probie Wan work the nozzle. Chunks of charred, sodden bedding blew out and stuck in the grass like malformed doughballs when Probie Wan hit the most heavily burned places. Smaller pieces were picked up and carried tumbling over the yard by gusts from the storm.

"Smoking?" Mick asked the captain.

Captain Buckman moved a step closer before answering, so he would be heard better. A pair of smoke ejectors had been started and were now adding their individual roars to the overall racket. The heavy-duty caged fans were stacked together and positioned a few feet back from the main entrance, feeding their flow of fresh air into the house.

"Smoking," the captain confirmed. "Guy works third shift.

Girlfriend woke him up, then went to the store. Came home, the house was full of smoke. He lit up a cigarette, then fell right back to sleep, looks like. Girlfriend got a real lungful getting him out. Medics have her in the ambulance, giving her some O2."

"No burns?" Mick asked.

"Nope," the captain shook his head. "At least none you can see. Can't say about her lungs. Probably take her in and check everything out good."

"Lucky," Mick commented, glancing back down at the mattress. After a moment he said, "Ate a big enough hole." He added, "Looks good, Wan. Think she's out."

Ron shut the nozzle off. He smiled a little inner smile to himself. Mick was the only one who ever dropped the Probie and called him anything close to his actual name, and even he didn't do it often. He wasn't exactly sure why Mick did it just then, but hoped it meant there was something of friendship developing between them.

"Understand why there's a hole burned straight down through it?" Captain Buckman asked him. The question left the rookie momentarily at a loss.

"Yeah," Probie Wan tentatively started to answer. Before he could go further, Sticks called from the front porch.

"Hey, Cap! See ya a minute?"

"Make sure he understands," the captain said, glancing to Mick before he turned to go see what Sticks wanted.

"Well?" Mick asked.

"It has to do with the way the fuel is positioned. There is a relatively small area exposed to heat when a fire is ignited on top of a solid fuel. Long as the mattress is horizontal, the fire will burn more or less straight down, with slow extension out to the sides."

"No shit?" Mick grinned.

"You asked," the rookie allowed himself to grin back.

A few seconds passed in silence. Then Mick spoke.

"First mattress fire, right?"

"Yeah."

"Won't be your last. When you get in a spot where you have to carry one out, if you can't get it wrapped up to keep the air from it, like the truck boys did here, don't even try until somebody's got a line ready. Flip 'em on their edge, all the heat is exposed to the mattress instead of rising free in the air. Go up like roman candles. Get everything around them burning, if you aren't careful."

"Understand," Probie Wan nodded.

"Me and D. J. threw one out a window on the top floor of Bartley Towers. Didn't make it 10 stories before she burnt slick up. Batman said all that made it to the ground was a handful of sparks."

"Wow."

"You two gonna stand there scratching your cracks and picking your noses all day?" D. J. yelled over the wind, having wandered down near them. "Let's get this line back on." Thunder boomed loudly, echoing down the streets. "Case you missed the bulletin, there's a storm coming."

Chapter 54

3:10 p.m.

I thought I heard a little birdie whistling. Something about I should check this out," Detective Boards said as he slid the humidor over to the edge of the desk. Boards was seated in James Henry's chair. He and Wilson had already searched inside the desk, through the books on the shelves behind, and everywhere else in the room, including the air vents, all to no avail. Only the humidor was left. Lifting the lid slowly, he looked inside. After a moment, he reached in and grasped several cigars. These he laid to one side on the desktop. Then he picked one back up and inspected its band. "Cuban. Didn't think you were able to get these in the States."

"Me either," Wilson agreed. "Ought to feed him to the Feds."

Boards nodded as he looked back in the humidor.

"Nothing else in here," he said, running his fingers around the inner edges, feeling for a catch. Pulling a pen from his pocket, he measured the humidor's depth, then the height of the outside wall. The outside was easily an inch higher. "Interesting," Boards noted. He turned the box onto its side, traced a fingertip around the bottom edge.

Nothing.

He set the humidor back down. Grasping the left-front leg, he gently tried to move it, but it held tight. When he tried the right-front leg it gave a little, then snapped back. A shallow drawer silently appeared, sliding out a couple of inches. Boards paused for dramatic effect, glanced up at Wilson. "Just like Christmas," he said, smiling a tight, mirthless smile as he slid the drawer out all the way with the tip of his pen.

Wilson leaned over to see. "Oh, thank you, Santa," he said. "You knew I've been a good boy." He straightened and met the other detective's gaze. "Life is good," he said, displaying a mirror image of Boards' mirthless smile.

"Yes, it is for some people. And for others, you might say they're having a bad day."

"Yeah," Wilson nodded. "A very bad day."

"Not as bad as the lady this prick ran over. But this might help even the score a little," Boards continued, his expression now serious.

"Guess we ought to see what Ms. Destiny knows about this."

Wilson stepped to the door and called her into the office.

"Ma'am, have you ever seen inside this box? This humidor?"

"Yes, on occasion. Sometimes when James Henry closes a big deal, he will get one of those cigars out," she nodded toward the pile off to the side, "and smoke it. Makes me about half sick. Things stink to high heaven," she concluded, batting her eyelashes.

As she explained she was also remembering how James Henry thought it funny to blow the filthy stench in her face. *What an ass*, she said to herself. *Well, where he's going, he won't be smoking any cigars. Ain't life a bitch?*

Boards was speaking.

"I'm sorry," Destiny said. "You were saying?"

"Did you ever see him put anything in this?" Boards asked, pointing at the secret compartment. "Or take anything out?"

Destiny seemed confused. Suddenly her face lit up, and she exclaimed, "That explains it!"

"Explains what?" Wilson asked.

"Once, I picked up this humidor—I was just trying to make room for him to spread out some project drawings—and he went ballistic. Told me to put it down and never touch it again. Guess he was afraid the little drawer might fly open."

"Secret compartment," Boards corrected.

"What?" Destiny's eyebrows went up with her question.

"The little drawer is a secret compartment."

"Oh," she answered, her mouth rounding with the word. "Well, I never."

Wilson and Boards looked toward each other, both thinking the exact same thing—*never* was unlikely. They held their tongues, though.

"Take a look. Be careful, don't touch anything," Boards instructed her. "Just take a look in the compartment, and tell me if you've seen Mr. Henry with any of these items before."

Destiny took a step forward and leaned over the desk. In a second, she glanced up at the detectives, her eyes huge with surprise. She took another longer look, then stood up straight.

"What in the world is all that?"

Wilson thought for a moment before answering.

"Hmmm. 'Bout a quarter ounce of marijuana. Pills look to be oxycodone. And the white powder, I'm not certain. We'll have to test it. Probably cocaine."

"My goodness."

"Did you ever see James Henry take any drugs?" Boards asked. "Ever see him act out of the ordinary? You know, spacey, little *too* happy, kind of hyper?"

Destiny appeared to be trying hard to remember for the next half-minute. All the time she was thinking, *The goofy bastard never acted ordinary in his life.*

She suddenly brightened. "Why, yes! Now you mention it. Once he brought some papers to my desk right after I saw him fiddling with the humidor, and he wasn't smoking a cigar. He was acting kind of giggly and silly like you said, and he had something on his face. I said, 'Dear me. I didn't know men powdered their noses, too.'"

The detectives managed to contain themselves. It wasn't easy. This gal had the *Gone with the Wind* stuff down pat.

"Okay," Wilson was able to say after a moment. "Thank you, Destiny."

Neither could help but watch as she walked away. As she entered the doorway, from somewhere to the front of the building a streak of lightning flashed, framing her in golden light. Thunder rumbled all around like a closing drumroll. Even after she was out of sight, both detectives continued to stare in the direction she had gone.

"Life is good," Wilson said at last.

"Ah, yes," Boards nodded. After a few seconds he turned back to the business at hand. "Well, guess it's time to get some photos and start working up a list of this stuff."

"Yep," Wilson replied, reaching for the small notebook inside his jacket.

Under his breath, Boards muttered, "She never did say if she saw him with anything in the compartment."

"Not a word," Wilson shook his head.

Chapter 55

3:12 p.m.

"Is it hailing?" Judge Hightower asked her bailiff.

The bailiff was looking out one of the courtroom's tall windows at the storm moving in. Hailstones were bouncing off the parking lot like kernels of popcorn popping. A pulsing bolt shot out of the black mass and hit somewhere close. The man flinched, blinked, backed away from the window as thunder rattled the panes. *Wow! This could get rough.*

"Yes, Your Honor. Looks to be small stuff. I'd say about nickel size."

"Let's hope we don't get any like a couple of years ago," the judge said, staring at the window, also.

She was remembering the baseball-size stones—stones which had beaten her roadster to a pulp. The car had been a dream realized, a mid-life crisis eased, until the storm. The memory, and the rumble from the avalanche of ice falling outside, was enough to stir concern over the same thing happening to her Escalade.

"I pray not," the court officer shook his head emphatically, turning back to face the courtroom. That storm had been something of a personal disaster for him, too, costing a new roof which took a month to finally get put on.

The bailiff scanned the pew-like benches behind the wooden railing. Wasn't much of a crowd left. It was usually this way by late afternoon on a Friday. He recognized a young lawyer, well-dressed and a bit anxious. Nice guy, it seemed, but still working on getting his sea legs. There was a lady seated next to the lawyer, 60s, her expression tired, sad, a grandmother, probably. He always thought they were the most pitiful, these poor, older women left to deal with the children of addicted or incarcerated parents. There was a rough-looking man in his 30s. The bailiff had caught the scent of liquor when this fellow came into the room half an hour ago. He bore watching. The final person was a lady on the opposite side of the aisle. She was about the same age as the drinker. It took someone with a practiced eye to recognize it, however. Her face was so lined, her jaws so deeply drawn in, she could have passed for twice her age. Bent slightly forward in her seat, her eyes had been constantly darting about the room since she sat down.

Yep, the bailiff thought, *something's going on with this one—pills, meth, maybe both.*

"Very well, Jerry. Let's get our little firebugs in here," the judge said.

The bailiff pulled a folded page from his back pocket and studied it a moment as he walked across the room. He swung a side door open and in a loud voice called, "Marvin Willis, Timothy Thomas."

Chapter 56

Should have called her, Captain Buckman thought as he looked out the windshield. Mad showers of small hailstones raked across the street, rebounding off every solid surface in sight, ripping at the rest. Virginia didn't like storms. He recalled the first bad one they went through together. It was around midnight. The wind was howling, lightning flashing, rain peppering the windowpanes. He was on his back, awake, enjoying Nature's show. Suddenly something heavy smacked the side of the house close to their bedroom window. In an instant she was in his arms, her hand grasping at his chest, her face pressed against his shoulder. She was shivering, as if a cold wind were blowing across her skin. He held her tight, whispered comforting words, and after a moment she became quiet again. A time later he came to realize she was asleep. Her breathing came in soft puffs against his shoulder, her hand lay relaxed on his chest. He had felt so many things then—strong, protective, loving.

Now, he felt a pang of guilt. He knew what was coming, but he hadn't called her. As soon as they got back to the station, he would take care of his oversight. She would be going home before long. Maybe one of the kids would come over. Probably not. Something she might interpret as watching over the defenseless female would make her fuss. She might not like storms, but she certainly didn't ever think she needed someone holding her hand, unless it was the dark of night perhaps, and he was the one doing the holding.

Ringgggggg!

A series of individual company tones followed. All the companies assigned to his station, plus one engine from another house, were being knocked out. The dispatcher recited her litany.

"—respond to a possible structure fire at 1227 Mockingbird Lane. Lightning has struck the house."

The captain turned the knob for the siren. He glanced over at D. J. who met his eyes in return.

"Gonna be an interesting ride, Cap," the engineer grinned, raising his voice to speak over the metallic roar of ice pounding the roof of the cab.

At that instant, half a block ahead of them, a car came out of a business lot, slowly skidded across the hail-covered street and bumped up sideways against a blue, post-office mailbox.

"Would appear so," the captain answered. Then he twisted his head around to yell toward the jump seats. "You hear?"

"Yeah," Mick yelled back, Probie Wan echoing him a split second later. Both men were already cinching the straps on their air packs.

"Rescue 1's right behind," the engineer reported, stealing a peek in his side mirror.

Captain Buckman didn't reply, though he glanced in the mirror on his side to confirm as he began buckling into his pack. Seconds later, D. J. slowed to pass the car against the mailbox. He and the captain were both looking when the car's driver hopped out, presumably to check for damage. Hail-stones were immediately bouncing off the man's head. For a couple of moments, he tried to ward them off, covering his scalp with both hands. Suddenly he dived back inside.

"Brain surgeon," D. J. observed dryly as they rolled on.

Their route was taking them around the base of Reservoir Hill, the highest spot in the city. Several streets traversed the hill. One of these, steeply sloped, intersected their street just ahead.

"Stop!" Captain Buckman yelled.

D. J. slammed on the brakes, risking a glance in the mirror to make certain Rescue 1 wasn't about to rear-end them. Then he saw it. Only feet from the intersection, a roiling wave, eight or 10 inches high, was racing downhill. Hailstones and gravel, sticks and leaves, tumbled over each other in the dark water.

The wave spilled out before them, fanning into a litter-filled delta on their street where its force was quickly spent.

After a quick scan to make certain nothing else was rolling down their way, D. J. started the engine forward again.

"Believe that's a first," he said.

"Yep," Captain Buckman nodded. "Don't see that every day."

Two minutes later Engine 4 came to a halt in front of 1227 Mockingbird Lane. Rounding the front bumper, Probie Wan didn't see anything out of place with the modest house. *No wonder,* he thought. *Like trying to look through a waterfall.* The hail had stopped, but he had never seen it rain like this. The drops seemed to have been shot from a cannon. They tore in at crazy angles, burning his bare cheeks. He fell in with Mick as they walked behind Captain Buckman toward the house.

"Slinging pitchforks and baby porcupines," a grinning Mick yelled over the roar.

"No joke," Probie Wan agreed, pulling his helmet shield down.

The residents, an older couple, met them at the door.

"Come in, boys, come in," the man said. "Haven't seen any fire, but it sure smells like it. Fried the TV, I'm sure."

"Yep, electrical, all right," Captain Buckman sniffed as he stepped inside. Then he brought his portable radio to his mouth and cancelled the other responding engine, as well as Battalion 1. With Rescue 1 and Ladder 1, they had all they needed on scene already.

Mick had already turned toward the living room. Probie Wan followed him over to the television. Together, they worked to slide the set away from the wall enough to see where it was plugged in. Mick pulled the plug. Seeing smoke stains on the outlet cover, he slid the back of his ungloved hand up the wall above it, searching for the heat of fire within.

"Can't feel anything," he said to Probie Wan. "Let's take a gander at the major appliances. Lightning loves them."

The man overheard him and said, "Utility room's right off the kitchen in the back."

Captain Buckman remained in conversation with the couple as they moved through the house, his gaze noting lamps and ceiling fans were working everywhere but in the living room. They were just inside the door to a bedroom, when Greg's voice called out from the hallway, "Got the attic yet?"

"No," Buckman called back.

"Stairs are right there," they heard Greg say, his voice softer. Then he called again. "Hey, Captain. Seen a sweet little lady in here? Might have an old, ill-headed codger with her."

"Greg!" the woman yelled, turning back into the hallway. "I thought it was you."

She hesitated. One firefighter was at the bottom of the pull-down stairs, holding them steady. A second firefighter was on the steps, visible only from the knees down as he checked the space for signs of fire. Greg worked his way past and into the woman's waiting arms.

"Hi, Aunt Aggie. Love you."

"Oh, I love you, hon," she answered, hugging him tight.

Greg broke free to shake the man's proffered hand.

"What have you been up to, Jesse, you old fart?"

"Dodging lightning bolts. Your aunt's been acting up again. Got the Lord after her this time, I reckon."

"Will you hush," she ordered, raising a hand as if she might slap him. She dropped it quickly. "We thought something was after us. Whew. We're okay, though; just a little shook up."

"Speak for yourself, woman. Think I ruptured my rectum."

This time she did strike, giving him a thump on the shoulder with her fist.

"You've always got to say something silly."

"Silly my wounded crack," the man complained, turning to Captain Buckman. "I was back in the kitchen, watching it hail, when lightning hit the transformer in the alley. Here she came, a ball of fire running down the wire straight at me. Boom! It hit the house, and I hit the deck. Thought I was back in Korea."

Captain Buckman and Greg chuckled along with the man. The lady, hands on hips, shook her head. A hint of a smile graced her face, however.

"Where's your electrical box?" Captain Buckman asked the man.

"Back there in the utility room," Jesse answered, waving his hand to indicate the way.

"Excuse me," the captain said as he edged past Greg and his relatives.

Mick and Probie Wan were in the kitchen, having already checked things over in the utility room. "Open the refrigerator door and see if the light comes on," Mick said as he bent down to do the same with the oven door. Both lights were working.

"How does it look?" Captain Buckman asked as he entered the room.

"Everything in here's working. Got the washer and dryer, though," Mick replied. "Little smoked up around the outlets, but the walls feel cool. Box is in the utility room over here."

The captain stepped between his men, then through the utility room doorway. He opened the electrical panel's door. "Kicked the breakers for both them and the living room," Mick continued. "Only ones tripped. Didn't see anything burned or melted."

"Okay," the captain nodded, closing the door. "I don't see anything, either. Let's take a peek outside."

A minute later the three firefighters were standing in a steady rain, staring at the spot where the electrical line fed into the building. Above the meter, the thin plywood of the eave was pulled loose where Ladder 1 firefighters were inspecting the void area. Two men from the crew moved in and began pushing the wooden panel back into place. Sticks was with them.

"It's clear," he said to Captain Buckman.

As the two officers talked, Probie Wan stared in awe at a grapefruit-sized hole in the gutter.

"See where it's scorched around the edges?" Mick said. "Lightning followed the wire till it hit the gutter. Then kaboom."

A couple of minutes later, Engine 4's crew was back at the front porch. Through the screen door, they could hear Greg's Uncle Jesse talking.

"This time I'm getting a TV big as the whole wall. Want everything life size. When they start up dancing on her show, I'm jumping right in there with 'em."

Captain Buckman moved close to the door screen and waved to catch Jesse's attention. Then he explained about the loss of the washer and dryer.

"No problem there," Jesse said. "She hasn't washed anything since Presidents Day. Ow! Y'all saw that. Spouse abuse."

As the laughter died down, Greg spoke to Captain Buckman. "Attic's clear and the boys did a second walk through. Jesse's calling an electrician here in a minute, so guess we're done."

Back in their jump seats on the engine, Probie Wan turned to face Mick.

"They sure didn't seem upset, did they?"

"Working people. Been getting hit by lightning all their lives. Just another day."

Chapter 57

3:15 p.m.

Robert managed to rise from his seat before the TV and make his slow way over to the sink to get a drink. *Why is it so dark? Have I been napping again?* Then he saw the rain running down the windowpanes. He leaned over the sink so he could see out better. The ground was white, which didn't make sense. With a mild start he realized it was hail littering the surface in a pock-marked quilt, as if it had snowed and the sun had melted a few widely scattered holes in the fabric. Strange, he hadn't heard the hail falling, and hail always made a racket. He must have really been out.

Won't last long 'fore it melts, he thought, the way the rain was coming down; and, of course, the ground was already warm. *It was warm, wasn't it?* For a moment he was at a loss as to what time of the year it was. Then he remembered. *Spring. Yes, it was another glorious May.*

She so loved spring. He had often joked no patch of their yard was ever safe this time of year, for she was forever tearing it up digging and planting. Spring was when they took little drives out into the country, just to see what was in bloom. She was crazy about the redbuds and dogwoods, each in their turn blanketing the hills in purple or white. They might go driving for a while every day then, frequently retracing a favorite path of the day before, returning until the blooms began to fade, and the trees were fringed with fresh, new green. How she enjoyed those drives. How he enjoyed seeing her joy.

It hit him for a moment as he stood there before the sink, watching the raindrops softly thump against the glass, just how alone he was. Those times with her were all in the past. The idea struck like a blow, low and hard in his stomach. He struggled a moment to get his breath. Finally, his lungs loosened. His breathing settled back into rhythm. The icy knot inside him, however, could never be melted away. Forever, with its terrible certainty, meant just that.

Feeling sorry for himself was not a luxury he long permitted. He pushed the weight of emptiness and pity away. The rain was slackening, perhaps only for a moment, for the sky was yet dark and heavy. Suddenly he could see much better through the window; see the rosebush, her yellow rosebush. For a moment he wasn't certain what he was looking at. Then it came to him as fast as the awful thought moments before about being alone. No bloom shone forth to catch his eye. Instead, in a small, ragged circle beneath the bush lay a mat of dirty-yellow petals, pounded into the mud by the hail.

What would he show Emily now?

A hot tear rolled down his cheek.

Chapter 58

3:16 p.m.

Cody waited for the hail to stop. It was killing him, but he sat there behind the steering wheel in the florist's parking lot, praying the avalanche of ice was not beating every speck of paint off his car and leaving it dimpled like a golf ball. He was on a tight schedule. Pick up her corsage and his boutonniere first, then swing by to get his tux. And he had to get gas, too. By pure accident his eyes had come to rest on the gauge as he pulled into the lot. There wasn't more than a wink between the needle and the empty mark. Man! This prom stuff was a lot to worry over. And expensive. He'd wiped out his puny savings and still had to borrow 20 bucks from his dad.

Everything was worth it, however, just to see her. All through lunch she had dropped hints about her dress, and her shoes, and how she would have her hair fixed. He had sat there giggling like he had half a brain and shoveling food in the whole time, his teenage body's need to refuel overriding any pretense of manners. He could not wait to see her. My God! She was already beautiful beyond anything he could imagine. Let his friends burn alive with envy when he and Angie took the dance floor. Of course, he couldn't dance a lick, but his lack of rhythm didn't worry him. With her in his arms, no one would be paying attention to his stomps and stumbles.

Then there was his tux: pale blue with black trim. He smiled, remembering how he looked like a million in it. Angie went with him to pick it out. He didn't know the difference between cucumbers and cummerbunds, so she made the final choice. It suited him, literally, just fine. The man at the shop even remarked what a stud he looked like in it. He would have taken it with him then, but she discovered a little spot on one sleeve where the trim was pulled loose. The man swore they would have it repaired in time. Cody guessed he would just croak if the shop didn't. What else could he do? A fellow couldn't go to the prom with his tux coming unraveled.

The hail began to let up. It was suddenly gone, replaced by a hard downpour of rain. The clock was ticking, and he had those other stops to make. His phone rang.

"Yes, Mom—okay—okay, Mom. I'll get it—okay. Yes, I think I've got enough money."

Now he had to stop and get milk!

Cody swung the door open and hopped out. He was instantly soaked. As he jogged toward the door to the florist's shop it dawned on him there was one of those little fold-up umbrellas under the driver's seat. He instantly dismissed the thought, however, being a teenage jock. Umbrellas were for sissies.

Chapter 59

3:23 p.m.

*T*hank goodness, Ms. Wood thought, looking out the door of the safe room. Across the pint-sized tables and chairs, she could see a window. It was raining now, instead of hailing. The wind had died down too, she thought, for she could see nothing blowing by, not even a few leaves torn from the trees.

"I'll be right back, children. Ms. Gina, why don't you lead them in their ABCs one more time."

Ms. Wood left the door ajar on purpose, so the children would know she had not deserted them. As she strode across the room, little voices washed over her, singing, "E F G, H I J K, L M N O P."

At the window she stopped and stared for a minute. It seemed millions of white marbles covered the ground. As she watched, the rain began to carry hordes of hailstones in ice-filled lava flows along low spots in the playground. The stones piled up, tumbled over each other, spilled out onto the banks—a far north winter breakup in miniature. She found it fascinating. *The children must see this.* She turned and called over the sound of their singing.

"Ms. Gina. Everything is all right. You can bring them out now."

Urged along by Ms. Gina, the children began to slowly venture from the safe room. They weren't quite certain it was okay, however.

"The storm has passed, children," Ms. Wood spoke again. "Come here to the windows with me. I want you to see something."

At her reassurance they rushed forward. They were instantly *oohing* and *ahhing*. If any had ever seen hail, the memory had probably slipped away. Just as unlikely was the idea any of them had ever seen anything quite like the little ice-laden rivers running through their playground. The sight left them mesmerized; all of them except Miriam.

Miriam clung to Emily's hand as they stood at a window. She was only now able to hold her tears back. The scene in the playground held little interest for her, for the fear she had felt at the height of the hail's pounding was so deep and real it could not dissipate as easily as it had with her schoolmates. Emily looked out the window for a short moment, then turned her head to face her friend. "It's okay now, Meer-e-um. That mean old storm went away."

Then, in the way children sometimes find the perfect thing to do, Emily leaned forward and kissed her friend on the cheek. Miriam gave her a timid smile in return, then kissed Emily back.

Ms. Gina saw it all and had to turn away, her tears sudden and unexpected.

The two girls stood at the window holding hands for a while, watching the rain come to an end. Eventually, Brandon, their red-headed classmate came to stand beside them. After a moment, he glanced their way.

"The wabbit is hopping 'round in my head. Wanna see?"

The two girls instantly stepped forward, each moving to one of the boy's ears.

"Oooh, I see him," Emily said.

"He's so pretty," Miriam added.

Ms. Wood smiled to herself, hearing their words. It was like turning a valve and relieving the stress brought on by the storm. She was proud of how she had responded, quickly, decisively, as she should have, being the headmistress. Ms. Gina had done well, too, handling the children with calm reassurance. Thankfully, the storm had not caused much in the way of true destruction. Now, glad for the distraction, she laughed to herself as she watched the rabbit viewing. After a few moments, she turned to go to the fridge to get a cold drink. Until then, she had not been in a spot to notice the limb poking through the hallway ceiling. Stopping only a couple of feet above the floor, its splintered end dripped water into a puddle. If a child— if she or Gina? Her hand flew to her throat. For the first time since the initial roll of thunder, Ms. Wood felt genuine fear.

Chapter 60

1536 Hours

They hadn't made it a block from the scene of the lightning strike when they were knocked out on another call. This time it was a lockout. Probie Wan was a little disappointed. There was no sense of urgency, no air horn blasting, no siren wailing. Since this was not an emergency, D.J. drove the engine with the flow of the rush-hour traffic.

Probie Wan had to admit, responding to a true emergency, with the air horn ripping the air over the screaming siren, was beginning to grow on him. Together they demanded everyone else move aside, as if the individual elements comprising the racket were commanding voices issuing an order. *Out of the way!* The sharp waves seemed to penetrate his being. They intensified his sense of purpose, which turned on a keen edge of anticipation with the dispatcher's first word. More than anything, he had a feeling he was a part of something important. How could he not be if they gave them an air horn to clear the way?

Conversely, the feeling heralded anything but an adrenalin rush. The necessity of maintaining a level head was something he had heard from the instructors dozens of times. As soon as he started on shift, he noticed how all the veterans seemed to avoid any appearance of excitement. Even the mouthier fire-fighters, though professional in their on-scene actions, exuded a laid-back aura of confidence. It was what Probie Wan wanted to be like—cool and calm. He glanced over at his mate. Mick seemed ready to doze off.

"Ever seen it like this?" Probie Wan raised his voice a bit over the roar of the motor.

"You mean all the calls?"

"Yeah. So busy? One run after another?"

"Oh, this ain't nothing," Mick answered with a shrug. "Bad weather gets you hopping every time. Of course, you've always got your service calls like lockouts stuffed in the middle of the craziness somewhere. They count, too."

"Maybe we'll set a record," Probie Wan offered.

"Doubt it. Hard to top the big freeze a couple of years ago. Right at Christmastime. Everybody out shopping. Front rolled in straight off the north pole. Sunny one minute, then set in snowing like crazy and didn't stop. Bottom fell out of the thermometer, and of course the power went off. Pipes freezing up and busting all over town. We're squeegeeing rivers of water out of all these businesses. People trying to light fireplaces that hadn't been lit in years and setting their chimneys on fire. And wrecks! Must have been at least a hundred. Town was one big slip and slide. Caught a good housefire late. Guy tried to refill a kerosene heater inside the living room while the thing was lit. Dropped the fuel can and spilled kerosene everywhere. Lucky everybody got out." Mick paused, remembering. "We got our first call about noon and didn't stop until we got off the next morning. Kind of an interesting day."

"Wow," Probie Wan said, trying to wrap his mind around the idea of staying on the go for such a long stretch. After a moment he shifted back to the present and admitted, "First time I've been on a lock-out."

"No big deal. Somebody left their keys inside or lost them. Probably won't take but a few minutes.

"Now lock-ins, those can be boogers. Got to treat them like the real deal. 'Member a three-year-old locked himself in a bathroom. Had every faucet stuck wide open and all the drains plugged up, one way or another. Could have floated the ark in there. Top it off, kid tried to flush everything from a bath towel to a scented candle down the toilet. Looked like a drowned rat time we got him out. Thing is, he could have been—drowned, I mean."

The engine began to slow down. Seconds later they came to

a stop in front of an older Cape Cod-style home. A wooden handicap ramp led from the walk up to the small, covered porch. There sat a woman in a wheelchair. She raised a hand in embarrassed greeting.

"Engine 4 on the scene." the captain said into the mic.

Half a minute later the crew approached the front of the house in a loose knot, Mick bringing up the rear. He was carrying a small toolbox. As they neared the porch, each firefighter was struck by the woman's appearance. Her long auburn hair was frizzy and windblown, her clothes wrinkled and damp. In contrast, her thin face was gorgeous, with deep dimples, a dusting of faint freckles, and sparkling blue eyes. A blanket covered her lap. She did not look over 30.

"I am so sorry to have to call you," she began, flashing a warm smile. As the captain came to a stop before her, she extended her hand and added, "I'm Sandra."

"Wayne Buckman," the captain replied, taking her hand briefly. "No problem. What we're here for." A second later he continued, "Say you're locked out?"

"Yes, I am so upset with myself. I just came outside to check my mail. Then the storm hit. First big gust of wind slammed my door shut. Afraid I'm in the habit of leaving the lock set even when the door is propped open. I have cerebral palsy, so fiddling with the lock can be a bit worrisome. Anyway, here I wound up, stuck."

"You were out here through all that mess?"

"Oh yes. Thank goodness it came blowing in from the back side of the house, so I was sort of shielded, at least part of the time. I'll have to say it was more exciting than anything I've seen on TV lately."

"Are you okay?" the captain said, shaking his head.

"I am fine. Mr. Preston across the street saw me about the time things started letting up. He brought towels and this blanket over. Such a sweet man. Gone home now to fix me a cup of hot tea."

As she spoke D. J. started around the side of the house to see if the back door was locked, too. Mick and Probie Wan moved onto the porch and eased past the lady to the front door. As they each knelt on one knee, the idea entered their minds of what it must have been like for her to ride out the monster. Then each shared another thought, a guilty one—sometimes lock-outs could be a very big deal.

Mick took a look at the door around the area of the keyhole. After a moment, he opened the toolbox and extracted a thin strip of celluloid. He tried to work it into the hairline crack between door and jamb, hoping to trip the lock. The space was too tight, however. For several minutes he tried other items from the box, some plastic, some long, thin pieces of metal similar to hacksaw blades without the teeth. Nothing worked.

"Having any luck?" Mick heard the captain say from behind.

"Afraid not. This thing's tight as Dick's hat band."

As he answered D. J. returned. "Back door's locked." he announced. "Got a window open on the second floor, B side, though."

"Oh, I forgot about that," Sandra complained. "Where my cousin sleeps. I'll bet there's water an inch deep in there, way the wind was blowing."

"We'll clean it up if there is," Captain Buckman assured her. "We're going to use a ladder to go in through the window. Okay? Then we can open this door from the inside."

"Whatever you have to do."

"Very well. Got any animals, booby traps, or anything else inside we might need to know about?"

"Just my baby doggie, Pookie," Sandra smiled a mother's smile. "He'll be so glad to see me. It's way past time for his afternoon gooey-chewy treat."

Three minutes later Probie Wan was climbing the 24-foot extension ladder up to the base of the second-floor window. On the ground between the ladder and the house, Mick was holding the ladder beams in his hands, leaning backward a bit and using his weight to keep the ladder firmly in place. The captain and D. J. watched from a few feet away in the yard.

Taking a leg lock through the rungs first to hold himself steady, Probie Wan worked to remove the window screen. Thankfully, it came out easily. He turned the screen at an angle and shoved it through the window, giving it a little toss when it cleared so he wouldn't step on it once he was inside. It turned out going in headfirst was the best way, for the window was fairly small. He untangled from his leg lock, then crawled straight through, catching himself with his palms flat on the damp floor inside. Standing up, he located the screen and started working to replace it in the window frame.

"Everything okay?" Captain Buckman yelled up at him.

"No problem. Floor's a little damp, but not bad," Probie Wan answered as he leaned far forward to snap the last corner of the screen in place.

At that moment, with his butt poised high in the air, something goosed him. The intrusion quickly withdrew. Probie Wan instantly slid a hand behind, felt hot air blow forcefully on his fingers, heard a low, menacing, *Grrrrrrrr!* Ever so slowly, he turned and met Pookie, a full-grown German shepherd with long strings of drool hanging from exposed canines the size of butcher knives. Apparently, this little doggie didn't like having someone stare at its teeth. It barked in protest, just once, loud enough to be heard a block away. Then it returned to growling, only much louder than before.

On the ground, the eyes of the other members of the crew all immediately doubled in size. Suddenly, Probie Wan was at the window, his face pressed against the screen.

"What's his name?" the rookie yelled, the dog's angry growls pouring out of the opening in waves, as if preceding the charge of some great mad bear from its cave.

It took a moment or two for those on the ground to say anything, for they found it difficult to speak while choking back laughter. Finally, Captain Buckman answered.

"Pookie! His name is Pookie!" A minute later he added, "Are you okay? Didn't bite you, did he?"

Probie Wan's response was immediate, its effect everlasting. From this day forward, each and every encounter of a Green Springs firefighter with a dog of any size or any temperament—and there have been many—included his words in the event's description.

"Hell no, I'm not okay!" he uncharacteristically snapped, his voice loud and excited. "The sonofabitch cold-nosed me!"

D. J. instantly bent double laughing. Mick fell on the ground, seized by a fit of shaking. Even the normally stoic captain had a couple of loud cackles blow past his lips before he could snag them.

Probie Wan's face disappeared from the window. His voice still carried out to the others, however.

"Nice Pookie. Good doggie," he said over and over, his voice growing fainter with each repetition.

"Okay, boys," Captain Buckman said, sounding slightly regretful, "let's pull it together and get back around front. Don't want the owner to think we've lost our marbles."

Pulling it together was easier said than done. The knowledge the rookie might be in real trouble finally kicked in after a few seconds. Then they hurried back to the porch. They could have taken their time. The front door was open. Probie Wan was stroking the dog's thick hair along its back. The dog, in turn, was licking Sandra's cheek as she held her hands cupped behind its ears.

"Oh, my sweet little, Pookie," she said. "You were scared of the bad ole storm, weren't you?"

Chapter 61

3:37 p.m.

Your Honor," the public defender began, standing before the bench with his client, Marvin "Chopper" Willis. "Mr. Willis has not been in trouble prior to this incident. He has maintained good grades throughout the school year. This is a smart boy who realizes his actions led to a costly accident. Nothing is to be gained by holding him over. His father is here in the courtroom," he paused to gesture to Marvin's dad. "He is prepared to take his son home and keep him under close watch. I ask, Your Honor, to please release this young man into his custody."

"Thank you, Mr. Garmon," Judge Hightower said. Then she lowered her gaze to study some papers. After a minute, the judge looked up at the court-appointed attorney representing Timothy "Hammer" Thomas. "Okay, Ms. Wilson, I suppose you have much the same to say about your client?"

"I do, Your Honor. Mr. Thomas also maintains the fire was an accident. There was no malicious intent, whatsoever. He, too, is a good student. His mother is here," she paused to lift a hand toward the lady seated alone. "She will confine him to her home until the court deems otherwise."

Without responding, the judge again looked down at the papers.

Mr. Garmon glanced over to the other attorney. Their eyes met. At best, the chances were 50-50—the percentage they had speculated between them—Judge Sharon "Hang 'em All" Hightower would release the boys.

Judge Hightower lifted her eyes from the papers, her gaze passing over the boys and their lawyers. The Willis boy's father sat slouched in his seat, toothpick in the corner of his mouth, both arms spread wide and draped across the seat's high, rounded back, glaring back at her. Mrs. Thomas, in contrast, appeared to be nodding off. The judge stared a long moment, her eyes coming to linger on the frazzled-looking woman's tangled mane. A question entered the judge's mind. *When was the last time you drug a brush through that mess?*

"Do you have anything to say to the Court?" Judge Hightower asked, suddenly turning her full attention to Marvin.

"Just tell the judge what you told me," Mr. Garmon said to Marvin, his hand momentarily resting on the boy's shoulder.

"We, uh—I, uh, I didn't mean to start any fire. It was an accident. I'm really sorry for what happened."

"And you, young man?" Judge Hightower shifted her gaze to Timothy.

"We were just smoking. It was an accident, I guess. I don't know how the fire got going, but we didn't mean for it to happen."

Judge Hightower stared at Timothy for a long, stone-faced minute. Then she turned her coal-black eyes back on Marvin and gave him the same uneasy treatment for another long minute. At last, she looked down and began writing on the papers before her.

"The fire," she began, looking up, "the result of actions by these two—these two young men—caused substantial damages and significant loss of property. But for the grace of God, and the timely response of the Fire Department, the losses could have been much greater. Of even greater concern to the Court, lives were placed in jeopardy."

The judge hesitated, her hard eyes resting again on Marvin for a moment, then moving to Timothy. No one but she knew when she looked at each boy, she saw a third young man who had stood before her some 20 years ago. She had shown him mercy. He had started another fire within hours of his release. The resulting tragedy continued to haunt her.

"I am most hesitant," the judge began speaking again, "to release these young men, not knowing if either or both have a predilection toward setting fires, until a child psychologist can evaluate them. "Tabitha," she said, turning toward her clerk. "Please see if Dr. Fathbruckner can meet with these two early next week."

Tabitha consulted a register, made a hushed phone call. She covered the mouthpiece a couple of minutes later and nodded to the judge.

"Tuesday, the 31st, at 9 and 11 a.m. are available, Your Honor," she said.

"Very good," Judge Hightower nodded. "Please schedule those times." The judge made a pyramid of her hands and rested her chin on her fingertips. She remained silent for a long minute, cutting her eyes first toward Timothy, then Marvin. Straightening, finally, she turned her attention to the two attorneys. "It is a good sign that a parent is here for each defendant. Though I have concerns, I have determined to release them to their custody. At all times, both defendants are to be kept under adult supervision until the Court reconvenes to review their evaluations. You will convey the importance of adhering to these requirements to the respective parents."

"Yes, Your Honor," the two attorneys replied together.

"Okay, Tabitha," the judge said, turning to her clerk, "let's see when we can reconvene. We need to ensure the doctor has time to prepare his summaries."

"Friday, the third, at 2:30?" Tabitha replied several seconds later, a quizzical expression on her face.

"June third it is." Judge Hightower glanced to the attorneys again. Please also inform the parents they are responsible for having their sons at Dr. Fathbruckner's Tuesday and back here in court next Friday."

Before the attorneys could answer, Marvin's father leaped to his feet.

"Now just a minute here," he said, his voice loud and angry. "I've done had to take off work this afternoon, and now you want me taking off two more days next week."

The bailiff had started in the man's direction at his first word. He was only a step away when the judge spoke.

"You are Mr. Willis, sir?" the judge asked him, maintaining an even tone.

"I'm Fred Willis." he snapped. "Marvin's daddy. No sense in all this running around. You just let me handle it, and I'll straighten him right out."

"I am afraid I can't simply do that, Mr. Willis. In the best interest of all concerned, your son must be evaluated. Then he must return to this court on the third."

"Then you're a whore-faced bitch!"

"Order!" Judge Hightower banged her gavel. "You will control yourself in my court, sir."

"Sorry, judge, I said that backwards. You're a dog-faced whore!"

"Bailiff, remove this man."

In an instant, the bailiff had Marvin's father by the arm. Willis slung the bailiff's hand off, then threw a wild punch at his head, which missed. A moment later the bailiff had him in a half nelson, but the man continued to struggle, sending them both dancing into the aisle, where they crashed in a writhing heap on the floor. The two boys and their attorneys stood watching, horrified, as more officers came hustling into the courtroom. Timothy's mother was screaming and crying, her hands pressed against the side of her face as she backed into a corner. Mr. Willis was quickly subdued, his hands shackled behind him. Two of the bailiffs caught an arm each and lifted him to his feet, facing the judge.

"I find you in contempt of court, Mr. Willis. You shall spend the night in the county jail."

"You're a stupid-ass piece of trash!"

"Make it two nights."

The gavel slammed down again.

Chapter 62

3:41 p.m.

Tom wondered how much longer he could hold it in, the explosion of nerves sparking inside him. He thought he was doing a fair job of maintaining his composure. Self-control was something he expected of himself. He was never one to show much emotion, especially in public. This, however, was the hardest thing he had ever experienced. If only someone would tell them something! He stared up at the clock high on the wall, thought of the old saying about time dragging.

It had been a long time since he had known this feeling. Since the early morning when Clarisse was born, he guessed. Katie had gone into labor about 10:30 in the morning, and Clarisse had not made her appearance until 5:15 a.m. the following day. Time had certainly dragged its feet all those long hours, though the anticipation of the birth of their child had taken the edge off in a good way. Of course, it was a different matter as far as Katie was concerned. Never once had she complained of what she had gone through to give birth. She smiled up at him as he held their daughter for the first time; simply smiled an exhausted happy smile and said, "Finally."

Now their baby girl sat next to him, his child, their wonderful grown daughter, and held his hand. It seemed the most natural thing in the world. Like her mother, she was a comforter, one who eased the pain of others with her touch, her voice. Like her mother, she would not complain, no matter how much she herself suffered.

Jack, though, was a chip off his own block. He hardly ever showed emotion. Like his father, he saw himself as the protector, the one who must remain strong in the face of any trial. This, however, was outside his experience. Since his arrival he had been unable to stay in one place more than a few minutes. He would be up and out of his seat before he had a chance to get settled in, pacing the room, going from window to window, seemingly on the watch for someone or something due to arrive at any moment to come hurrying in from the storm. Then he would stride back over to Tom and Clarisse, first ask his father, then his sister, if they needed anything. Now he sat staring at the television, apparently much interested in the progress of the baseball game.

"Who's winning?" Tom asked him.

"What, Dad?" Jack answered anxiously, ready to leap up and do his father's bidding; to do anything but sit there.

"Who's ahead?"

"Oh." For several long seconds Jack was not certain what his father was talking about. Then he realized a baseball game was on the television. "Oh," he said again. "Uh, Cards—I think." A moment later he asked. "Want a cup of coffee, Dad?" He hopped to his feet.

"I've got enough caffeine in me now to stay up all night. Thanks, though."

"Clarisse?"

"I'm fine," she whispered softly, a smile turning the corners of her mouth up a hint. Her brother was a good person, but this had to be a record for him trying to do nice things for others. He had always been a bit self-centered. It hit her like a gust of wind, clearing her mind. Perhaps she had always been mistaken.

Across the way a black woman of indeterminant age—she could have been 60 or 85—rose slowly from her seat. She and Tom, because of where they were situated, were facing directly at one another. For some time, she had been staring at him. Taking a moment to first smooth the wrinkles from her dress, she turned and walked the few feet along the row of chairs separating them. Rounding the end of the row, she slowly made her way down their aisle until she came to a halt before

Tom. Then she turned and began trying to move a chair out of the opposing line, to slide it closer to him.

Jack appeared to help, easing it forward until she said, "That's good. Thank you."

It took her a moment longer to get settled in place. At last, she looked up into Tom's face.

"These are your children?"

"They are," Tom answered. "This is my daughter, Clarisse, and my son, Jack. And I'm Tom."

All three smiled at her.

"My name is Mary," she answered, smiling in return. Her expression quickly became serious again. "You have been here a long time."

"That we have, Mary," Tom acknowledged, "and so have you. I saw you over there when we first came in."

"Your wife?"

"Yes. She was in a car accident. She's in surgery now."

Mary nodded.

"And you?" Tom asked. "Who do you have here?"

"My husband. William had a stroke."

"I'm sorry." Tom replied. He heard his children repeating his words.

Long, quiet seconds passed, then, "Tom is my son's name. Thomas Brinley Shobe."

"How about that?" Tom smiled, glad to have the connection, no matter how tenuous. "Is he, uh, here? On the way?"

"No," she said, looking him directly in the eye. "He moved to California many years ago. He called once, then we never heard from him again. The police could tell us nothing, but they seemed to believe the worst."

"Oh my," Tom said, nonplussed. It took him a moment to speak more. "I am so sorry. I—I don't know what else to say. What a loss you must—" He could go no further. The idea of never again hearing from either Jack or Clarisse, and worse, thinking they might be dead, was overwhelming. Then he felt a touch on his hand. Looking down, he saw her hand resting on his.

"I'm sorry means everything. I thank you."

Tom could only smile.

"William and I were blessed. Our son came to us later in life. We did not think we would ever have children." She paused a moment before continuing. "He is a good man. He is a wonderful son."

"I am certain he is," Tom replied, turning his hand slightly so he could gently clasp hers.

He sat for a few moments, Clarisse holding one hand, his other held by Mary. All were silent.

"Our lives have changed this day," Mary spoke at last. "It is very unsettling to think of how much might be different from now on."

"Yes," Tom answered. "It is very troubling."

They grew quiet again, each staring out into the distance at something no one else could see. After a bit Mary sighed softly, an unconscious act punctuated at the end by a barely audible, "Ah me." She glanced up at Tom, surprised by her words.

"Worry makes for a hard wait," she said, managing a weak smile.

"Yes, it does, my friend, it certainly does," Tom replied with a little smile of his own. He gave her hand a slight squeeze and leaned forward so their faces were but a foot apart. "Having you with us helps."

She softly bit her lower lip, then slowly leaned her head to one side so she was looking at him at an angle.

"And likewise, I'm sure."

Their eyes held one another in place for a time. No words were necessary. In the other's sight, alone, each found something much needed: something of understanding; something of kinship; something of a hint of courage. At last, Tom felt her squeeze his fingers hard.

"I was wondering," she said, for the first time the tiniest quaver in her voice. "Would you mind praying with me?"

She did not wait for his answer. Instead, she closed her eyes and bowed her head. Tom and his children closed their eyes and bowed their heads in turn.

Chapter 63

3:48 p.m.

Robert stood on his front porch looking out across the lawn toward little Emily's house. He could not see the rosebush from there, nor did he care to. He had already seen enough of the denuded plant from the window. At least the rain had finally stopped. Now water dripped along the length of the gutter into puddles beneath it in a loud symphony of irregular plops. *Guess it's time to have the gutters cleaned*, he thought, remembering how he used to do it himself, her on the ground holding the ladder steady. They were a good team, always working together, but those days were gone.

He took half a step forward to rest his hand on the wrought iron railing and lifted his eyes to stare at the stretch of open ground across the road. The stream cutting along its front edge usually wasn't much, its sharp banks no more than six or eight feet apart, its flow about what one might expect would spill from a garden hose left trickling in the grass, more a drainage ditch than creek. Today, however, it was rolling down from the hills, full-banked and angry, rumbling like a locomotive. Thousands of gallons of water cascaded in rapids and roils, threatening to leap out into the street. He hadn't seen it like that more than a handful of times in all the years they—he— had lived here. The storm must have dropped several inches of rain, so no wonder. Soon the little creek would start falling, however, since the rain had at last ceased.

After a time, he made his way slowly down the steps. He ambled a short distance along the front walk, then stepped out into the grass. The ground gave beneath him, a sodden sponge which sucked at his shoes with every stride. He paused a moment and looked all about, aware suddenly he was in the midst of a loose gathering of robins. A regiment of robins covered not just his lawn, but Emily's lawn, and the lawn of his neighbor on the other side of his house as well. The rainwater had flushed loads of earthworms to the surface. Now the robins were on the march, gathering them by the buckets. It bothered him to think he might be interrupting the harvest.

A memory flashed—her, in this very spot, laughing at a robin trying to pull an earthworm from the ground, the poor worm stretched out half a foot like a rubber band. Her laughter was a sweet memory, a warm, sweet memory. He stood there and allowed it to flow around him, to wrap him in its loose embrace for a while. Another memory drifted up against him. A warm blanket. He was ill, wracked with chills. She warmed a blanket in the dryer, laid it over him ever so softly. It felt as if she had caught a thread and drawn a sun-baked cloud down upon his skin.

Some time passed. At least he supposed it had, for he suddenly realized he was still standing in the middle of a parade ground of robins. They were paying him no mind, too busy in their work to be bothered by an old man, unmoving as a statue in the soaked grass, the brown water oozing up through the thin, cracked soles of his shoes and between his toes, the ground bubbling out to the sides when he shifted his weight.

He found his way eventually to the rosebush. There was no surprise, of course. From the kitchen window he had seen the damage, knew there was nothing here of the morning's beauty. He did not cry now, which surprised him a little, for he seemed to cry so easily of late. Perhaps it was because he was at last growing accustomed to disappointment. Perhaps, on the happier side, it was because he noticed the signs of promise, of renewal. There were buds, fat and ripe, at least a dozen poised to open, on the thorny branches. He would bring Emily here to his wife's favorite rosebush when she came home this afternoon. He would teach her of the wonder to come when these buds warmed to the sun and reflected its light back in unspiraling knots of brightest yellow. Together, he and Emily would check every day for that transformation. It was something to look forward to, especially because he knew his wife would ever be beside him, her hand squeezing his arm with Emily's every *ooh* and *ahh*. The thought made him smile.

He looked up, turning to follow the wisps of dark cloud speeding across the sky. Suddenly he stopped, stood frozen in place, his smile broadening until he felt the old thin skin growing taut across his cheekbones, staring at the rainbow arched over the eastern hills.

"Good afternoon, dear."

Chapter 64

3:49 p.m.

Attorney-at-Law Stephen Grimes showed his credentials to the guard. He hoped to be in and out of the jail in 15 minutes, tops. He had a big night coming with the Barristers' Ball. It was the no-miss event for any member of the bar in Green Springs, and he, Stephen Grimes, was the emcee. He needed to be there no later than 6 p.m., and he had to shower and shave first. Before cleaning up, he had to swing by the cleaners and get his tux. Before the tux, he must appear in court with his client, and finally, first of all, he must complete this visit with James Henry here in the Watkins County Detention Center.

It would not be a pleasant meeting for his client. The location guaranteed James Henry was already unhappy. How he might react once Stephen gave him the latest news would likely make his mood worse. Minutes earlier, he had picked up word detectives were executing a search warrant at James Henry's office, as he had suspected might happen. Certainly, no one would be glad to hear such news, though telling James Henry did not greatly bother Stephen. Bearing bad news was an element of his occupation. The client simply must be told, and that was that. Stephen's job as the attorney meant he must always strive to stay on an even emotional plane, to maintain intellectual detachment. This part was easier for him than most not in the profession might expect. It was an important element of what made him a good lawyer, and after all, it was not his tit caught in the wringer.

Speaking of wringers, James Henry looked like he had been through one when the guard led him into the visitors' area.

"It's about damn time!" James Henry spoke into the phone as Stephen raised the receiver on his side of the partition.

"I got here as soon as I could," Stephen replied smoothly. "I suggest we get right to brass tacks. They'll be coming to get you to appear before the judge in 10 or 15 minutes."

James Henry glared at him a long moment before replying, "Alright."

"I have a few questions I need to ask, and you must answer straight with me. Do you understand?"

"Yeah," James Henry replied, his glare not quite as mean.

"Did you use drugs before the accident?"

James Henry hesitated.

"James, we don't have time to play with."

"Yes. Yes, I did. I snorted a line of coke."

"Where did you do it? In your office?"

"No. Reservoir Hill Park." James Henry's glare was gone. He dropped his head before he continued. "I was in my car."

"Why were you at the park?"

"Met my connection. Made a buy."

"In broad daylight?"

"Yeah," James Henry replied softly, all the fire gone out of him.

Stephen resisted the impulse to shake his head. This was not good. The police were keeping an eye on things at Reservoir Hill. He had another client who had been busted there two days ago. At least that man had enough sense to make his transaction in the dark of night.

"Okay," Stephen went on, scribbling on his notepad as he spoke. "So, you were high when you had the accident?"

"I don't know. Maybe a little."

"Did you run the red light?"

"Not sure. Probably. Hell, I don't think so."

"If the judge asks, that's what you say: 'I don't think so.'"

"Okay."

"Did you, or rather, do you have any illicit drugs in your office?"

"Why?" James Henry snapped. The glare was back.

"The police are executing a search warrant at your office this instant. I need to know if there's anything they might find to complicate your situation further. Now, do you have anything there?"

James Henry hesitated so long Stephen had to prompt him again.

"Is there anything there?"

"Yes," James Henry finally answered, squirming like he was in a dentist's chair. "A little blow. Some pills. A bag of weed."

"What kind of pills?"

"Oxy, mostly. Maybe a few ludes."

Stephen resisted the impulse to say something about being up shit creek. Instead, he asked, "Anything else?" James Henry shook his head.

The attorney moved to questions related to the incident.

"Did you get into it with the police? What I'm hearing."

"No," James Henry seemed genuinely surprised. "Whoever said I did is lying."

It was Stephen's turn to glare. At last he said, "The truth, James."

James Henry waited a few more seconds before answering. "I might have had a few words with a couple of firefighters—one of them was a real smartass—but I don't remember anything about a problem with the cops."

"You argued with firefighters?"

"Well, uh, yeah—maybe a little."

Stephen shook his head.

"What's the big deal?"

"Don't want firefighters testifying against you. Most respected public servants. Jurors don't like it when a lawyer challenges them. Might as well smack a baby."

"Shit."

"Yeah," the attorney nodded.

When Stephen didn't say anything more right away, James Henry asked, "When are you going to get me out of here? I've got places to be tonight. Things to do."

Stephen simply stared at him for a couple of seconds before responding. The news was about to get worse.

"Did they take you for a blood test?"

"Yeah, at the ER."

"I doubt you are going anywhere till at least tomorrow, then. I fully expect the judge will hold you overnight, maybe longer, pending developments."

"Bullshit! It's just a car wreck."

"Yes, it was a car wreck. A wreck in which you have already admitted you were on cocaine. The blood test will confirm it. A wreck which has led the police to search your offices, such search, by your own account likely to turn up further illicit drugs. There's one other thing."

"What else?" James Henry asked, some of the heat gone from his tone.

"The lady in the other vehicle. A friend at Memorial tells me she's been in surgery since. If she dies—if she dies, we will be looking at a whole new set of very serious worries. With all these aggravating circumstances, a charge of manslaughter is not out of the question."

"Henry!" the voice belonged to a big burly guard. "Let's go. Can't keep the judge waiting."

"See you in the courtroom, James," Stephen said, then hung up the phone. On the way out the door he glanced at his watch: 4 p.m. on the nose. Appearing before the judge shouldn't take but a few minutes. The proceeding would be wrapped up by 4:15, 4:20 at the latest. Judge Snodgrass wouldn't dally, not on a Friday, especially on this Friday. He would be in a hurry to get home and get ready for the Barristers' Ball, too. His Honor was appearing in the opening skit.

Chapter 65

1601 Hours

Things finally began to slow down. Every company in the department had been running like crazy since the storm hit. Now they were working their way through the backlog of automatic alarm activations. Per protocol, Dispatch shuffled those calls to the back of the list whenever the number of runs exceeded the available companies, the idea being buildings equipped with automatic alarms also usually had automatic sprinkler systems. Because sprinklers are highly effective at extinguishing fires—or at least holding them in check—some response delay during a heavy call volume situation was acceptable. Besides, at this hour on a weekday, it was likely employees would be on the scene to confirm if there was an actual fire. Nevertheless, rather than waiting to receive confirmation all was well, Dispatch had been laboring throughout to make phone contact. Individual companies were now simply touching base at these locations, primarily to determine the status of alarm and suppression systems.

D. J. steered the engine along the access road to a modest-sized factory. With the lull in new calls, he was in a reflective mood.

Maybe it's time to make a little change in things, he thought.

He really liked Tina, the woman he had spent the night with. They had been seeing each other for a year and a half. That had to be some kind of record for him. She was a nice lady, happy and fun-loving. Being truthful with himself, his feelings had started to run deeper than simply liking her. Tina was different from his usual companions. She could talk on any subject, it seemed. The woman could cook up a storm, too, not to mention she was very easy on the eyes. To top it off, she was a wonderful lover. He could do a lot worse. Hell, he *had* done a lot worse! Any number of times. *As a matter of fact*, he chuckled to himself, *I have always done worse.* Maybe he would give her a call tomorrow morning, invite her to dinner at a really nice place, sound her out on the idea of making things a little more permanent. *Yeah*, he decided after a moment's reflection, *I'll give her a ring as soon as the shift ends.*

Wayne was thinking of Virginia. She would be getting home before long. He imagined her kicking off her shoes, taking a seat in her recliner in the den, opening the paper. It struck him just how much he missed her, a thought he usually managed to keep suppressed on duty days. The thought was out there now, however, so he went with it. He knew they had something rare. Between juggling their jobs, keeping up with the kids and the grandkids, and helping out whichever member of their extended family happened to need their help at the time—seemed there was always one of their gang in something of a bind—the two of them still had the old spark. It was time they did something a little special, like take a couple of days off and go down to Gatlinburg. She loved the Smoky Mountains. She also loved him. Of this he was certain, as certain as he was of him loving her. *Yeah, sliding out of town for a while was just the ticket.* The idea made him smile.

D. J. noticed the smile when he checked the mirror on the captain's side. He didn't say anything, however, assuming the man was simply happy. Busy days like today always put everybody in a better mood. It was preferable to be dealing with problems rather than waiting and wondering what was about to fly apart in someone's world next, he figured.

Mick was thinking of business—fire department business. As soon as they got back to the station, he would have to fly into getting supper ready. That would keep him hopping for at least half an hour. There was no quicker way around it. And the guys would be hungry, too, all of them having put in a hard afternoon. Maybe, finally, tonight he could get back in the books. The promotional exams were only a month away. It was time he really got to cracking if he wanted to have a hope of making rank this year.

Probie Wan rode quietly in his jump seat, listening to the low growl of the diesel, feeling the vibrations of the truck thrumming into his thigh as he rested it up against the engine cowling. Like after this morning's garage fire, he was hot, sweaty, grimy dirty, and becoming more satisfied with himself with every passing minute. *What a day!* He counted the runs in his head. This milk-run made seven, and it was only 4 p.m. *Wow!* Most of his other days on shift had been rather calm, with only a handful of runs getting his blood pressure up. *But today!* He imagined this was how a veteran felt. He couldn't wait to tell Caroline about it tomorrow. She always wanted to know what he had seen and done on the job. Then the memory of her standing before him this morning, so exquisitely beautiful, came flooding into his mind. Like the captain, he began to smile.

D. J. guided the engine into a spot before the main entrance to the factory. The other members of the crew swung down to the ground, then walked together toward the building's main door. A maintenance man appeared outside the entrance as they neared. Everything was okay, it seemed. The alarm system had reset. A water-pressure surge had triggered it—a common problem with this facility. As the crew turned back toward the engine, Captain Buckman stole a quick glance toward the west. A long black line, thick and angry, was draped across the horizon. The second round of storms was approaching.

Chapter 66

4:06 p.m.

Probie Wan's wife could not have explained why she had to look in her purse to see if it was there. Of course, it was. No one would steal a pregnancy test kit, and she had just looked five minutes ago. Caroline dropped her purse back to the floor. A car was at the kiosk. She recognized it; recognized the small, elderly man behind the wheel—Mr. Granitelli. He was so cute in his little golfing hat.

"Hi, Mr. Granitelli," she said into the mic. "How's my favorite customer today?"

"Wonderful, my angel. Able to be out and get around. At my age it's about the best you can hope."

The container came swishing in through the air tube. She opened it to find a single $100 bill.

"Want the usual, Mr. Granitelli?"

"Yes, please. And how are you today?" he added a moment later.

"I'm fine," she answered as she counted out the change: four $20s, three $5s, five $1s. "Thank you for asking."

"Wooo, was that a storm or what?"

"Yes, sir. I was frightened," she answered as she placed the bills in the container.

"Is your young man on duty?"

She punched the return button. "Yes, he is."

"Bet he's run his legs off today. He must be a good boy if he's married to you. Tell him I'm proud of him."

"Thank you, Mr. Granitelli. I'll be happy to tell him. I'm proud of him, too."

"You have a good evening, my angel."

"I will. You too, sir."

Caroline certainly hoped to have a good evening. She hoped

to have a great evening. Otherwise, she would not have bothered to buy the kit. When she stepped out to get a sandwich for lunch, she suddenly had this feeling, so powerful, so true, like she had felt at the house earlier. Her woman's intuition was really kicking in. She found herself in the aisle at the drug store down the street, looking at pregnancy tests. Ever since, it had been all she could do to keep from slipping into the bathroom here at the bank to find out. What if it were positive? She would scare the customers and her fellow workers half to death, screaming and jumping for joy. Such a reaction simply would not do, however. Her stern, pinched-face manager might have the big one. Somehow, she would hold back, wait and take the test when she got home, take it the very first thing after walking in the door. And it would be positive. She didn't have a doubt. The only question would be could she wait until Ron got home in the morning to tell him? Or would she end up rushing down to the station tonight?

Chapter 67

4:10 p.m.

Odell had never given much thought to the fact his home faced west, other than when the late afternoon sun ran him off his front porch. Today the storm quick marched in from that direction, carried forward by hard, angry winds which sent the porch swing to bouncing on rattling chains. Those winds pushed on through double windows left a few inches ajar, cooling the living room where Odell lay sprawled on the couch, asleep, and cooled him, too. Though he did not waken, in response he crossed his arms, hugging himself, and pushed his head a tiny bit deeper back into Letha's embroidered pillow.

The wind would have been of minor consequence but for two other factors. Odell had not closed the main door when he came in, leaving only the screen door to guard the opening. Second, he had not bothered to shut the back door in the kitchen, either. This opening was protected only by a screen door, also, so both front and back entrances allowed the wind's full force to pass unimpeded through the house. The gaps at the bottoms of the double windows served to intensify this effect by increasing the incoming pressure. In hot weather like today this arrangement was desirable, for the home was not air-conditioned.

When the storm hit, however, and the rain came hammering in horizontal sheets, enough water blew through the front screen door and windows to form little puddles on the floorboards of the living room. Odell did not notice. In fact, he never woke up, so he noticed absolutely nothing about the storm—the rain, the booms of thunder, the bright flashes of lightning, the drum rolls of hail on the roof, and certainly not the hard wind which sent papers flying off the end table and scattering down the hallway. He was too drunk to lift his lead-filled head from the pillow had he noticed.

Though he was never aware of the wind, the invisible force did perform one great service for Odell. It gave him a chance at survival.

No one ever lays down to sleep expecting their house to catch fire. Odell surely did not that day. All he wanted was the peace of sleeping off what for him constituted a wonderful afternoon. Indeed, up until he fell from the barstool and Joe closed the tap to him, Odell would have declared it a perfect afternoon. He had a most pleasant buzz, he was laughing it up with the other guys in the bar, and of greatest significance, Letha—torment's own whip cracker—was nowhere to be seen.

Then, as he dreamed of a heavenly place where a man could keep a tap forever in a keg of cold beer, flames erupted only a few feet away—flames which grew in strength and intensity with unbelievable speed to anyone other than a firefighter. They gnawed at the walls and ceilings of the bathroom, the hallway, growing ever bigger and meaner and hungrier. In the kitchen they shot toward the screen door with blow torch intensity, threatening to devour every splinter in one searing gulp. The flames were pushed to the opening, fed a constant dose of fresh oxygen that increased their strength, while they remained held in abeyance in the hallway just outside the living room, all by the wind.

Odell slept on with nary so much as a twitch of an eyelid as the rear wall of his house was incinerated, inch by charcoaled inch, during those early moments. Then the wind shifted direction, quartering in from the south as a section of the gust front broke free and raced ahead at an angle. Instantly the air moving through the house was hardly more than a breeze. Its power dropped further, until it no longer possessed the strength to hold the flames back in the hall. The smoke came into the living room first, a black, oily concoction, silent, stealthy, defying gravity to slip across the ceiling in softly rolling waves and swirls borne along by the heat. It quickly formed a layer only a foot or so thick from the ceiling down. In moments, the layer had grown in depth to two feet. It grew thicker with alarming speed, dropping ever closer to Odell. In seconds it would cover his nose, his mouth, the carbon monoxide poison right there for his taking, so potent it was as if the dark angel himself were whispering death. Only a breath or two and it would all be—

Bam!

The explosion did it, finally. Odell's head shot up from the pillow and plunged into the smoke. Had he jumped to his feet, had he even managed to sit up just a little toward straight, he would have died right there, for the heat, too, was layered in the smoke, hundreds of degrees hotter only a handful of feet higher, far more than his throat or lungs could have withstood without fatal damage. As it was, he was again fortunate, for the old couch with its sagging frame and worn-out cushions sat close to the floor, where the heat was the lowest and the smoke the thinnest. He half fell, half rolled onto the rug, vomiting, coughing so hard at the same instant it ripped and tore at things down low in his gut. Everything in his sinuses and a gallon more broke loose, came pouring from his nose. He tried to hold his eyes open, but they teared up immediately, burning with the acrid smoke. Frightened beyond any semblance of reason, he crawled alongside the coffee table, unthinkingly shoved it aside with a forearm, a pitiful, tortured animal, his face pressed to the rug, propelled by primal instinct.

He heard the flames crackling, popping, objects somewhere close falling, breaking, knew without thinking the fire was in the room with him now, searching, reaching after him with blistering talons. Suddenly there was a glimmer of light, low, rectangular, shrinking. He slithered toward it, toward the doorway, the scorching heat pressing down upon his back. Then Odell was on concrete, cool stone against his belly, the flames chasing out the top of the doorframe behind him, crackling louder, mocking his weakness, him coughing, coughing, coughing, as if he must expel every atom of his inner being.

The coughing was what alerted his neighbor, Vernon, who lived two houses down. Had Vernon not been late going to the box to get his newspaper he never would have heard those awful retching sounds. But he was out of iced tea and had taken the few minutes necessary to brew a new pitcher before he stepped outside, so he did hear Odell's coughing. Trying to focus in on the source, he discovered the smoke. An instant later he spotted Odell lying face down at the head of the porch steps. Yellow fire lapped out in sharp waves across the ceiling above him. One of Odell's hands was extended, his fingers scratching at the lip of a step, a poor soul drowning in an inverted sea, desperately trying to grasp something, anything, to pull him away from his horrid pursuer.

Vernon leaped forward. Later he would remember the main details: sprinting down the sidewalk; dragging Odell off the steps, his hands under the older man's armpits; the fire flashing over in the living room in a bright burst of orange that sent flames shooting out through broken windowpanes to attack the porch from a new angle and drive him to his knees with their heat. Suddenly he was half-dragging, half-carrying Odell, across the yard, slipping and stumbling on the wet grass, low waves of hot smoke chasing, not stopping until they reached the curb; rolling Odell onto his back, trying to remember the CPR sequence, on his knees bending down to share his breath.

He did not have to, though. Odell coughed so hard his knees bent almost to his chest, and he brought up something squishy filthy. Vernon turned the man's head to the side, raked a ball of soot-filled gunk away from the corner of his mouth. Odell sucked in a sharp breath, looked up at Vernon through red, watering eyes, trying to focus, his blackened lips at last moving.

"Beans," he said, and the next coughing spasm began.

Chapter 68

4:13 p.m.

Darlene couldn't believe what she was seeing when she stepped into the day care. In the hallway up ahead, a large limb protruded from the ceiling. She stopped and stared a moment, an involuntary shiver icing her spine. Finally, she moved forward and carefully worked her way around the new obstacle. Somehow, she managed not to step in the puddle growing on the floor beneath.

All the children were in the play area in the rear section of the building. Brandon, her Emily's little red-headed friend, was standing stoically, his back to the big window on the left side. Grayson, another little friend, was peering in one of Brandon's ears. Miriam and Emily were on Brandon's other side. Emily was looking in this ear. Two more or less equal lines of children—all the remaining boys and girls, it appeared—extended from Brandon's ears across the room. The group was most uncharacteristically subdued. Ms. Woods was standing off to the side, watching and biting her lower lip to keep from laughing out loud. She noticed Darlene and came walking over to her.

"What in the world?" Darlene asked, glancing back toward the hallway.

"Oh, my Lord," Ms. Woods replied, instantly serious. "The storm was so noisy we didn't even hear it when the limb came through. I didn't see the thing until later. Scared me to death."

"I imagine. If one of the children, or you—"

"Yes," Ms. Woods nodded solemnly. After a minute she added, "I've already called a roofer and the insurance company. We should have things fixed by Monday."

"Good, good," Darlene replied, her attention shifting to the children. "I have never seen them this quiet. What in the world are they doing with little Brandon?"

"Oh, they think there's a rabbit in his head," Ms. Woods laughed. "Something they saw in a cartoon yesterday. They've been looking inside his ears half the day. He doesn't seem to mind."

At that moment Brandon cut his eyes toward the women. Indeed, his expression did not convey the least aggravation. If anything, he seemed happily resigned to having his head examined by his classmates.

"Okay, children," Ms. Gina called out in a commanding voice. Then she bent down to grab a toy off the floor. "Let's get our things put up. Mommies and daddies will be here soon."

The two ear lines dissolved immediately as children went scurrying about in every direction. Emily and Miriam managed to stay close to each other in all the confusion. After a few seconds, however, Emily spotted her mother and came flying to her.

"Mommy! Mommy! Mommy!" she yelled, wrapping her arms around her mother's legs.

"How's my baby girl?" Darlene asked, bending to kiss the top of her daughter's head. Miriam had followed Emily. She stood a few feet behind her now, her expression a mixture of anxiousness and sadness. Suddenly she took a couple of running steps forward and threw one arm around Emily. With the other she grasped at Darlene's knees. Reaching down, Darlene patted the child on her back. This was something new. She looked in confusion to Ms. Woods.

"They always stay close together, as you know, but since the storm they have been absolutely inseparable. Poor Miriam was so scared. Emily comforted her the whole time. You have a brave little girl."

"Aw, thank you," Darlene said, her smile one of a knowing and proud mother. Then she bent down and gave Miriam a kiss on the top of her head, too. A moment later she turned back to the teacher. "That storm was horrible. All that lightning. It just would not stop."

"Oh, I know. It must have hit a lot of things. We've been hearing sirens all afternoon."

"Yes, me too," Darlene paused, seemingly lost in thought. "Hope no one was hurt."

"I pray so."

Darlene stood there a moment longer, then she bent down to her daughter again. "Time to go, Emily. Tell Ms. Woods and Ms. Gina goodbye."

Emily released her hold on her mother and looked up at the headmistress.

"Goodbye, Ms. Woods." She craned her head around to find Ms. Gina. "Goodbye, Ms. Gina."

"Bye Emily," the ladies answered one after the other.

Her friend continued to cling to her, however, hugging her with both arms.

"It'll be all right," Emily said, hugging her back.

Chapter 69

1614 Hours

The captain waved to Lester, the maintenance man at the factory, and swung up to his seat in the cab. As soon as he was buckled in, he keyed the mic on the truck radio.

"Engine 4 to Fire Dispatch."

"Engine 4."

"Engine 4 is 10-8.

"Engine 4 is 10-8, 1615 hours," the dispatcher replied.

"Fire Dispatch to Battalion 1."

Batman answered a couple of seconds later.

"Battalion 1."

"The backlog of calls has been cleared. All units are now in service."

"10-4 Dispatch. Well done."

It wasn't standard protocol to compliment anyone over the radio, but Batman thought the dispatchers deserved it. The storm had triggered an avalanche of calls onto an already busy afternoon. They had managed the communications end of the response to the onslaught in an efficient, professional manner.

"Thank you, Battalion 1."

In the cab of Engine 4 Captain Buckman listened to the exchange. He was glad Batman had complimented Dispatch. The dispatchers had earned it. It was also a relief knowing the backlog had been cleared. He looked over at D. J. and smiled. "Home, James," he ordered, and eased back against the seat. A little break would be welcome. He had to admit to himself he was feeling it a bit. The old bones were aching.

"Yes sir," the engineer grinned, already pressing his foot down on the accelerator. The truck surged forward.

After a short distance, the access road made a half loop, so they were facing due west. In the few minutes since they first passed along this stretch the sky had changed. The dark line on the horizon of moments before was now a much closer high, black wall. Lightning ripped and sparked along the front in sharp stabs and fractured webs which shifted and reformed with each new pulse.

"You see that mess?" D. J. asked.

"Yeah," the captain answered, sounding as tired as he felt, sounding resigned to being even more fatigued shortly. "Moving this way in a hurry. Better grab a breath while we can, cause this one looks as bad as the—"

Ringgggggg!

The tones started, one set following hard on the heels of another.

"Our lucky day," D. J. said, his voice as flat, as resigned as Captain Buckman's. "Playing our song," he added, recognizing the tones for their company before the dispatcher began speaking. He reached over on the console to flip the warning lights on.

"Attention Battalion 1, Engine 4, Rescue 1—"The dispatcher continued reciting the companies being knocked out, then, "Respond to a structure fire at 1322 Shannon Way. Repeating—"

"Not too far," the engineer noted, raising his voice over the dispatcher's voice. He reached down to turn the knob on the siren. "Four or five blocks. Should be first in."

Captain Buckman was already looking out the right corner of the windshield in the direction of the address. The instant the dispatcher concluded the knockout, he brought the mic up, keyed it, "Engine 4, 10-6. Break. Engine 4 is in the area. We have smoke showing."Then he twisted his head around toward the jump seats. "Saddle up, men. Looks like we've got one."

A minute and 35 seconds later Captain Buckman keyed the mic again.

"Engine 4 on the scene, one story frame residence. We have a working fire. This is Shannon Command."

"Engine 4 on the scene," the dispatcher repeated. "1322 Shannon Way. One story frame residence. Working fire. Designated Shannon Command."

Captain Buckman swung to the ground. Facing the house, he could see fire and smoke billowing out the open front door and through some broken windowpanes onto the porch. The open door was key. Might be an indication of people inside. Glancing to the left, he saw a car in the gravel drive. That added to the people at home worry. Mick and Probie Wan appeared next to him, their masks already on.

"Preconnect."

The two firefighters turned back to the engine. Probie Wan reached up first and began pulling off the nozzle half of the hose load.

Captain Buckman lifted an ax from its bracket on the side of the truck. Striding across the yard, he brought the mic of his portable radio to his mouth.

"Engine 4 to Battalion 1."

"Battalion 1."

"Need a supply line."

"10-4. Battalion 1 to Rescue 1."

The captain didn't need to hear which company Batman was designating to bring them a five-inch supply line. Nor did he need to know what would inevitably follow—the assignment of a company to pull a second attack line. Providing backup was standard procedure. Having managed a look at both the right side and the front of the house as they rolled up, he moved to the left, between the house and car, and made his way toward the rear. Fire was not venting along this side, so he kept going until he reached the backyard. Heavy fire was blowing out the back door, however. He turned back the way he had come, having covered the four sides, completing his size-up.

Returning to the front, the captain met his firefighters a few feet from the porch steps just as the skies opened again. They ignored the downpour. Probie Wan and Mick finished shaking out the last kinks in the line as the hose began swelling and jumping, charging with water. Captain Buckman rested his ax handle against his thigh, then pushed his helmet back from his head. In seconds, his mask was in place, straps cinched tight, hood up, helmet back atop his head. Connecting the mask to the regulator, he reached behind and turned his air bottle on, took a breath just as Probie Wan hit the front of the house with a straight stream. As the exposed flames darkened down, Probie Wan and Mick moved forward and up the steps, Probie Wan directing the nozzle to keep the fire pushed back inside the doorway. On the porch they dropped to their knees. Captain Buckman joined them.

"I'll search as we go," the captain said to Mick, clapping him on the shoulder. Keying the portable's mic, he called Dispatch. "Shannon Command to Fire Dispatch."

"Shannon Command."

"Engine 4 is making entry. Command is in offensive mode," meaning he would guide his crew's fire suppression efforts from inside the building.

"Engine 4 making entry. Shannon Command in offensive mode. 1622 hours."

From Vernon's front porch, he and Odell watched the fire-fighters disappear into the smoke, both too winded, too shaken to realize it might be important for the crew to know that no one was inside the burning house.

Probie Wan had already switched the nozzle to a shield of narrow fog to give them some protection from the heat. He swept the stream around the inside of the doorway, blacking out all the fire he could see. Steam and smoke rolled back over the men in a hot cloud which raced along the concrete floor of the porch and spilled out onto the grass behind them. As one, they began crawling forward.

"Kick this mother's ass!" Mick growled in his mask.

Probie Wan stopped just inside the doorway. Mick moved up tight against him, braced his back with a shoulder. The smoke was incredibly thick, the flames no more than a dull, orange glow that came and went through the blackness. Things were popping, cracking, falling. The rookie worked the stream around the room systematically, locating fire by hearing as much as sight. Pivoting at his waist, he switched to straight stream and shot where he thought the hallway might be. Another wave of steam drove the men lower, confirming Probie Wan's aim. They crawled forward once more.

"Right-hand search," Captain Buckman said into Mick's ear, telling him he was going to check the room for victims, keeping the wall on his right side as he went. It was a two-man job when you had enough personnel. Since they didn't, the best he could do was a primary search on his own. If he didn't return quickly, his hose team would know which way he had gone as they searched, in turn, for him.

"Right-hand search," Mick acknowledged.

On the left at the beginning of the hallway was a partially open door to another room. There was fire here also, though not as extensive as it had been in the living room. Probie Wan and Mick crawled to the doorway, pulling the line along with them. Probie Wan settled on his knees, felt Mick pushing against his back again, and opened the nozzle on narrow fog. Working the stream about in a wide circle, he quickly knocked down the fire inside.

"Search complete," Captain Buckman said in Mick's ear, reporting about the living room.

"Got a room on the left here, Cap."

The hose team crawled a yard into the hallway, the officer making his way over the line behind them and into the second room.

"Right-hand search," Captain Buckman called again, and once more Mick echoed his words.

The captain moved out into the room as far as he could go and maintain contact with the wall on his right. Holding his ax by the blade in his left hand, he extended his arm and swept the handle across the floor, seeking to find a victim—or victims—who might be lying there. In this manner, he quickly crawled around the walls until he came to a bed. He swept the ax underneath, a place where children and pets sometimes sought refuge, then lifted it and swept across the covers. Nothing. Moving forward again, he was soon back at the doorway.

"Search complete," he said, just in time to feel like he was in a pressure cooker.

The captain knew instantly what had happened, though he was powerless to do anything about it, powerless to do anything but flop around on the floor as he and his crew were scalded. Up until then, Probie Wan had been working the nozzle as he had been trained, alternating straight stream blasts of water along the hallway ceiling to break up the thermal layering, then switching to fog to push the flames and heat ahead of them. There was only one problem with fog: it readily converted to steam. With the nozzle on a fog setting, Probie Wan must have directed it into a small tight room. The resulting boiling wave, with nowhere to go but out the doorway where the hose team crouched, had enveloped them in a flash.

"Hellfire!" Even through his mask, Mick's pained yell was loud.

Fortunately, the steam bath ended after a few seconds and the firefighters regained control of their bodies. They went back to work as before, the captain quickly searching what turned out to be a bathroom as the hose team systematically made its way toward the rear of the house. Probie Wan and Mick soon came to the edge of the kitchen and found it filled with fire. The blaze was particularly intense around the back door, the walls and ceiling there a mass of flames. Probie Wan worked the area with a straight stream, ceiling first, blacking it down and sending what remained of the screen door flying into the back yard. He moved his aim right and blasted the glass panes out of the window over the sink—a window he had not known was there because he could not see it through the smoke. Switching to narrow fog, he worked the spray around the cabinet-filled walls until he could neither see nor hear anything else burning. Suddenly, there was light—not orange-flames light—but daylight coming through the thinning smoke at the doorway and the window.

Meanwhile, Captain Buckman had found the closed door to another bedroom on the left. He called out, "Left-hand search," and entered. The fire had not made its way into this room because of the closed door. There was only light smoke. The captain was back in seconds, closing the door behind him. "Search complete."

Probie Wan took a hard thump on the top of his helmet.

"By God, you're turning into a regular smoke eater!" Mick congratulated him.

Probie Wan grinned like a kid inside his mask. He didn't answer. He didn't need to. Then, for the first time, he heard other voices coming from inside the house. More firefighters had entered. A radio crackled with Batman's voice as he assumed command.

Captain Buckman spoke from just behind Mick, "I don't see any more fire. Do you?"

Sweeping his gaze across the jumbled chairs of the scorched, half-melted dinette set, the scattered pots and pans and broken crockery, the jigsaw-puzzle-shaped chunks of drywall lying about in pancaked heaps and wrinkled slabs, the alligatored face boards of the backdoor's frame, the heaps of soaked insulation and black-charred, steaming splinters and slivers of wood and ashes littering every surface, Mick answered as only a firefighter could answer, "Looks good to me."

Captain Buckman keyed his radio.

"Engine 4 to Command."

"Shannon Command," Batman answered.

"Fire is knocked down. Primary search completed."

"10-4. Primary search completed. Ladder 1 is conducting secondary search. Engine 7 is entering with a second line. Have you some relief in a minute."

"10-4."

From the front of the house came the sound of smoke ejectors. The air inside began to flow toward the back door and the broken window, carrying smoke and heat outside. In moments, they were able to stand. Probie Wan had choked the nozzle back and was wetting down hot spots when Sticks appeared in the hallway, a couple of pike-pole-toting truckies behind him.

"Take a break, Cap," Sticks said. "We got this."

Captain Buckman raised a gloved hand, his thumb pointed up. A moment later he spoke into his portable's mic.

"Engine 4 to Command."

"Engine 4."

"Engine 4 is exiting the building, C side."

As Sticks instructed his men on where to start pulling ceiling to check for fire extension, the crewmembers of Engine 4 made their way down the detritus covered steps to the backyard and into the refreshing bath of a torrential downpour.

Chapter 70

4:19 p.m.

Finally, Cody made his last stop. The tux was hanging in the back. He had already filled up the gas tank. Her flower sat in its clear plastic case on the floorboard behind him. And now, at last, he had the gallon of milk, wrapped in a yellow plastic grocery bag, laying on the passenger seat. He gunned it out of the store parking lot. In the back of his mind, he knew there was plenty of time for him to shower and change into his resplendent outfit. He could even be slow and careful shaving, which was a good thing. When he rushed, he always wound up looking like he had been in a sword fight, dripping blood from half a dozen cuts. He might even have time to go through the automatic carwash. Driving the wet streets was spotting his fine, hand-rubbed wax job, especially around the fender wells.

Without realizing what he was doing, Cody was suddenly on the bumper of a green minivan. He could see the long, black hair of the female driver. "Come on, lady," he said aloud. This feeling he needed to hurry was making him ever more anxious. Then he saw a small arm point out to the side from a blob—a child's car seat behind the driver—and he braked lightly, allowing the minivan to get ahead a few car lengths. That made things safer, of course, but did nothing to settle his nervous system. He knew he would not relax until he had Angie in the car, and they were on their merry way to the prom.

The minivan turned off on Shallowford Lane, which was the way to where Angie lived. His route was at last clear, not another car for two blocks. He gave it the gas. Up ahead a cop pulled out from a side street. Cody tapped the brakes as he glanced at the speedometer. Sixty in a 35 zone would get him a serious ticket, and who knew how many points off his license. He braked a little harder, settled around 40. Suddenly the police car turned on its blue lights and went speeding away. Cody relaxed—a little.

All at once he realized he was right on top of his turnoff. He cut hard, mashing the brake pedal at the same time, tires squealing on the damp blacktop. The driver's side wheels went off the road, plowed through the wet grass and mud, threatening to spin the car sideways. He jerked the wheel hard and found the rough edge of the pavement, went bouncing across the street at an angle, noisily slinging mud and gunk off his tires and onto his car. One mud pie somehow splatted against his door window, hung for a moment, then slid downward, leaving a brown trail to mark its path. Looking at the nasty glob almost made him run off the street on the other side. He jerked the wheel again, got the car headed more or less straight at last, though the sharp maneuver set the gallon of milk to bouncing up and down on the passenger seat. It finally went flying out of its slick bag and landed on the floorboard with a sodden thump which seemed to signal a fatal rupture.

"Rat shit!"

Without slowing further, Cody leaned over sideways, stretched, and managed to catch the milk jug by the handle. He held it up to check for leaks.

"Thank God!" he said, following the exclamation a half-second later with, "Oh, crap!"

He was on the wrong side of the street, headed straight for a parked car. Swerving out to miss it, he overcorrected, running a wheel onto the opposite sidewalk. He quickly got straight. There was his driveway. He zipped into it and came to a hard stop with a short squeak of rubber grabbing concrete.

It took Cody a moment to look over the mud-streaked mess—going through the carwash was now a necessity—and another moment to gather up the milk, and his tux, and the goofy flower for his lapel, and, most important, Angie's corsage. Then he trotted toward the door, propelled by the doomsday clock ticking inside his head.

Chapter 71

4:21 p.m.

Jack got to his feet and strolled over to the bank of windows facing west. It was clouding up again. The sky seemed to grow darker, more ominous, as he stared. After a few moments he turned back to face his family. Tom, Clarisse, and Mary continued to sit close together, his father still holding hands with the two women, though their time of prayer had ended several minutes earlier.

Now Tom and Mary spoke in soft tones, the hint of a smile first gracing one face, then the other, as if they were friends reminiscing about better times. A young woman entered the waiting room, coming through the automatic doors leading to the emergency treatment area. Dressed in pink scrubs, a clipboard cradled in the crook of her arm, she exuded an air of self-importance. She halted at the edge of the seating area and glanced down at the clipboard.

"Johnson family. Katie Johnson family."

Clarisse and Jack were instantly moving toward her. Tom started to jump up, then he hesitated. With a squeeze of her hand he said to Mary, "May God be with you."

"And with you and your family," Mary replied, squeezing back. Suddenly she pulled her hand from his. "Go." Tom was on his feet in a flash. Seconds later he was standing before the young woman, flanked by his children. *Surely to goodness if it were bad news—* he said to himself. *If she—no, they wouldn't tell us here before everyone.*

"My name is Shelia," the woman in pink introduced herself with a perfunctory smile, like people give who have become accustomed to breaking hard news. "They have moved Mrs. Johnson out of surgery and into the recovery room. If you will come with me, we'll go to a conference room. The surgeon should be out to see you in just a minute."

Recovery room, Tom thought as he and the kids fell into step behind Shelia. *She is alive! Thank God.* All this time and no word. The awful worrying thoughts had found their way inside him and scoured out a raw hole, left his stomach empty and aching. Just inside the double doors leading to the ER, Shelia made a turn to the left. After a few strides she stopped and opened a door, then held it as she motioned them inside.

"Dr. Phillips is her surgeon. He is the very best," she added from the doorway, smiling her practiced smile as each found a seat, Clarisse and Jack flanking Tom. *She says that to every family,* Tom imagined, a little white lie she employed, hoping it would hold family members back from peppering her with questions before she could make her escape. In this instance, Tom prayed she was telling the full truth. "He'll be right here," Shelia promised, pulling the door to behind her.

Two minutes, two interminably long minutes dragged by like rainy-day mornings. They sat there quietly, hands clasped together before them on the tabletop, staring straight ahead. At last, Clarisse ventured, speaking to no one in particular, "She must have been terribly injured."

"Yeah," Jack agreed after a moment's hesitation. "They had her in there forever."

"She is alive," Tom said, not cognizant of the relief in his voice as those three words came out.

There was a soft knock on the door.

"Come in," Jack practically shouted.

The door swung open. A tall, lanky man came stepping inside, a surgeon's cap askew atop his head. Fatigue lines darkened the areas around his eyes. He walked straight to Tom, who was coming to his feet.

"Daniel Phillips," the doctor said, shaking Tom's hand.

"Tom Johnson," Tom grabbed the doctor's hand with both his. *He's smiling! Got to be a good sign,* he thought. "My daughter,

Clarisse. And Jack, my son," Tom continued with the introductions as the doctor shook each of their hands in turn.

"Please, have a seat," the doctor gestured, then walked around to the opposite side of the table. "Believe I'll have one with you," he added, plopping down heavily on his chair's worn vinyl.

"Katie is going to be all right."

Tom exploded in tears. He had not had a clue they were coming. He could not have held them back even if he had known. Seeing him, both his children were instantly crying, too. Each placed a hand atop his nearest shoulder. The stress of waiting and worrying if Katie would live at last released, all three quickly recovered. The doctor began speaking again.

"She is going to be all right, but she will have a long, and often painful, recovery. Her injuries are very serious. She had significant internal bleeding." Tom heard Clarisse catch a sudden breath. "What took us so long. We had to make certain we had it under control."

Dr. Phillips paused a minute to allow his words to sink in.

"Her spleen was ruptured. There was no choice but to remove it. She has four broken ribs. Her left leg is broken—the femur, her thigh bone. The femoral artery was damaged, which led to major blood loss. Dr. Gilbert, an orthopedic specialist, joined me in setting the break. He will take an active role in guiding her recovery.

"She also complained of neck pain. Fortunately, her extremities are responsive, and we have not found anything to indicate major trauma to the spine. She received some strain / sprain-type injuries to her neck, no doubt, but we didn't find anything of concern in the scans. Of course, we will watch it all very closely for the next several days. I am optimistic she will not have any paralysis. We have called in Dr. Ramsi to consult on her case. He is a specialist in spinal injuries. You can have every confidence in what he tells you. Okay?

"We did a CT of her head, also, just to make certain there

was no sign of brain injury. She has developed a real shiner around her left eye, so she took a lick there, but we did not find any significant internal swelling or any fractures of the skull."

Dr Phillips paused a few moments, moved his gaze to linger a moment on each family member, finally settle on Tom.

"Katie is very fortunate. I will be frank. Things were touch and go for a while. If not for the first responders—they did everything right."

A silence enveloped the room for a few moments. Tom spoke at last.

"We realize how fortunate my wife is, doctor. There are many people we must thank for working to help—to help our special gal. You are the first. I want you to know how grateful we feel to have you as Katie's surgeon."

Dr. Phillips flashed a smile.

"Just one of the team, sir."

"Please extend our—our—" The words just would not come.

"I will tell them," Dr. Phillips said, sitting upright in his chair. He paused a moment before changing course. "Now, do any of you have any questions?"

Clarisse and Jack each echoed the other, their curiosity lost in relief.

"No, doctor. Thank you."

Tom simply shook his head at first. Then he found his voice.

"I'm sure we will think of at least 1,000 things as soon as you leave. For now, I'd just like to know how long before we can see her?"

"She will be in recovery for quite a time, I'm afraid. Could be as much as two hours, perhaps even a bit longer. You may stay in here until you can go in if you wish. It's not a problem. Or there's a cafeteria in the main building."

The doctor rose to his feet. Tom sprang up. He leaned across the table and grasped him by the hand.

"Thank you."

Once Tom was done, Jack offered his hand, too. Clarisse

stepped to the other side of the table and hugged the surgeon around his neck.

The doctor had not quite pulled the door closed behind him when they heard a female voice in the hallway.

"Hi, Doctor Phillips. Is the Johnson family in there?"

The door swung back open an instant later, and a young lady stuck her head in.

"I have Mrs. Johnson's personal effects here."

Clarisse was nearest the door. "Oh, thank you," she answered, taking a large plastic bag with white handles from the woman.

"Can I get you something to drink? Coffee? A soft drink? Some water?"

No one wanted anything, so the woman pulled the door softly to behind her. Clarisse placed the bag on the table and began pulling things out: her mother's cellphone first; her purse; a small, zip-lock bag holding her rings; a little flip-top box with Hendershott Jewelers emblazoned on the top. She opened the lid, hesitated a long moment, then turned and extended her hand to show her father what rested inside. Seeing his watch, the second hand ticking forward, Tom burst into tears again.

Chapter 72

4:34 p.m.

James Henry sat on the edge of his cot in the jail dormitory, a blanket draped over his shoulders and pulled tightly together in front to cover him. His prison issue clothes lay in a pile on his left. To say James Henry was steaming would be an understatement. He was close to blowing apart at the seams.

Stephen had been right. Judge Snodgrass had flat refused to consider releasing him.

"Given the results of Mr. Henry's blood test, this Court orders that he be held overnight."

The judge's order was bad enough, but the conversation that transpired between the attorneys and the judge was more troubling. There seemed to be a lot of concern for the other driver, the victim. *The victim!*

Apparently, she was in bad shape. As Stephen had explained, if she died, he could be looking at a manslaughter charge. The facts he was on drugs and had drugs in his vehicle, not to mention whatever the search of his office might have yielded, and of course, speeding and running a red light, were all aggravating circumstances. As his lawyer had tried to explain, one did not want aggravating circumstances when one stood before a judge.

At last James Henry had come to realize he was well and truly in it deep.

He glanced at the pile of prison garb, his childish sign of protest at his convoluted and troubling circumstances. He had rather wear a feed sack than this outfit. Please! Orange jumpsuit? Orange boxers and white socks? Cheap plastic, open-toed shower shoes? He had quickly stripped it all off and wrapped himself in the blanket from his cot when he thought no one was looking. Now, so what if the guard said to put it all back on? He would get around to it when he felt like it, and not a minute before.

"If you need help," the guard said as he came to a halt before James Henry again, "it won't be a problem to arrange." A second guard came wandering over, stopping to stare at him from a few feet off to the right, then a third officer joined the group on the other side.

"Gentlemen, if you don't mind me saying, the outfits here leave something to be desired."

"Take it up with the taxpayers," the first guard told him.

"I had just as soon wear what I have, thank you. Even here, since we are in America, I am entitled to some freedom in selecting my clothing. This blanket, my robe of choice in this sartorial desert, keeps me perfectly warm."

When the guard continued to stare back without comment, James Henry thought his silly protest might have a chance of working. He decided to push it a little farther.

"Perhaps you don't understand. I'm a very successful business-man, with many important and influential friends in this town."

"Oh, I understand just fine. You are a detainee in the Watkins County Detention Center. You absolutely will wear the detainee uniform while you are here."

James Henry heard a short series of pops from the right. He glanced over. The second guard was cracking his knuckles. His knuckles weren't what caught James Henry's eye, however. Though the man was of less than average height, his upper arms were as big around as fence posts. He had a chest to match. This guard casually glanced toward the first officer, his expression seeming to say, *Want me to snap this twig for you, boss?*

Movement off further to the right caught James Henry's attention. He cut his eyes toward it, saw other inmates beginning to gather in a loose line along the wall. All were staring at him.

"Now." The first guard's voice was not loud, but it carried real force in its tone just the same.

"Okay, okay," James Henry said, relenting at last. It had dawned on him the other inmates were lining up to watch something happen—to him. "I get the picture."

He reached over to the clothing pile and picked up the boxers. Glancing up, for the first time he noticed two particular inmates back behind the guards. A Mutt and Jeff pair—one big, one small—they were slouching against the wall just outside the doorway to the showers. The one on the right was a giant, easily six foot seven, thick and burly, his pumpkin-sized bald head sporting a large swastika tattoo on top. In contrast to his bare scalp, a tangled thicket of red hair protruded above the collar tabs of his jumpsuit. The second con was much smaller than James Henry. He had jet-black hair slicked straight back. There was something about him, a meanness, tight-coiled and grotesque, visible even in his laid-back stance, and further enhanced by an expression on his face that somehow appeared both empty and evil. On their arms and necks, the inmates were covered with enough ink to print the Sunday funny papers.

James Henry tried to stare back, to look as hard and tough as them. Suddenly, both blew kisses his way. Then the little one flashed a wink and began nodding. A smile like Satan at a barbeque spread over his face as his tongue traced his lips.

Trying to appear nonchalant, James Henry swung a foot up to slip through the boxers' leg. The movement made his blanket part down the middle a few inches. Though he doubted anyone could have seen much more than his foot, it didn't stop the little greasy con from whistling. The sound threw James Henry off. Snagging a toe on the underwear's waistband, he pulled too hard and lost his grip. The boxers sling-shotted off his toe to the floor.

"Come on," the head guard said. "We don't have all day."

Hurrying, James Henry stood, then bent over to pick up the underwear. In his haste, distracted by the attention aimed his way by the other prisoners, he failed to hang on tight to the blanket. In a flash gravity took over. The cover cascaded into a heap at his heels. James Henry froze, bent over, fire seemingly dancing across every naked inch of his skin.

"He's sure got a purty tan," the giant con remarked to no one in particular, "and the cutest little white butt I've ever seen."

James Henry snatched angrily at the boxers and the blanket. Inmates and guards alike were all roaring with laughter. Finally, somehow, he had both items in his hands at once. He snapped upright. With a twirl he swung the blanket over his shoulders, caught the front edges and pulled them together to hide his nakedness. Then he flopped down on the cot before anything else could happen. From somewhere out of all the racket he heard a singular voice—the little bastard with the slicked-back hair?

"Oooh! Drop 'em again, sugar."

Chapter 73

4:35 p.m.

Darlene unbuckled Emily's car seat. It was like throwing a switch. Her daughter was out of the car in an instant.

"Mommy! Mommy! It's a water slide!" Emily exclaimed, bouncing on her toes.

"No, it's not. The little creek is just up from all the rain," Darlene answered as she slung her purse over her shoulder. She moved back to the open driver's door, leaned in, reached across to the passenger seat, and grasped her laptop. Hopefully, she could get a jump on updating her quarterly records over the weekend.

"Water park! I want to go to the water park, Mommy! Please! Please! Pretty please!"

"Not today, honey." Darlene had to smile. One thing was certain about her daughter, she was always enthusiastic. "Looks like it's going to storm again," she added, stealing a quick glance at the darkening sky.

On cue, a low boom of thunder came rolling over the hills. She grabbed Emily by the hand as the first heavy raindrops began falling.

"Come on, baby. Let's get in the house before we get wet."

Darlene released Emily's hand as soon as they were inside the door. Then she went straight to her office in the spare bedroom and dropped her purse and laptop on the desk. When she came out, she saw Emily at the door, staring out the storm glass.

"Want some juice, baby?"

Emily shook her head without turning back to face her. *Odd*. Emily always drank one of her fruit juices as soon as she got home.

"Come away from the door, Emily. It's starting to lightning."

Emily flinched at a bright flash, the bolt seeming to strike only a block away. The sharp boom of thunder came half a second later.

"I'm scared, Mommy. I don't want it to storm no more."

So that's it. She walked over to her daughter and squatted down beside her. "Everything will be okay, honey," Darlene reassured her, placing an arm around Emily's small shoulders. "It'll be over in a few minutes."

"I'm scared for Meer-e-um. She's afraid of storms."

Darlene didn't answer, Emily's lesson in compassion having silenced her.

Chapter 74

4:36 p.m.

Virginia slammed the car door shut and began walking hurriedly toward the grocery. She had parked what seemed a mile away—on the back row of the lot—but it was the closest space she could find. Friday afternoons were always a mess getting in and out of this place, but she needed a few things: bread, milk, and eggs, for sure, a pack of bacon. Wayne Buckman always had to have his bacon. Besides, she didn't want to have to go out again this weekend. And once she got home, she was taking these new shoes off and kicking back in her recliner. It had been one of those days. A bolt of lightning flashed from somewhere off to the side, and she began to trot; not an easy thing to do in those blame shoes.

She was a good 50 feet from the door when the first drop splashed on her hand. Suddenly she heard it coming, the roar of a hard rain charging toward her. She sped up, just made it under the awning when Niagara Falls came washing across the parking lot. Of course, she had left her umbrella in the car. *Maybe this won't last long,* she thought. Hopefully, it would be over by the time she was done shopping.

As she stepped past the sliding door a thought of Wayne crossed her mind. He was somewhere out in the city now, she knew, responding to an emergency of one sort or another. Storms always got them rolling, he had told her many a time over their years together. And this afternoon had been something out of the ordinary, already. The hail wasn't bad at her workplace, but it must have rained two inches on top of it. Now it was pouring again.

It was a bit like riding in a bumper car at an amusement park, she imagined, as she made her way through the throng of people. Most had carts loaded to their brims, all waiting to head to their cars when the rain let up. As she grasped the handle of a cart in the row of empties, a sudden feeling, an unfathomable need, made her pause. Then she did something completely out of character. She closed her eyes and said a quick prayer for Wayne.

"Father, please hold my husband in your arms this day. Protect him from the tempest."

Though Virginia could not have explained where *tempest* came from—she never used the word—offering the simple prayer made her feel better. She rolled her cart into the shopping area. This weekend he would be off both Saturday and Sunday, an event that occurred only one weekend in three because of the shift schedule. Maybe they could do something special; just something for the two of them, alone. She could fix him one of his favorite meals on one evening, at least. *Lasagna!* It came to her in a flash. Oh, he loved her lasagna. He would be so excited. She smiled to herself just like a little kid. Of course, it didn't hurt it was one of her favorites, too. She paused in the aisle, ticked off the things she would need, then set out pushing her cart with a purpose.

Chapter 75

1638 Hours

Cinders paused just inside the front doorway, the intermittent sounds of a hose stream splattering against something hard coming from the rear of the house. An individual drop plopped loudly on his helmet. He paid it no mind, having just stepped out of a monsoon. Besides, dripping water went with the territory.

The investigator's practiced eye moved over the living room. Everything—furniture, walls, ceiling—showed severe damage. Even the floor itself had been on fire. *Flashover.* Hot gases had poured in until room and contents all simultaneously ignited, the temperature instantly soaring to 1,000 degrees. He slowly moved his gaze about the room again, turning the opposite direction of his first inspection. It helped him keep from overlooking something he might have missed on his first survey. He was at last satisfied. There was nothing of the deeper charring in one spot to indicate what he was seeking: the source of ignition.

He stepped across the width of the room, debris crunching beneath his boots, and stopped at a bedroom door on the left. There had been great heat. It had been high, extending across the ceiling and down a couple of feet on the walls, the line marked where scorched wallpaper had peeled away. No flashover, but full involvement could not have been more than moments off. A small television resting atop a chest of drawers was warped and twisted, its screen like a fun-house mirror. Tails of miniature monsters, melted strings and ropes, drooped into the open air from plastic figurines on a nearby shelf.

The investigator turned his attention to the hallway. Damage was heavy here. Fire had scorched the walls from top to bottom. Chunks of drywall had fallen from the ceiling, or been pulled down by firefighters, so the roof rafters and boards were visible. Torn bats of insulation draped over exposed joists dripped water, like pink Spanish moss shedding raindrops. The floor was a jumbled, thick mess of drywall, stained gobs of drenched insulation, and black chunks of burned wood, with flakes of wallpaper and broken glass—the glass likely from a ceiling globe—mixed in.

He made his way across this gunk, felt his foot scraping the floorboards as he reached the bathroom door. With one hand braced flat against the wall, he lifted his foot. A nail—an eight-penny—was stuck in the sole of his boot, bent when his weight drove it up against the steel plate inside. Reaching down with a gloved hand he tugged and twisted it by the head until he worked it free, then dropped it into his coat pocket, another souvenir.

Standing flat on both feet again, he looked up at the doorframe. "Well, what have we here?" he mouthed. There was heavy charring at the top of the frame, the wood deeply alligatored with hash-tag cracks. Most significantly, the damage extended from the bathroom into the hallway. He expanded his inspection. Except near the top, there were no deep burn indicators along either side of the doorframe on the bathroom side, but he did discover a thin metal disk, a couple of inches in diameter, stuck edgeways in the door just below the knob. "Hmmm," he said to himself. "Been a while since I've seen one of those."

He leaned his head inside the room, took a slow look around. The left-hand corner of the countertop around the sink was the last place he looked. Eureka!

"Find anything interesting?" Captain Buckman's voice came to him from the far end of the hallway.

"Yep, believe I have." The investigator leaned back and looked down the hallway to see a soot-speckled face nodding at him. The officer stood framed in the rear doorway. Past him rain fell to the ground in sheets. The investigator started walking toward him, the debris crackling and rolling beneath his feet. "What are y'all doing back here? Cooking supper?"

"I wish. 'Bout ready to call it quits," Captain Buckman replied. "Just hitting a couple of hot spots first."

There was the sound of water splashing again as Probie Wan wet down a steaming rafter above the rear window. When he closed the nozzle, the rafter wasn't steaming any more.

"Ought to do it, kid." It was Mick's voice. "Hey, Cap, is that worthless Cinder Dick goofing off over there as usual?"

The investigator stepped into the kitchen's entranceway. He looked over to see Mick and Probie Wan staring up at what remained of the ceiling.

"I don't see anything else," Mick said, then glanced over toward the investigator. "I heard you popping off about supper. Got some beans here if you want."

Moving over to the stove, the investigator looked inside the large pot resting on top of a burner. Along with flecks of insulation and a handful of blackened splinters, a chunk of fatback floated atop a sea of brown beans.

"Smells good," Cinders lied. "I'd get a bowl, but the wife's taking me out tonight."

"Picky," Mick grinned.

"Let's break it down boys," Captain Buckman told his hose team. Speaking into the mic of his portable, he instructed D. J. to shut off the line.

As the two firefighters dragged the line out the back door to drain it, the captain and the investigator made their way back along the hallway to the bathroom.

"You are about to make the occupant, at least one of the occupants, very happy," Captain Buckman said as Cinders followed him inside.

"Oh? How's that?"

"Poor guy passed out on the sofa, drunk. Got a good dose of smoke. Lucky to get out. Anyway, thinks he left the beans on too long and set the house on fire."

"You didn't explain it?"

"Nope. I tried, but he was so torn up he couldn't tell day from night. Kept saying she would kill him when she got home. No doubt he believes she might."

The investigator chuckled a moment.

"Well, let's see if we can give him some ammunition to shoot back with." He bent down closer to the vanity top. "Unhuh. Looks like bits of fabric left underneath; towels or washcloths; maybe both." Reaching in his pants pocket, he pulled out a knife. He opened it and slipped the wide blade tip under a blackened rectangle, then carefully slid the piece to one side.

"Seem to be about the right size for a tissue box? Might have been one of those decorative cases."

"I'd say so," Captain Buckman nodded, "if you count the burned-up fringe."

"Had another towel on the rack here. Some of the hemmed edge still hanging. And a medicine cabinet on the wall there, what's left of it. Wait a second. I didn't notice this at first. Rubbing alcohol comes in plastic bottles about the same size, doesn't it? I think this melted chunk is what's left of the bottom of one of those bottles."

Captain Buckman leaned in and stared at the piece of shriveled plastic a moment. Looking toward the investigator he said, "That'd get the party started."

"Sure enough. Anyway, burn pattern runs straight up the wall and out the door."

"Like an arrow."

"Hey, did you see this?" The investigator asked, pointing at the metal disk wedged in the door.

"Yeah. Rest of the can is over here in the bathtub. Hairspray. Suckers blow there's no telling where they're going."

"Leave a mark, for sure. Y'all close when it went off?"

"No," the captain said, shaking his head. "Happened before we got in here, I guess, but that reminds me. Old boy said something blowing up is what woke him. Probably it."

"Might be." The investigator was bent close to the counter-top again. "Huh. Looks kinda burnt where it connects to the back there. Might have shorted out. Doesn't matter, though. It's our source of ignition. Time to pay the man a visit. Know where he is?"

"Second house on the left, this side. Name's Odell. Odell Ledbetter."

"Okay. I'm going to head down there and ease Mr. Odell's mind. Tell him his wife shouldn't leave her curling iron plugged in and lying on a towel."

Chapter 76

4:39 p.m.

It was a good thing Cody decided to shave first, otherwise he might have cut his own throat. He was absolutely beside himself. The reason he waited till the last minute to pick up his tux was because they needed to fix a piece of the black trim where the thread had come unraveled. Angie was the one who spotted it when they went to select his outfit, so, of course, there was no choice. It must be repaired. Well, they said the job was done, but it most certainly was not. His entire outfit was laid out on his bed: patent leather shoes, socks, frilly shirt, pants, belt, cummerbund, goofy flower for his lapel, even goofier looking bow tie, clean underwear, and the coat with its unhinged trim on the left cuff. The piece of trim was worse than when she first noticed it. He couldn't go to the prom like that, one sleeve with a black band around the cuff, the other with a strip flopping loose at the end, like a ripcord made of felt. It would embarrass her, for certain, and make him the target of his buddies' jokes all night long. Something must be done, like right now.

He plopped down on the end of the bed. His mom could sew it back on, but she wouldn't be home for another 30 minutes. The clock was ticking. He needed to be dressed and out of the house in an hour, and he hadn't even had a shower yet! It wasn't like he had a choice. He would have to sew the strip back in place, himself. His mother kept her sewing kit on a shelf in the den. He hopped up and went striding after it.

Two minutes later he came rushing back into his room. He practically dove onto the bed, clutching the sewing kit to his chest. The clock's awful ticking inside his head was now just a decibel or two on the short side of painful. He found the spool of black thread easy enough, though finding a needle was more difficult. After a moment he realized he was looking at an array of them, all stuck into some little whatsamadoojer cushiony thing. He selected one that looked about the right length and reached for it. It took him three tries to snag it by the end, but he at last pulled it free. He laid the needle atop his thigh. *Tick. Tick. Tick.*

Finding the end of the thread was every bit as great a challenge. At last he dug it loose with a fingernail. He stuck it into his mouth to moisten it, like he had seen his mom do, though he wasn't at all sure why it was necessary. Then he glanced down to pick up the needle. It was gone. Real panic was just about to take over when he spotted it on the bedspread. The anxious moment didn't exactly leave him steady of hand when he started trying to guide the thread through the eye. It took him six attempts and several decidedly bad words spat out under his breath, but at last the thread was inserted through the eye of the needle. Then he pulled what he thought was enough thread off the spool to get the job done, which amounted to something in the upper neighborhood of a yard. In the pulling he set the spool to rolling. It managed to fall off the covers and went spinning silently across the floor all the way to the hallway, where it ran out of thread and clicked up against the baseboard, naked.

"Rat farts!" He pinched the thread at a spot he thought was close to the original length he wanted and bit it off with his teeth. He managed to tie a clumsy knot, though both free ends hung about three inches past the jumble. He pulled the coat sleeve onto his lap, then spent a moment trying to determine the best place to start sewing. *Ah heck!* he thought, jabbing the needle into the strip of material at the end where it lay loose and floating. Saying a silent prayer, he started trying to push it through, praying most of all this sewing job would work out better than his last: the repair of a hole in a sock heel which closed the hole so well he couldn't get the darned sock on his foot.

The needle did not want to move. He pushed harder. The needle still did not want to move, but the ball of his thumb did, giving just enough for the thread end of the spear to penetrate the flesh.

"Damn it!" Cody yelled as he danced across the floor. Now he was bleeding!

Chapter 77

4:55 p.m.

Charlotte Montgomery sat in the Suburban, primping her hair in the visor mirror, while her cameraman lugged his stuff onto the sidewalk in front of the little house. There was no sense getting out in this rain again until she had to. Thankfully, it appeared to be letting up. Now that the second fire truck had started backing up the street, a group of firefighters working to reload the thick, yellow hose in the hose bed, she could see the side of the house all the way to the back yard. This side did not look too bad. The front was a different matter. The windows onto the porch were broken out. Shattered glass was scattered across the concrete. Burn marks and smoke stains splayed from the openings and across the ceiling in a fan pattern. A similar overlapping pattern extended out from the doorway. All the damage would do nicely for her backdrop. There might be a better shot at the rear of the house, but damned if she was trudging around through the rain and mud to find out.

They had some good stuff on tape already. Under cover of her umbrella, she had sprinted through the downpour to a neighbor's house—a man named Vernon Pillow. Was that it? Oh, it was on tape, and in her notes, too, so why worry? Charlotte had interviewed him about rescuing the old man. The victim, however, was adamant about not showing his face or mentioning his name. *Good grief!* And she got a sound bite with the paramedic after he finished administering oxygen to the victim, a nice bit about the dangers of smoke. She was disappointed, however. There were few things in the business as dynamic, as eye-catching, as a structure fire in progress, and they had arrived too late. The fire was out.

Ed Cecil, her camera operator, turned to face her and raised both hands as if to say, *What now?* She hesitated a moment. The rain had almost completely stopped. Nevertheless, she reached down on the floorboard and grabbed her umbrella. What was left of her hairdo needed protecting. She stuck the umbrella outside the door of the SUV and popped it open. Instead of stopping beside the cameraman, she strode on toward the two firefighters talking on the front porch. She made certain to put a little extra sway to her hips as she walked. *It helps loosen lips*, she thought. At the foot of the steps, she came to a halt.

"Excuse me," she said, trying to sound official, but coming off more like Destiny would have sounded, a little too sugary. "I'm Charlotte Montgomery, Action 19 News. May I please speak to the officer in charge?"

The firefighters looked at one another.

"Battalion 1 just went 10-8," Greg replied. "Leaves Engine 4 in command. Just a second, ma'am, and I'll get him for you." Before he went looking for Captain Buckman, he spoke a few last words to the fire investigator. "Hope I don't see you anymore this shift."

"Same to you, Greg. Be careful," the investigator added, turning to step off the porch.

A few moments later Greg was back with Captain Buckman in tow. The captain wore a resigned expression. Some things he had rather not do—like giving interviews before a camera—but they went with the job.

Two minutes later Captain Buckman and Charlotte Montgomery were standing together in front of the camera. The rain had finally stopped, so she put aside the umbrella. Charlotte was done with the interview after another five minutes and seated once more in the Suburban. The car shook as the cameraman slammed the hatchback closed, having already loaded his equipment. She punched in a number on her phone.

"Vick," she spoke to the news director when a male voice answered. "We've got some good stuff on the fire. Interviews with a fire officer, the rescuer, and a paramedic," she said, working to make it more than it was.

She listened for a few moments as the news director spoke.

"No, I'm afraid not," she bit her lip. "It was pretty well out when we got here."

Charlotte listened a quarter of a minute more.

"Okay," she finally answered, and hung up.

She glanced over at Ed Cecil, who was staring back at her, eyebrows raised in question.

"He said go on to our original assignment. Just send everything in from there. Probably put both stories on at six."

"Shallowford it is," Ed Cecil said, turning the key.

"Be glad when they do something about that area," Charlotte complained. "Floods every time it gets cloudy."

"Yep."

"Be my third piece on it since I started last fall. Same old stuff."

The cameraman simply nodded, not bothering to mention he had been filming there for a long time before Miss Charlotte—destined to be a star—Montgomery burst onto the scene.

Chapter 78

5:22 p.m.

After putting the groceries away, Virginia took a bottle of mineral water from the refrigerator door. As she walked into the den, she twisted the cap off and took a long drink. It was *sooo* good. Her mouth was dry as dust. And her feet were killing her. She had been on them all day.

Slipping her shoes off first, she sat down in her recliner. The chair had been part of her Christmas from him last year. She had given him an identical chair of his own. The kids had made fun about the lack of surprise, of course, though it didn't bother her or Wayne. They had reached the point where practical was the primary concern in their gift-giving. The exception had been a gold pinky ring. He had wrapped it in a box big enough to hold, well, a recliner.

Virginia laughed to herself, remembering his excitement as she tore into the box, for excitement was uncharacteristic of him. He was like a little boy when she finally found the ring hidden in all those piles of tissue paper. First, he had rushed to find her glasses, then the magnifying glass when they proved to not be enough for her to make out the inscription. "Forever My Love," she read at last, her lips whispering the words. She looked up and saw that same boyish grin, that same certainty in his eyes she had seen on a long-ago day when he stepped in front of her and announced they were going to be married.

Smiling a soft smile of contentment, Virginia grasped the lever and tilted her chair back. With her other hand she slowly spun the pinky ring one full revolution around her finger. It had become her touchstone; her confirmation all was right with her world. Then she drifted off to sleep.

Chapter 79

5:23 p.m.

Yes! Yes! Yes!" Caroline sang as she danced down the hallway. She glanced at the test strip, then looked at the box once more to make absolutely, positively, 100 percent certain. It was right there in black and white. The instructions said blue was positive. There was no doubt.

"Yes! Yes! Yes!" she sang again, twirling into the living room. She spied her purse on the sofa, where she had tossed it in her rush to get to the bathroom and take the test. Snatching it up, she frantically dug her phone out, thinking to call Ron. Her fingers went flying over the keys. Halfway through the station number she stopped. No. She would not call him now. Telling him this wonderful news should be done in person. She hesitated a few seconds, the pressure to tell someone the test results building until she thought she would explode. Of course! She had to tell her. Caroline punched a number on her speed dial.

"Mom!" she screamed moments later. "I'm pregnant!"

Chapter 80

5:28 p.m.

"Mommy! Mommy! Mommy! I wanna see Grandpa Bob," Emily begged, bouncing up and down on her toes. "Can we go now? Can we?"

Darlene looked out the window on the storm door. The rain had stopped. She saw Mr. Robert come around the front corner of his house, heading toward the rose bush.

"I guess so," she answered. They might as well get it over with, the little daily afternoon trip to visit Mr. Robert. She really didn't mind. He and Emily plainly loved each other, so it was good for grandpa and grandchild.

"Goodie! Goodie! Goodie!" Emily exclaimed, her words stumbling over each other as she reached for the door handle.

"Just a minute, young lady," her mother ordered. "We are not going to ruin our good socks and shoes. It's wet and muddy out there. Get your flipflops on. I'll wear mine, too."

In just a few moments mother and daughter were trudging across the wet grass, their flipflops flipping and flopping, the ground squishing with their every step. *My, we've had a soaking,* Emily's mother thought, a wave of slimy mud washing onto her left foot. It left a slick gumbo coating between her shoe and the bottom of her foot, with the leftovers extruding between her toes. To refrain from falling, she stopped and wiped her shoe, then her foot, across the grass. That got most of the mess off.

In the meantime, Emily broke away and went running toward the elderly man as fast as her little legs would carry her. She had the advantage of lighter weight, so she didn't sink down in the mud like her mother.

"Grandpa Bob," Emily exclaimed while they were still 40 feet apart. A few seconds more and she reached him in a half-crash, half-hug, her thin arms flying around his knees. Robert tottered precariously for a moment.

"Emily, be careful," Darlene yelled a warning. "Don't knock him down."

"Hello, my angel," the elderly man cooed, bending to pat Emily on her shoulders. "I couldn't wait to see you. Did you have a good day?"

"There was a really bad storm, and Brandon had a bunny in his head, but it wasn't hopping all the time, and Meer-e-um was scared, and we all fell down and got tangled up, and ice cubes came out of the sky, and we sang songs with Miss Gina, and a tree went through the roof, and I hugged her. Then Mommy came and got me. It was a kinda good day."

"Oh, my goodness. It certainly sounds like you had an interesting time." He glanced up toward Darlene, who had finally caught up just as her daughter stepped aside. "And hello to you, too."

"Hi, Mr. Robert."

"Grandpa Bob," Emily corrected, bending at the waist to look at something in the grass.

"Excuse me. Grandpa Bob. How are you?"

"I'm fine as a feather. Think I slept through most of the afternoon's festivities." Canting his head toward Emily and lifting his bushy eyebrows, he asked. "A tree through the roof?"

"Not a whole tree," Darlene nodded emphatically. "But a large limb came through the ceiling in the hallway. No one was hurt, but it scared me to death when I saw it."

"I imagine so." Those wonderful eyebrows shot up again. "I hope things at work weren't nearly as exciting as Emily's day."

Both adults were temporarily distracted by the sight of Emily piling earthworms on top of dandelion blooms. There were scads of worms all around them, driven to the surface by the rain. Darlene was the first to speak, remembering Grandpa Bob's last comment.

"Pretty dull, actually. Busy, though. Fridays are always a bit frantic. With Frank gone, I slipped out early; left it to Betty."

"Glad business is good," Grandpa Bob smiled.

Just then, Darlene's phone rang in her pocket. She dug it out. Glancing at the screen, she said, "Excuse me just a moment. It's Frank."

As she talked, Grandpa Bob interrupted Emily's worm gathering and led her over to the rosebush.

"See these buds, angel?" Grandpa Bob asked her, touching one with his fingertips. Emily started to reach for one. He gently caught her wrist before she could touch it. "Careful, child. The thorns will stick you. They are all over the branches. See?" he asked, pointing at a couple.

"Will they hurt?"

"Oh, yes. You have to watch for them. They will grab you if you get too close."

"But I want to touch a bug."

"They are *buds*, hon, rosebuds. Soon they will turn into gorgeous flowers. Let's see if we can find you one down lower."

Taking her hand, he guided it to a bud. He continued to hold on loosely as she touched the young flower.

"It's got yellow stuff inside."

"Yes, that's a tiny bit of a petal."

"What's a petal look like?"

Grandpa Bob looked down to the petals from the desiccated bloom plastered on the soaked ground. Only the faintest flecks of dirty yellow were visible. He studied them a moment, then using Emily as a crutch to cling to he managed to bend a little with his back, and a little more with his knees, until he could just reach an upturned corner of a petal and carefully peel it free of the mud. A couple of swipes against his pants leg brought some of the original yellow back. Standing straight again, he held it out in the palm of his hand.

"You like this color, angel?"

"Ooooh, its boo-tee-ful," Emily answered, pulling his hand close to look at the petal.

"I wanted you to see the bloom it came from, but the storm knocked it down."

"I wanna keep it," she said, her tiny finger pressing the petal and through it, his palm.

"It's awful muddy," Grandpa Bob replied. Glancing up he noticed a narrow flow of rainwater coursing down the ditch alongside the street. Across the pavement, the creek was leaping and bucking like a mad bronco, the brown water threatening to wash over its banks. "Give me your hand," he said. She did as he asked, reaching up to wrap her tiny fingers around his old, crooked ones. "Let's see if we can rinse this off better."

It took a couple of wobbly, slippery minutes for the pair to reach the ditch. Once there, Grandpa Bob again used Emily as a brace, resting one hand on her shoulder. The bit of slope at the edge of the yard also helped. Between the two, he finally managed to get to his knee. Then he held the petal by the edge, allowing the rushing flow to rinse the mud away. A sudden ripple almost jerked it free. On reflex, he let loose of Emily's shoulder so he could grasp the petal with both hands.

Emily lifted her face at that moment.

"Water slide!" she squealed with excitement.

In an instant she was out in the street, her little flipflops slapping the pavement as she flew toward the wild creek.

Chapter 81

1729 Hours

Captain Buckman continued to stand on the sidewalk after the reporter and the cameraman walked away. It was as good a spot as any to watch everything going on. As usual, though, at this stage little needed watching. All the firefighters knew what needed to be done. There was something scratching at the back of his mind, however, that said, *Take this in and hold it.* Perhaps it was because the idea of retirement was beginning to settle in. He could not deny the thought was there, especially now when his knees were complaining about all the crawling around on this job. The aching brought another undeniable thought—a fact, to his mind: *This was a young person's work.*

Okay then. The time had come to have a serious talk with Virginia about him hanging it up. Maybe they could decide what time would be best when they went to the mountains, like he was thinking about earlier? *No. It would spoil the romance.* He laughed to himself. Surely, he wasn't so very far over the hill if romance was on his mind. Guess this old bull could still charge. The idea, as out of place as it seemed here, helped frame the issue in his mind. He wanted to leave on his own terms, not when he could no longer carry his weight. It appeared the time to make that move was at hand. He and Virginia would discuss the particulars over the weekend.

For now, he, Captain Wayne Buckman, had work to do. His eyes focused on how the firefighters were progressing. As he watched, he automatically went about assessing their physical condition and the readiness status of each unit. One never knew when the bell might ring again.

Rescue 1 had laid the supply line. The crews of Rescue 1 and Ladder 1 were just now completing the reloading of the five-inch hose. With the last section folded in, the firefighters up in the hose bed began snapping the canvas cover back in place.

Engine 7 had been assigned the backup attack line, which the crew pulled off Engine 4. This was in accordance with policy—better to have a lot of equipment off the first-in engine than a little off several trucks, when the needs of the incident permitted, of course. It resulted in a higher state of overall readiness for the department.

The captain noted his company would be without inch and three quarters until they could get back to the station and reload with clean, dry hose. As he watched, Probie Wan placed a dirty roll on one of the hose stacks on the tailboard of their engine. Then D. J. came walking around the front bumper with a towel in his hand. He paused a moment, looked about, and found the ax the captain had used, leaned up against the front wheel. After giving the ax a quick wipe, he set it back in its brackets on the side of the cab.

At last, Captain Buckman came striding down the walk to D. J.

"Know we don't have any inch and three quarter. How we stand on everything else?"

"Air packs are all changed out. Booster tank's full. Just need to clean up a few hand tools and the packs. Handle that little bit at the station. About it."

"Good," the captain nodded. "Let me see if everybody else is ready to go." He walked around to the far side of the engine and stopped at the edge of a group of grinning firefighters. They were listening to an animated conversation between Mick and Greg. No one noticed him.

"Did he crap his pants again?" Greg said to Mick. "All I'm asking."

"Not sure," Mick answered, his expression as dead pan as Greg's. "At least he don't smell as bad as he did after the garage job."

Probie Wan smiled broadly, realizing the men wouldn't

be talking about him at all if they weren't pleased by his performance.

"Well, got to admit you're telling the truth. I can tell from here, and I'm grateful. Long as he's improving, I guess," Greg finished his inquiry with a shrug. "On a different note, when do you aim to fix some supper? My stomach's growling like a bear."

Mick gave a look which said, *One more word and—*

Greg was dancing on thin ice again, being an officer, and he knew a misstep could send the surface cracking beneath him, not to mention sending his dinner into the trash can. The danger was what made it fun, playing on the edge. He was careful to simply ask what Mick's intentions were and not make any derogatory comments about his cooking.

"I've been just a little busy," Mick said at last.

"Okay, I'll give you that much." Greg conceded after a moment's thought.

"Here's the deal," Mick added. "Beef was already half turned to leather back at lunch, it got left out so long. Probably make tractor tires out of it by now. So, my advice is, you boys better like pizza, 'cause I'm making a call as soon as we get in quarters."

"I love pizza," Greg smiled. "Make mine pepperoni," he added as he turned toward his truck.

"No special orders," Mick yelled after him. "Getting all supremes. You can pick off what you don't like, just like you always do."

"Let's head to the house," the captain said over the heads of those closest.

"Take care, Wayne," a hand waved to him from across the group.

"See you, Harv," Captain Buckman nodded toward the officer on Engine 7. As he moved back to his side of the truck, he lifted a hand toward Cinders and Odell, both seated on the rescuer's porch. Odell, in stark contrast to what he had seemed earlier, didn't appear the least bit upset. In fact, as he waved back, a broad smile spread across the older man's face.

Engine 7 led the way from the scene, followed by Engine 4. Rescue 1 and Ladder 1 were supposed to come next in the convoy, but when Rescue 1's engineer glanced in his mirrors before moving he noticed a compartment door standing ajar. Greg hopped out to shut it. In the few seconds it took him to walk to the compartment, close the door, then get back to his seat and buckle in, Engine 7 turned left at the first intersection, heading back to its house, and Engine 4 went straight through. A couple of minutes later Rescue 1 stopped at the cross street, caught by a red light. Ladder 1 eased to a halt behind it.

Up ahead, D. J. slowed down as Engine 4 neared its turn onto Shallowford.

"Wow, Cap, will you look at this? Hail's piled up like snow."

"They got the big stuff up here, for sure," Captain Buckman replied, looking out the side window at the drifts of golf-ball-sized stones along the road. Rafts of them jammed the surface of the little creek just a few feet further beyond. "Crazy weather. Two hailstorms in one day. Different parts of town, though, thank goodness."

Chapter 82

5:42 p.m.

Y ou look so nice," Cody's mom said to him after she stepped back to look. "My handsome son." She moved back in and pinched the stem of his boutonniere between her fingers, twisted it the tiniest fraction, and stepped back once more. "Perfect! Now let me get your picture."

"Mom! I've got to go. I'm gonna be late."

"Won't take but a second. Got the camera right here," she said, walking over to the coffee table.

It took Mrs. Cox a minute or two to get the focus adjusted—she wasn't used to this new camera—but she finally got it to suit her and took the shot.

"Just one more to make sure."

"Mom!"

"Say cheeseburger."

Cody slid in behind the steering wheel a minute later, flustered and nervous. He might just make it to Angie's house on time, after all, even with making a quick run through the car wash to rinse the mud off. Thank God his mom finally got through taking pictures, and thank God she came home in time to stitch the loose piece of trim back on his jacket. She had even helped him get his tie on straight. *Who came up with such a silly looking thing, anyway?* He turned his rearview mirror so he could see himself and took a few moments to check that every hair remained in place. They all were, just like they had been two minutes earlier when he stopped to check his appearance in the hallway mirror; and three minutes earlier when he checked his appearance in the mirror on his dresser; and five minutes earlier when he checked how he looked in the bathroom mirror right after he put a fresh band-aid on his thumb. The semi-final check done, he repositioned the mirror, placed the key in the ignition and started the motor.

He was at the stop sign before he remembered Angie's corsage was in the refrigerator. A shift of gears, a squeal of tires, a bat-turn, and he was headed home. Back up the drive he came in a burst of speed. He stopped with another short squeal of tires, flung the door open, and sprinted into the house, leaving the car idling in place. In exactly 33 seconds, he came flying back out through the front door—the sound of his mother's wild laughter chasing after him—and dove back behind the steering wheel. All that and he managed to be careful with Angie's corsage, gently placing it to rest on the passenger seat. He wasn't as careful, however, as he should have been backing out this second time, but the neighbor on his way home from work saw him coming and came to a halt in time. Cody shot across the street in reverse and managed to miss this neighbor's garbage can. With a wave to the first neighbor, whom he had just spotted, he shifted gears, and the car jumped ahead.

Heading down the street, he glanced at the clock on the dash. 5:49. If he didn't run into heavy traffic, and if all the signals were green, and if there wasn't a line at the car wash, and if he pushed it a bit past the speed limit, and if he didn't do something stupid that made him stumble and fall walking up to her house—a walk which must be measured and digni-fied to his way of thinking, because her mom or dad might be watching out the window—he would be fine. The trip, which he had timed each and every time they had gone out during the last six weeks, took anywhere from 13 to 16 minutes. She had said be there no later than 6:15. He ought to have several minutes to spare—if.

The car wash was just ahead. No line! He whipped in and stutter-stopped at the selection machine. Bills in the slot, basic-wash button punched, and he was headed into the bay.

Chapter 83

5:42 p.m.

Emily. Emily. Come here," Grandpa Bob called to the child, hurrying the best he could across the pavement after her. "Don't, angel!" he warned as Emily stepped onto a large flat rock at the very edge of the wild stream.

"I love you, too, darling. Call us before you go to bed. Bye," Emily's mother said as she concluded her call to her husband. Grandpa Bob's shout made her spin around, the breath already leaving her. She saw them then. Emily stood, her arms swinging loosely at her sides, only a few feet away from the elderly man. He was doing his best to run, stumbling and almost falling as he reached out for the child.

"No, Emily!" her mother screamed.

Remembering how she did it at the water park, Emily stared down at the racing flow and swung her arms forward as high as her head. "Water slide!" she yelled as she jumped, pulling her knees up toward her tiny chest.

1743 Hours

The captain and the engineer both saw her jump, saw her head bob up for a moment then disappear, as Engine 4 rounded the curve not 100 yards away. Captain Buckman yelled to his firefighters, "Water rescue!" as he reached for the radio mic.

"Break! Break! Engine 4 to Dispatch. Swift water rescue 2000, check, 2100 block Shallowford Road. Child! Knock out a full response."

With his free hand, he reached across his body for the seat belt button as the engineer gunned the rig forward. They both saw Grandpa Bob launch himself into the water where the child had gone in.

An instant later a woman came flying across the road in front of them and leaped into the water beside the old man. "Rescue rope!" Captain Buckman called over his shoulder to Mick and Probie Wan.

D. J. brought the rig to a hard stop a moment later. The captain hopped to the ground, grabbed at the mic on his portable.

Ringggggg! The dispatcher was starting to call out more companies.

"Break!" Captain Buckman interrupted. "Shallowford Command. We have one child and two adults in the water." He was quick marching along the embankment now. Stopping at the rock where Emily had stood, he did a quick survey. Maybe 15 yards away the old man was clinging to a low-hanging limb, his body rising and falling atop the rolling waves. A few yards further downstream, the woman held onto a bush near the water's edge with one hand. With her other hand, miraculously, she grasped the child's hand. Captain Buckman sidestepped down the bank, working his way along until he was in position across from the child.

If I was in the water, he thought, *I would be able to reach the girl.* It wasn't the way to do it—no rope, no harness—but his firefighters couldn't be ready with both for another minute or two. He could grab the same bush the woman held onto. A calculated risk and no time to waste. He dropped and slid down the steep slope on his backside and into the stream. The water reached his knees, its mad power threatening to sweep his legs from under him. He braced himself against the incredible push, grasped a branch with one hand and reached for the child with the other.

In a flash she was gone, her tiny hand trailing behind her as she rushed away atop the roiling surface, each joint limber and bending with each new undulation. Captain Buckman could only follow her with his eyes as the woman's screams pierced the air. At a footbridge, about 25 yards distant, the child disappeared. He leaned to his left as much as he could and watched for her to show on the far side. Seconds passed. Nothing.

For an instant, he thought of diving headfirst into the icy stream and going after her. But there was a woman in the water only an arm's length away—a woman in mortal danger. He glanced at the expression on her face and thought she was about to do the same thing he had been considering. Without warning, she released her grip on the bush, the flow catching her immediately. On instinct, he reached out and somehow managed to catch her by the arm. The new weight almost toppled him forward into the mad current.

"Urrraahhh," he grunted, leaning backward. The muscles in his back burned with the effort, but he had her. Somehow, he managed to get a hand under her other arm so he could keep her head above water. Then it was all he could do—just stand there and hold her.

The rope bag was in a compartment on Probie Wan's side of the engine, so it fell to him to get it out. He grabbed it quickly and headed around to the front of the truck. There he met Mick just in time for them to see the girl disappear under the bridge. As with the captain, neither saw her reappear on the far side. Halfway between them and Captain Buckman, D. J. was hustling toward the creek. Without stopping, he turned and looked back their way.

"I gotta help the captain!" the engineer shouted. They glanced over to see Captain Buckman holding the woman, obviously struggling to stay upright. A few feet upstream, an elderly man with his arms hooked over a limb whipped back and forth in the rushing water like a kite on a string. "Get the kid!" D. J.'s voice came to them over the sounds of rushing water.

Probie Wan turned the bag upside down, dropped a coil of heavy rope, two rescue harnesses, and an assortment of pulleys, carabiners, and lengths of webbing on the ground. He immediately snatched up one of the harnesses, began putting it on.

"You sure?" Mick asked, catching him by the elbow. Their eyes met.

"Yeah. Already been in it twice today," Probie Wan answered, then glanced down to start cinching the straps.

"Okay. I'll belay you from the truck." Mick said, not expecting an answer.

Mick eyeballed the distance to the bridge, estimating how much rope it would take to reach there, then gathered up what he thought were enough coils and moved close to the truck. He dropped a loop of webbing with a pulley over one of the thick hooks in the bumper, then slung the excess line to one side where it wouldn't be under foot, and he could easily feed it out. Done, he turned to see Probie Wan finishing a figure 8 with the far end of the rope.

"Ready," Probie Wan announced, snapping the knot into the carabiner on the front of his harness.

"Let's see," Mick answered in a calm voice. He stepped in front of Probie Wan, did a quick inspection of the knot. His fingers pulled at every strap, checked every buckle on the harness. "Okay. Look at me," Mick said. The two men locked gazes once more. "Give me a moment to get the slack pulled out, once you're at the bridge. Do not go in the water till you see my thumbs up. Got it?"

"Got it."

Mick didn't bother to say, "Be careful," though the idea shot through his mind he was sending one kid to save another. He shook it off. No time for questioning here. As Probie Wan stepped away, Mick stole a glance toward the captain, saw D. J. at the edge of the bank take the woman from him, start hoisting her up out of the water. A few feet upstream, the old man was still clinging to the branch, for now. Captain Buckman was already pushing toward him. Mick turned back to make certain the loop on the hook was secure. Satisfied, he grasped the rope several feet past the hook on the truck side and draped it across his hips. Then he raised his eyes, looking for his partner.

Probie Wan was just stopping beside the bridge. He turned his head toward the truck. Mick took a couple of sideways steps to pull out the few yards of slack. Then he lifted a thumb.

"Hold on! Hold on just a minute longer!" Captain Buckman shouted to Robert. "I'm coming."

"Let me keep my feet. Just let me keep my feet." The captain kept mumbling over and over to himself, praying as he tried to work his way over to the elderly man. God the water was powerful! And cold! The feeling in his legs was fading fast.

"I got you, Cap."

From behind, a hand grasped his. It was D. J. He was in the water. With his other hand, the engineer held onto an outcropping of rock protruding from the bank. Their bent arms began to straighten, like an accordion unfolding, stretching out as they edged their way across to the elderly man. Suddenly the captain had Robert by a drenched sleeve. His fingers crept up the bony arm until he neared his shoulder. A quick release and snatch and he had him by the collar.

"Got ya."

"So cold," Robert managed to answer through chattering teeth.

"I know. On three I want you to let go. Okay?" The captain could feel his feet starting to lose purchase on the bottom. "One two three!" But Robert didn't let go. "Arrrhhhh!" The captain exclaimed, straining with everything he had. Suddenly there was a loud snap, and he was moving back toward the bank, Robert in tow, the old man skipping across the water's boiling waves like a fishing float being reeled in, clutching the broken limb to his chest. From behind came D. J.'s long cry of agony as his shoulder joints threatened to pull apart from the weight of both men, from the force of the water shoving against them. Then another sound, a primordial roar of power, like a charging grizzly, as D. J. summoned the strength to pivot and swing the others in against the bank. A quick breath, and the firefighters lifted and rolled Robert up on the grass. Helping each other, they made their way out of the water and collapsed beside him.

Probie Wan sat down on his rear end near the edge of the steep bank, then slid across a patch of grass and into the cold water. Though it was only knee deep, he didn't know how he was even able to stand up, the current was so strong. Rafts of hailstones, limbs and assorted trash were piled up against the ends of the footbridge here, like barges marshalled for a tow. He put out his left hand to brace himself against the side of the wooden arch and began to inch toward the clear channel in the middle of the creek, the rafts clinking and shedding stones as he waded through them. Then he saw it, a tiny bare foot protruding from underneath the structure. Two steps and he would be able to reach her.

He took the first step. The water's force seemed no greater. Swinging his foot forward a few degrees, he took the second step. Suddenly his boots were sliding along the bottom, threatening to lose all traction. He was being carried into a deep hole—the water was chest high now—so he pushed down with his feet as hard as he could, pointed his toes as he felt for purchase on the bottom, surprisingly found uneven rocks. A quick breath. A word of thanks panted. Then—

He knew he was in trouble the instant it happened. His left foot slid an inch or two and caught in something. A smaller, deeper hole? Between rocks? And it was right there. Stuck tight as anything. He tried a moment to pull his foot out of the vise, but it wasn't moving. *Okay. What to do?* He still had to get her. Digging into the deck of the footbridge with the fingers of his left hand, he leaned as far to the right as he could.

He had her! He had her by the ankle. Thank God! He strained to pull her to him, but her tiny body would not budge.

He tugged. She did not move. He jerked then, but nothing happened. Suddenly he became aware of the terrible force pushing against him. What if his foot popped free? Would he be swept under the bridge before he could stop himself? Be trapped and drown beside her?

Chapter 84

5:43 p.m.

Charlotte Montgomery and Ed Cecil were on their way to their next assignment when they heard the call for a water rescue come over the scanner.

"You know where that is?" she barked out to the cameraman.

"Of course. Shallowford's where we're headed to shoot the flooding. Remember? It's just a couple of blocks ahead," he added, swerving left through a gap in traffic and gunning it beneath a yellow light.

"We need to hurry up." Her words sounded like an order.

"What do you think I'm doing," he snapped back. They were all the same, these hot-shot young reporters, men and women both, ready to be the big boss, the director. Not a one of them could find their way across the street. Well, he certainly could. He had been recording the good and the bad around this town for 20 years, putting the vision in the local television news. There wasn't a street he couldn't find his way to in his sleep.

She paid him no further mind, her thoughts racing ahead. It had been a busy day for the Green Springs Fire Department, and a busy afternoon for her, chasing them. This would be her lead in. They had tons of tape already, but it was practically all after the fact. Firefighters rolling hose, reloading equipment; police talking to witnesses, directing traffic around an accident scene; ambulances rushing away, lights and sirens going. She would get everything edited in plenty of time for the 10 o'clock news. Better late getting on than never.

Her phone beeped.

"Montgomery," she answered with her last name because she thought it sounded more important, more official. "Yes. Okay. Okay."

She pressed a button, ending the call.

"That was Vick," she said across to Ed Cecil, an edge of excitement in her voice. "We're doing a live feed from the scene. They'll break in whenever we're ready."

"Okay. I'll have us up in no time," Ed Cecil replied, swinging left onto Shallowford Road. "We'll be there in a minute," he added.

"Great," Charlotte said, pulling down her visor and checking her hair in the mirror. *Not bad,* she thought, considering the wind and rain she had been out in this afternoon. At any rate, it would have to do. No time to primp now.

She forced herself into what she called her on-air frame of mind, concentrating on slowing her breathing, her face becoming a mask reflecting a mix of professional detachment, with a modicum of humane concern. This could be the one to launch her out of this burg and into the big time. The network was always begging for live-rescue stuff.

Chapter 85

1749 Hours

Captain Buckman and D. J. didn't stay down but moments. The captain was the first to push to his feet. He was striding toward Probie Wan in an instant. D. J. quickly fell in behind, leaving the two adult victims unattended. *No choice.* As they hurried along, both had the same thought—*At least they're breathing.* Each man dropped a hand onto the rope, felt it stiff as a steel bar with the weight of the young firefighter in the water. They followed it to the spot on the bank where he had slid in. The air suddenly carried the distant sounds of sirens, of help coming, as the other companies neared.

"We're here, Probie Wan. Right here."

The rookie glanced over his shoulder at the captain but didn't answer. He quickly turned back to face the bridge. Leaning forward slightly, he tugged at the little foot again, pulling down, hoping to pop the child free of whatever it was that held her. No use. She remained caught fast.

"Find her?" Captain Buckman shouted over the roar of the water.

"Got her by the foot," Probie Wan answered over his shoulder.

The captain and D. J. grasped the rope with both hands, readying themselves to pull.

"Whenever you're ready, we'll haul you in. Okay?"

Instead of speaking or at least nodding in reply, Probie Wan turned his head toward them and simply stared back.

"Did you understand what I—"

"She's stuck," Probie Wan yelled, not because he was panicked, but because he wanted to make certain the captain heard. His words hit the other men like a hard fist. His next remark knocked the breath out of them. "So am I."

For a few seconds there was only the sound of the water.

"What's got you? Hung up in branches or what?" the captain called to him, imagining a twisted mass of limbs caught beneath the bridge.

"My foot—wedged in the rocks."

Silence again, though only for moments.

"See if you can reach down with your free hand and pull your boot out."

Still holding onto the child, he tried like Captain Buckman said, but he couldn't reach his boot without ducking his head under the water. The force of the current against the brim of his helmet felt like it would rip his head off. He stood up quickly and released the chin strap.

"Toss it," the captain instructed, waving his hand.

Probie Wan slung his helmet toward the officer and immediately ducked back under. This time he was able to reach the boot top. He dug his fingers in and yanked over and over, but the boot didn't move. Bobbing back up, he sucked in a quick breath. Then he cut his eyes toward the captain and shook his head.

"Can you wiggle your foot out?"

"I'll try."

And Probie Wan did try, but his foot was so numb he couldn't seem to get it to move.

"Can't feel my feet," he shook his head after a quarter of a minute. "Going down again."

"Okay," the captain nodded.

Probie Wan inhaled deeply, his chest puffing out, then bent under the water. This time he caught a fistful of pantleg near the top of his boot and jerked as hard as he could. He kept trying until his lungs were screaming for air. Finally, he popped back to the surface. Once again, he looked at the captain and shook his head.

The silence between them stretched out longer this time. The captain fought against the urge to jump in and help. Just because he and D. J. had gotten away with it upstream didn't mean he could do it here, though. They had gambled and won, but the flow narrowed at this bridge, became deeper and swifter—a much meaner animal—and he didn't have a harness. It wasn't fear holding the captain back. It was the knowledge that without the proper gear he would likely add to the problem, maybe cause yet another case of a firefighter perishing trying to save a fellow firefighter. But by God, he couldn't stand there and watch his man die. He could think of only one other thing to try. If it didn't work—

"Can you hear me?" The captain's voice was loud, although there was a calmness, a certainty in his measured speech.

"Yes."

"Here's what I need you to do." Captain Buckman paused a beat. "Turn her loose."

"I can't do that!"

"Yes, you can. You have to help yourself before you can help her. Let her go. Then you can use both your hands to work yourself free. Okay?" In a lower voice he spoke to D. J. "Keep an eye on the far side, case she washes loose."

"Right," the engineer replied.

Probie Wan glared at the captain for a few moments, then reluctantly nodded. He continued to hold on, however, tugging at her foot to no avail, breathing deeper with each breath before suddenly releasing his grip. In one motion he squatted, forcing his head and shoulders down into the flow. The mad current had him at its mercy, smashing against him like a bulldozer blade, threatening to press him to the bottom. Things unknown banged into his body, his head, rebounded away. His hands found the boot, pulled and jerked and twisted frantically. No use. It held fast. When he couldn't ignore the burning in his chest any longer, he straightened his back. A sharp inhalation and down again, grabbing fistfuls of pantleg, pulling and jerking until his lungs seemed to be ripping apart. Finally, popping back to the surface.

Probie Wan was aware of voices shouting encouragement.

He didn't acknowledge them, however. Two breaths, the first inhaled sharply, the second slower, deliberate, air drawn in and compressed until his chest seemed to be ripping down the middle. Down in the water again. The current buffeted him, but he went deeper than ever, until his hands could meet underneath the back of his bent knee. He locked his fingers together and jerked. No! Pulling hard and steady then, focusing every drop of strength, howling like a demon within. Movement! Now or never. Bubbles crackling across his lips. Screaming into the water, "Stand! Stand! Stand!"

"I'm out!" he sputtered in the open air.

Probie Wan's bare foot came alive with the rush of water across it. The boot, however, remained submerged, stuck in the rocky bottom. *To hell with it.* He risked half a step forward, feeling with tingling toes before resting his weight. Then he reached for the child's foot. She was gone!

He lunged forward, sending dozens of hailstones spinning free, his hands sweeping wildly beneath the freezing stream. Nothing. *God help me!* he screamed inside his head. *Slow. Slow down*, he said to himself a moment later, remembering how the instructors had said sometimes you have to talk yourself through the problem. He started inching along, moving under the bridge, took one more great breath, ducked under again. Blind emptiness, then something, something that gave way when his hand brushed against it. *Grass?* he wondered. Between his fingers now. *No! God Almighty! Hair!* The rope snapped. They were pulling him out! *Not yet!* He squeezed his fist tight and jerked, popped up into the air two feet out from the bridge. A small body shot to the surface beside his chest. He instantly had both arms around her, holding her in a vise, her face just clear of the surface. The harness straps cut into his flesh as they were pulled across the flow.

"Good job, Ron." Captain Buckman's voice remained calm. He was knee deep in the stream at its edge, D. J. holding him by his belt from behind. Other firefighters' hands grasped the rope, reached for the officer. "That's it. Swing her over. Let me get a good grip. Okay. I've got you, baby." Suddenly, the captain and little Emily were up the bank and gone.

Chapter 86

1753 Hours

Aragdoll. She was but a ragdoll, like his daughter had when she was little. It was Captain Buckman's first thought as he cradled the child in his arms. Limp and lifeless, the tiny girl didn't seem to weigh anything. Wet hair lay across his arm, clung to his skin. An image flashed in his mind, the doll's head, with its stringy red hair splayed out just so, resting on a fluffed-up pillow on his little girl's bed. *Not now!* He bent his head forward, covered the child's mouth with his, and breathed a prayer into her lungs.

Hands had him by the belt, by the shoulders, pulling him—them—up the bank. *D. J.? Greg? Yes.* He heard their voices, recognized them. More. How many? Didn't know. Didn't matter.

"We've got you, Cap. We've got you."

He was free of the water, Greg at his shoulder, guiding him. The child cradled in the crook of his left arm, the fingertips of his free hand found the spot, pressed down on her chest. The numbers and rhythms of CPR came to him without thought. It wasn't his first time to do CPR, although the others had been adults. How many times had he practiced this on a child mannequin? The mannequin didn't have long wet hair that caught at his elbow, however. His mouth covered hers again and again, his face barely lifting between breaths.

"Ambulance is right ahead," Greg said. "Almost there."

A clatter of wheels, movement, something out of the corner of his eye. A gurney.

"Lay her on here," a female voice gently commanded.

He didn't want to let the baby go. She was his responsibility. He would bring her back. Any second now she would take her first gasp of air, rise up, throw her arms about his neck. And he would carry this precious child to her mother, place her daughter in her waiting arms.

"It's okay," the female voice spoke again. "Just lay her here."

This time he did as the voice said, bending close over the white sheet and carefully allowing the child to slip from his arm. Somehow, he did it without breaking rhythm with his breathing, his pressing of the small chest.

"I've got the breathing," the same female voice said. He glanced up to see Shaneesha—the paramedic from the wreck that morning—with a child's ambu bag and mask. She seamlessly slipped the mask over the girl's mouth and nose as he lifted his head, then gave the bag a squeeze. "Keep doing compressions," Shaneesha told him.

He slowly became aware of the others around them. Donnie laid a folded sheet across the child, covering her from the waist down. Greg and Biceptual placed straps across her, bound her safely to the stretcher. The second paramedic was at the gurney's foot. She released the brake with a metallic pop. Following her instructions, they all moved as one toward the ambulance. He was scarcely aware of climbing the steps. In seconds they had the wheeled stretcher and its precious burden secured inside.

Shaneesha continued squeezing the bag, even as the other paramedic connected an oxygen line to a port on the mask and started the flow. In an instant she had a stethoscope, began listening to the chest, then the stomach, and sliding the disc under, the back. Donnie appeared across from him, dropped down beside the stretcher.

"I've got compressions," Donnie said.

The captain paused, felt Donnie's fingers touch his, finally lifted his hand, reluctantly moved half a pace toward the rear door to get out of the way. As he stepped down from the tailboard, Greg caught his elbow, steadied him. He started to jerk his arm away. Since when did he need a hand? Then he realized how tired, how cold, he suddenly was. Someone threw a sheet around his shoulders. He caught at the edges, pulled it together at his chest, like a robe. Sticks approached the rear of the ambulance, his slender arm wrapped about a woman who was also draped in a sheet. *Is she the same one I had pulled from the water? Must be. Her hair is dripping wet.* A question, Sticks speaking.

"Yes, let her in," he heard Shaneesha say. "We'll make room."

Seconds later the ambulance door clicked shut.

Chapter 87

5:57 p.m.

Darlene witnessed the entire operation. After one of the firefighters wrapped a sheet around her, he stayed at her side, his arm embracing her shivering shoulders, as they watched Engine 4's crew pull Emily from the tumbling waters. Darlene screamed then, something incomprehensible, a cry of both relief and anguish. Together with the firefighter, she had followed close behind the man carrying Emily. Did she thank God then? She could not say. But she did quietly mouth words of thanks as they loaded her little daughter into the ambulance, then followed those words with the most earnest whispered plea.

"Dear Lord, please help my baby live."

Everything seemed so detached, so unreal. The firefighter remained with her as she moved to the rear of the ambulance. She stood there on the pavement watching the paramedics working over her Emily as if it were all something on a television screen. Seconds masquerading as hours dragged by, and she came to realize in a vague, far-off kind of way, her shivering had ceased. The firefighter still had his arm about her shoulders. The full meaning of this simple act suddenly became clear. He was sharing his warmth. She heard him speak without comprehending his words.

The paramedic working to squeeze air through the mask, to breathe for her child, glanced up.

"We'll make room," Darlene heard the paramedic say in return.

The firefighter helped her climb inside, then stepped back and closed the ambulance door behind her. In the crowded interior, Darlene found a spot to kneel beside the foot of the gurney. She reached across the small, quiet legs and took her daughter's hand in hers.

"It'll be all right, baby. Mommy's here."

Chapter 88

5:58 p.m.

Robert could not remember the last time he had thrown a fit; when he was a child, perhaps. He had certainly thrown one just now, however, when they tried to take him to the second ambulance. He argued and fussed as they attempted to fasten the straps across him, slung his legs off the gurney, somehow pushed his way up to a sitting position so he could see the rear doors of the first ambulance, the one they had carried little Emily into.

"Sir, please lie down."

A woman's hand appeared on his shoulder, gently pushing back.

"No!" Robert barked, twisting away from her. The determination in his voice surprised him. It surprised her, too. She pulled her hand back quickly, like she had touched a hot skillet, and stood up straight before him. "I'm not leaving until I know about my grandbaby."

"You are soaking wet and shivering, sir," the paramedic tried to reason. "Let us get you into the ambulance and out of these clothes."

Robert reached up suddenly and snatched at the damp, crumpled sheet hanging across his upper half. He jerked, and it fell away. In an instant his hands were clasped together at his collar. He jerked again, hard, buttons flying until his shirt was open all the way to his waist. Then he started trying to pull the shirt off his shoulders, wiggling and twisting and tugging at the waterlogged fabric.

"Just a minute," the woman said again, surprised at how fast he was moving. "Let me help."

From a couple of paces away, Biceptual saw what was happening.

"I'll get you some stuff, Diane," he said, grinning as he moved past her. He hopped up in the ambulance. Seconds later he reappeared, a bundle of linens in his hand. Stepping down, he placed the pile on the gurney beside Robert.

The paramedic grabbed a towel and quickly worked it over Robert's upper half, drying him off. Then she peeled a hospital gown from the stack.

"Let's get this first," she said, guiding one of Robert's hands through a sleeve opening.

She had it on him quickly, a knot tied in the strings at the back of his neck. Biceptual leaned in and draped a doubled sheet over the elderly man's shoulders. Then together, Diane and Biceptual wrapped a doubled blanket over the sheet.

"Want me to drop my trousers, too," Robert asked her, reaching for his belt buckle.

"I do not," Diane said, moving around to face him. She took a towel handed her by the firefighter and used it to wipe at Robert's damp hair. Meanwhile, Biceptual pressed a towel along first one of Robert's legs, then the other, squeezing as much water out of the soaked material as he could. Next Diane draped a towel over Robert's head to form a hood reaching to his shoulders. Then she and the firefighter quickly doubled a final sheet over his thighs from waist to knees. Moving back half a step, she asked, "Better? You all snug?"

"Like a bug in a rug. Thank you," he added, his eyes locked on the ambulance holding Emily. "Sorry," Robert spoke softly a minute later. "Didn't mean to bite your head off."

Diane leaned in and patted his shoulder in reply. After a moment she said, "Let me get your shoes and socks."

"Whatever," Robert answered absentmindedly.

She quickly bared his feet and toweled them dry. Biceptual hopped up in the ambulance and emerged with a pair of hospital socks. Each taking a foot, they put them on him.

That was the scene for a time—an old man, wrapped up like a mummy, his tousled hair peeking out from under a makeshift hood, sitting midways on a gurney in the street at the rear of an ambulance. His gaze never moved from the vehicle's back doors. His lips moved, though, in the constant recital of silent prayer for his adopted granddaughter.

Chapter 89

6:03 p.m.

Charlotte waited a full five seconds before exhaling after she said, "Back to you, Renai," to the evening news co-anchor.

She had been on the air forever it seemed. They arrived while the rescue of the little girl was underway. Ed Cecil pulled into a driveway across the street, not knowing it was where the child lived. He was set up and broadcasting seconds after she positioned herself at an angle to the action. Her spot didn't block anything, though it ensured she would be in the frame as she described what was happening to an audience requiring no description. The picture told it all—a raging stream; a firefighter in the water; another firefighter doing CPR on a child; the door to an ambulance closing.

Charlotte thought she had done great: professional, with just a hint of the dire situation finding its way into her voice. A bit of anxiousness was to be expected. A child's life was at stake. Ed Cecil even thought she had done a good job, giving her a nod and a wink when she sent it back to the studio.

Ed Cecil had seen a lot in his years of filming all kinds of trauma and destruction. He, too, was proud of the job he had done. It didn't take him but a second or two to push the thoughts from his mind of his own daughter when she was little. It had happened before when he was filming an incident, so he was ready to deal with it when it flashed in his mind this time. When it came to what his camera captured, he was a compassionate professional. Only he—and the relative handful of others who made their living filming disasters—would know how he was careful not to show the child's face as the firefighter carried her to the ambulance, would realize he had done the same with the distraught mother, would note how the shot widened to take in the group of firefighters moving toward the ambulance as the doors closed behind mother and child.

Now the firefighters—several as wrung out and bedraggled as the mother—were gathered in a loose knot a few feet behind those ambulance doors. Ed Cecil aimed his camera at this group and began taping once more, just in case something newsworthy happened.

Charlotte was watching this group, too. She suddenly realized the oldest firefighter—the one who had carried the child in his arms up the bank, who had pressed his lips over her tiny mouth again and again as he rushed to the ambulance—was the same one she had interviewed at the scene of the house fire not 30 minutes ago. He was a good interview: articulate and straightforward, nothing but the facts. *Captain something. Buckman!*

As she watched, the young firefighter who had been in the rushing creek, sidled up to Captain Buckman's side. The older man turned and glanced down at the young man's feet. Then he smiled, laid a hand on the younger's shoulder briefly. Charlotte peered across at them, finally noticed the young man only had one boot. His other foot was bare.

"I want to speak to that captain again," Charlotte said, turning toward Ed Cecil.

The cameraman was slowly panning across the scene now, zooming in close, then back out, taping everything: the firefighter's bare foot; someone wrapped in blankets and towels sitting on a gurney; the swollen creek and the little footbridge; the ambulances; the fire trucks; the police officers holding traffic back at each end of the scene; the rope in a loose pile along the creekbank; settling at last on the group of firefighters gathered behind the one ambulance.

"Sure," Ed Cecil finally replied. "Might give them a minute. Looks like they're waiting to hear about the child."

Chapter 90

6:03 p.m.

Darlene didn't have any concept of time. The paramedics seemed to have been doing CPR for hours, their words coming to her as if spoken inside a barrel. There must be something more she could do, but what it might be would not come to her. All she could think of was to hold her daughter's hand and repeat softly, over and over, that it would be all right.

One of the female paramedics cut Emily's top down the middle from neck to waist, began attaching electronic leads to her chest. Quickly done, the paramedic reached for the defibrillator control and commanded, "All clear."

Everyone stopped what they were doing, Darlene included, and leaned back from the child. The jolt from the defibrillator caused Emily's body to jerk, but otherwise there was no effect. Shaneesha and Donnie immediately returned to administering CPR. Darlene struggled to hold herself together as the second paramedic said something about trying another shock.

The sudden turn stunned them all. Emily coughed. Shaneesha hesitated the briefest moment, then yanked the mask to the side. Emily coughed again. It was wet and loose. As one being, the medics erupted into a flurry of activity, unlocking straps, moving things out of the way. Then, Shaneesha supporting the child's C spine, they quickly, efficiently, turned her onto her side to help keep her airway clear. Her partner kept one hand on Emily's back in support, shoved a pillow up against her to keep her there as Donnie leaned to his right, reached for the suction. Another cough. Water. Shaneesha with a light, checking inside the mouth, taking the suction wand from Donnie. Before she could use it a cough. More water. More than before. A lot more, spilling out on the pillow. Suction. A bit of fluid gurgling in the plastic tube, then gone. Tiny fingers wrapping around Darlene's forefinger, tight, tighter, clamping down hard now. A raspy whisper?

"Mommy."

One of the rear doors cracked open on the ambulance. A hand appeared, gave a thumbs up, then disappeared as the door closed again. Smiles flashed across the waiting faces in the small group of firefighters. Moments later the door swung open again. A firefighter stepped out, exchanged waves with a white-helmeted officer, then hurried around to the cab. With the firefighter behind the wheel, the ambulance pulled away in seconds, its siren wailing. The group began breaking up, individuals moving off in their own independent directions.

"Oh, my," Charlotte gasped, her hand at her throat. "Did you get the thumbs up?"

"Yep," Ed Cecil answered. "I never miss a happy ending."

Chapter 91

1807 Hours

Thought you were getting too old for this stuff, Wayne," Batman said, grinning.

"Damn skippy," the captain nodded tiredly, plopping down on the front bumper of Engine 4.

Scattered out in front of them, a mix of firefighters from the three crews were gathering up equipment. Biceptual had a couple of PFDs—personal flotation devices—draped over one arm, and in his other hand, a pike pole long enough for pole vaulting. All had been unneeded, brought off Rescue 1 to the stream's edge moments before the child was pulled from the water. Mick held a worn canvas bag open, tossing in the pulleys, carabiners, and webbing dumped in a pile earlier by Probie Wan. Greg came walking through the group, stopped by Mick and said something which made both men laugh. Then Greg clapped his friend on the back and sidled over to join the other two officers at the front of Engine 4.

"How about the old dude?" Greg asked Batman as he sat down beside the captain.

"Think he'll be all right," Batman replied, leaning out to the side so he could look back up the hill. Two firefighters from Ladder 1 were helping load Robert into a second ambulance. "Do you believe it? Wonder the poor guy wasn't froze stiff. He threw a fit. Wouldn't leave until he knew the little girl was gonna make it. Finally got him out of his wet clothes—part of them anyway—and wrapped up good in some blankets. Taking him in now. Give him the once over."

"Good deal," Greg nodded. A few seconds passed before he added, "Never know with a drowning. Cold water makes a difference. And that water was cold, wasn't it, Cap?"

"Like ice," the officer nodded.

Half a minute passed in silence. At last, Batman spoke. "Think I'll head on in."

He made no move to leave, however. Instead, his gaze settled on Captain Buckman. Their eyes met, stayed locked for a time. Neither spoke. They didn't need to. They had shared a lot of years and a lot of rough scenes together. Too often these officers had felt the emptiness of knowing nothing could be done to help those they had come to help. And yet, the men had shoved that knowledge down inside a dark place and tried anyway.

This was not one of those times. The hint of a smile crept across Batman's face. Then the same thing happened with the captain. Sometimes, once in a blue moon, everything went right. It was what the job was all about.

Batman turned to walk away, he hesitated a moment at the corner of the truck and turned back, his eyes meeting his friend's gaze once more. "If I'm ever in trouble, I'm calling you, Wayne," he said.

"Sometimes you're just lucky," Wayne replied.

"And sometimes you're just good."

The battalion chief's right hand rose to his brow and fell away again in a soft salute. Then he turned his back and went striding up the hill toward his command car.

Seconds later Probie Wan came trudging along, the one foot still bare, coiling the wet rope.

"What about your shoeless probie there?" Greg asked in a voice deliberately loud enough for Probie Wan to hear. "He worth keeping?"

"Yeah," the captain answered in a voice equally loud, a broad smile spreading across his face. "He'll do, I reckon."

"Come here, Ron," Greg said, waving the grinning young firefighter over. "Look at you, stomping around in your bare feet. Let's get you out of this wet harness." As he undid the straps, Greg paused to look Ron in the face. "Captain Buckman says you might amount to a bump on a gnat's ass yet." The officer's hand came to rest on Ron's shoulder as he helped him shuck out of the harness. Done, Greg gave the shoulder a little squeeze. In that instant, Ron knew what it was to be knighted.

"Anything different about this rope now?" Greg asked, taking the soaked coil.

"Never use it for rescue again," Ron replied, "'cause it's had a load on it."

"Right. You can use it for utility," Greg explained, ever the teacher. "But nothing else," he concluded the lesson. He stood quietly for a moment before speaking again. "Have a seat with Cap there. You've earned a break. I'll find you something to put on your naked toes, so you don't embarrass us any further," he added as he started to walk away.

Ron followed Greg's suggestion, dropping down on the engine's wide chrome bumper. Mick came up after a few moments and squatted down a few feet away, facing Ron and the captain. Seconds later D. J. joined them, rounding out the crew, plopping down to sit cross-legged on the grass.

Captain Buckman relaxed back against the sun-warmed metal of the truck. The heat helped, for he was close to shivering in his clammy clothes. Worse, he could feel the ache of strain digging into every muscle. His age came to him in that ache like he had never known it. He could not remember being so tired. At the same time, he had never realized a greater sense of satisfaction. A burden had been lifted; an oath fulfilled. He closed his eyes, allowed the sweet stream of relief to flow through his veins. Some time passed. Seconds? Minutes? He opened his eyes to find the other three staring at him. To his mild surprise, he found himself speaking.

"Been at this a long time, boys. Seen a lot. Done a lot. Worked side by side with some hellacious firefighters, but I've never seen a crew who could hold a candle to this bunch."

The quiet stretched out for a few moments before D. J. answered for them all. "We kinda think the same thing about you."

A woman's high-pitched shouting interrupted.

"Captain! Captain Buckman!"

They all turned toward the voice. Across the street the television reporter—Charlotte something—was waving their way.

"Can we talk to you?"

He nodded back and began pushing to his feet.

Chapter 92

6:11 p.m.

Cody was beginning to relax. Leaving the carwash, he had not anticipated catching every light red, but he had. Nor had he counted on water blocking one lane of Oakland Avenue just before his turn-off. That cost him several minutes, dealing with the backed-up traffic, working to get around it. But now he was on Shallowford Road. Shallowford was about a mile and a half long, with traffic signals only at its start and at its end. Without the interruptions of red lights, he was making some time up. He felt confident, a bit cocky, certain he could handle driving on the wet pavement, thinking he knew just how far to push it. He gunned it harder coming out of a curve, felt the tires grab and sling him forward. A block ahead was another bend in the road. *No worries,* he thought. *At this rate I'll be at Angie's house in three or four minutes—right on time. We'll be dancing within the hour.*

He couldn't dance a lick, but man, Angie could. It was all that mattered to him. With her in his arms, no one would be looking at him anyway. As he steered into the turn, he popped the console open and stole a couple of quick glances inside, searching. In a moment he found what he was looking for. He slipped the disc in the player. David Bowie came through the speakers. "Let's dance." Oh yeah, she loved this one. "Put on your red shoes—"

Coming out of the curve, he saw the cruiser first, then the patrolman beside it, directing traffic. He hit the brakes, but he was too close and going too fast to do anything but swerve around the screaming officer. Just ahead there was a young woman at the edge of the pavement on the righthand side. He swerved again. Suddenly there were flashing red lights in his face, a fire truck. He stomped with both feet on the pedal, for an instant thought the brakes were holding. Then the skid began. It felt like he was falling sideways.

Chapter 93

6:21 p.m.

The commercial ended, and the picture switched back to the local news. Renai Richmond, the anchor, was turned at an angle to the news desk and holding her hand to her earpiece. Suddenly, she nodded and swiveled back around in her chair to face the camera.

"We will go to our Sports Wrap-up in a moment, but first we are returning to Charlotte Montgomery, our Action 19 reporter live on the scene of the dramatic water rescue of a child only minutes ago. Charlotte, we understand there have been some tragic developments at that site on Shallowford Road since your last report."

The picture of an obviously distraught Charlotte appeared on screen. Her red eyes cut back and forth for a moment before she found her composure enough to focus on the lens. With an obvious effort, she seemed to pull herself together. Quickly clearing her throat, she began.

"Yes, Renai. As we reported earlier, only minutes ago members of the Green Springs Fire Department carried out the incredible rescues of three people, one of whom was a small child, from the flooded creek behind me. This reporter had just concluded an interview with one of those directly involved in saving those lives when there was a horrific accident. A speeding vehicle entered the area, slid out of control, and struck a firefighter. This hero was killed instantly."

The camera panned quickly to a group of firefighters standing in front of an engine. Ed Cecil was careful not to show their faces. He was also careful to avoid the bloody sheet or any hint of the outline of a body beneath it. Just a bit of white edging was enough. However, the fire truck's door, with Engine

4 painted on it, clearly appeared in the frame for a second. FIREFIGHTER KILLED suddenly filled the crawler line at the bottom of the broadcast picture, as he swung the camera back to Charlotte.

"The young driver involved does not appear to have been seriously injured. Firefighters here on the scene were quick to administer to him. Fortunately, there were no additional victims."

"Oh, my," Renai replied, the picture splitting to show both her and Charlotte. The anchorwoman paused an appropriate moment. "That speaks to the professionalism of our public servants more than anything I can imagine." She paused another instant before adding, "Charlotte, I assume names are being withheld pending notification of next of kin. Correct?"

"Yes, Renai."

"Thank you for what has to have been a most difficult report, Charlotte." The reporter gave a quick nod as the picture went back solely to the anchor. "We are so thankful the child and the others were saved," the anchor woman continued. "We shall certainly keep all those involved in our thoughts and prayers, especially the members of the Green Springs Fire Department and their families. We will return in a moment."

Chapter 94

Tina stopped just inside the doorway to O'Connor's. To her left, the dining room appeared to be nearly full. Though she expected they would be dining there later, the bar was where she needed to go. "God, I hate blind dates," she whispered. And she was early! That practically shouted desperation. "How did I let Peg talk me into this?" But she knew how. She really liked D. J., maybe even felt something akin to love for him. If he had only offered a word, a hint, of committal to her she would not be here now. She turned to the right, toward the bar.

He saw her coming—her date—and jumped up to meet her in the doorway.

"Tina?"

"Drew?"

She allowed herself to be led back to his table. Drew seemed nice enough. He even held her chair for her. He was 50, maybe, a little too dressed up with the tie, his haircut a bit too neat, his smile sort of oily, overly polite. She tried to concentrate, but the experience was almost otherworldly, as if she were watching someone else seated at the table instead of her, trying to find a few safe words of small talk to keep the conversation going. Worst of all, there was nothing there, no connection, no click of anything promising between them. Boring. Without thinking, she glanced up, her eyes moving quickly from one of the TVs to another scattered high around the walls of the bar. Baseball. Golf. The local news. A picture of a fire engine, D. J.'s truck. The words superimposed along the bottom of the screen.

FIREFIGHTER KILLED.

To Drew's shock, Tina burst into tears.

Chapter 95

6:22 p.m.

Marge gathered the empty burger wrappers and French fry sacks into a pile atop the kitchen table, then scooped the pile up in one armful and carried it to the trash can.

"Like a pig sty," she muttered to herself as she turned to the small TV on the counter.

"Please let there be no storms tomorrow," she pleaded as she hit the power button. "If I can't keep these heathens out of the house—" The local news was on, as she had hoped. It always ended with a recap of the weather forecast.

The words Shallowford Road registered. It wasn't far away. She saw the same picture Tina was seeing, the door with Engine 4 in gold-leaf letters, the horrible words on the crawler line.

Moments later, without any clear recollection of how she got there, Marge found herself in the driveway, purse in hand. The loud shrieks and yells of boys at play jarred her into the present. "The boys?" she asked herself, alarmed. "Where are they?" She quickly spotted them in a far corner of the yard, running and sliding on their bellies through a large puddle in the grass. Marge struck out marching their way.

"Michael Alan, come here right now!"

The 10-year-old froze in mid-sprint, then, head down, started slowly across the lawn to where his mother was pacing. It didn't dawn on him she was at the edge of the place where the ground became too squishy to walk without sinking. He was too torn up by her use of his middle name. Trouble.

"Michael, hurry up," she said as he neared, dirty water washing up over his shoe tops. "Oh, just look at you all. Soaking wet and covered in mud."

"I'm sorry, Mama." Michael was having a hard time meeting her eyes.

"Never mind." Her hands were suddenly gripping his shoulders. Marge bent down so their faces were only inches apart. "Michael, I need you to listen close. Understand? I need you to be my little man now."

"Yes, ma'am," the oldest son answered, fear instantly stabbing its way into his belly.

"I have to go somewhere. Something has—Mama has to leave right away. Okay?"

"Yes, ma'am." *It must be bad.*

"I want you to take your brothers inside and clean up a little. You don't have to take showers, just towel off. Everybody put on dry clothes. Then get on your bikes and ride over to Aunt Jenny's. Keep Mark out of the middle of the street. You know how he is. Got all that?"

"Yes, ma'am."

"I'll come and get you later. Okay? You're my little man. I'm depending on you." Then she kissed him on the forehead.

It was all Michael could do to keep from crying like a baby as his mother turned and hurried back toward the van. Whatever was going on must be horrible. Mama never kissed him on the forehead.

Marge hesitated at the end of the driveway half a minute later. Which way? Right would take her toward Shallowford Road. A voice inside her said no. She absolutely should not go to the scene. Left led to the station. She would head there, where she would be able to find out something from the other firefighters. And if the crews were all gone on calls, she would sit and wait until someone came in and told her about Mick. That's it. She would sit there and wait, ripping her hair out by the roots, until someone told her something.

Chapter 96

6:22 p.m.

Oh, I don't care if it's a boy or a girl, mom! It doesn't matter! Not to me, and it won't to Ron, either."

Caroline listened at the phone to her mother then. This was their fourth call since Caroline broke the news. She was deliriously happy and so fidgety nervous her feet would not stay in one place. She didn't know if she could wait until the morning to tell Ron. Maybe she would call the station and tell him to meet her outside.

"Yes, Mom. I know, Mom. I'll eat right. No more junk food, I promise."

Caroline listened again for a few seconds.

"Names! Oh, yes. We will have to work on that—make lists for boys and girls both until we know. Oh, I'm so excited! Aren't you? You're going to be a grandmother! What do you want to be called?"

Caroline fell silent as her mother spoke.

"Yes, we will have to make a list of names for you, too. Okay, Mom. I'm going to let you go now and call Becky. You can get back to your show."

Caroline listened for a moment. Then she said, "The news is on? I didn't realize it was so—"

Her mother's scream tore through the receiver.

"Mom!" Caroline yelled back.

"Oh, dear God! Oh, dear God! The TV," her mother yelled into the phone.

Caroline rushed to grab the remote. The set was already on. She managed to punch in the local station in time to see the engine number on the door. Okay. This had happened once before. She had seen Ron's truck on the news when he was at his first house fire. Then she noticed the words on the crawler line. They tore the air from her lungs.

Down below, down deep inside her, Caroline felt something give way. She bent over double, then started to fall. Her mother heard the crash, heard the phone tumbling across the floor, heard her daughter's muffled moaning, "No. No. No."

Chapter 97

6:23 p.m.

The phone ringing woke Virginia. It took her a moment to get her bearings. She was kicked back in her recliner, shoes and glasses both off.

"Oh, shut up," she fussed, fumbling to grab her cell off the end-table. "Hello," she finally answered, the fog not quite gone.

"Virginia, are you alone?" her best friend, Lizbeth, asked in a rush.

"Yes," she replied, trying to blink the sleep out of her eyes.

"You haven't heard?"

"I haven't heard what, Lizbeth?" Virginia asked after waiting a moment for more. She was still struggling to wake up. The questions confused her further.

Several seconds went by before Lizbeth commanded, "Don't you move. Hear me? I'll be right there."

The phone went dead. Now Virginia was thoroughly confused. She laid the phone on the table after a moment. Then she pushed the lever forward, bringing the recliner upright. Her shoes were there next to the chair, but she hesitated to put them on. *It's just Lizbeth coming over, so why bother*, she thought.

So now, what was the latest hot gossip Lizbeth had to tell? That had to be it. The phone was not good enough, obviously. It meant it had to be red hot. Lizbeth always had to tell the really juicy stuff in person.

Virginia had left the TV playing with the sound turned down low. The droning helped her doze off when she needed a nap, like she had today. The local news was on. She caught a glimpse of a fire truck, but without her glasses she couldn't make out if it was his or not. Where were they? Virginia was curious now, hoping to catch sight of him. Every now and then she would see him on television, which was sometimes a bit scary, but always special.

Here were her glasses in her lap. She put them on. A young female reporter was talking, her back to a raging stream. "Lord. Why are they showing her?" she whispered. "She looks awful, like she's been crying."

Virginia lifted the remote from the end table and tried to turn the sound up. She didn't raise her finger off the button in time, however, so the TV was suddenly screaming. Finally, she got the sound back down to a reasonable level.

"—pending notification of next of kin," were the first words she understood clearly.

Oh my, Virginia thought. Some poor family has suffered a tragedy.

The anchor was speaking again. "—so thankful the child and the others were saved." *Wonderful. There's some good news.* "—in our thoughts and prayers, especially the members of the Green Springs Fire Department and their families."

What a strange thing to say.

More words were suddenly pounding in her ears, though they didn't come from the TV. They were his words: *—or I won't be coming home.*

Why did that pop in my head now?

A bell was ringing somewhere. The doorbell. Virginia got up to answer it. *Must be Lizbeth.* A voice, a man's voice, however, called her name. Could it be? She hurried, ready to run to her Wayne, but when she turned toward the door there stood Batman, instead. Tears were streaming down his face. He rushed forward and caught her in his arms as she started to fall.

Chapter 98

6:23 p.m.

Robert was warm now. Once in the ambulance, gentle hands had quickly removed his wet pants and underwear, toweled him dry, covered him with more sheets and blankets. He had fussed about going to the hospital, for he wasn't hurting anywhere, just tired. The medics had insisted, however. His heartbeat was irregular, they said. It would be wise to let the doctors check him out. *Whatever,* he thought. Now that he knew Emily was alive, nothing else was worth a pinch of worry.

It was quiet in here. Since they were going to the ER only as a precaution, the paramedic had explained, was why the siren wasn't on. She went about her business now, seated to the side of his gurney, listening through a stethoscope to get his blood pressure reading. As she leaned close, he made out her nametag, Diane. Finished checking his pressure, Diane left the depleted cuff on his arm, moved the disk over his heart, listened again for a minute. At last, she took the earpieces out and laid the scope to the side.

"Still a little out of rhythm, Mr.—oh, I'm sorry. Your last name just slipped my mind. Got it right here on the chart. Where is—"

"Robert is fine," he said, looking up into the young face. The paramedic ceased her search for his name on the paper, smiled down at him. She was but a child, in her late 20s, perhaps. At his age, that was a child. "Bob. Call me Bob."

"Excuse me?"

"You can call me Bob," he said, smiling back at her, back at this caring child. "No. I would rather you call me Grandpa Bob," he told her, suddenly remembering his first meeting with Emily, her bestowing of his new name. "What my *grand* daughter calls me." He spoke slowly, breaking the term into two words, stressing the first.

"Okay, Grandpa Bob. I'm honored," she nodded, then glanced away, hoping to keep him from seeing the sudden tears welling in her eyes, remembering her own sweet grandfather who had died only a month before.

"Emily's all right, isn't she?" Robert blurted out, lifting his head off the pillow. He had seen the look of distress on Diane's face.

"Yes. She's going to be fine. My partner spoke with the other crew. Said she was talking to her mother." The paramedic placed her hand on Robert's shoulder, softly pushed him back down against the warm sheet. "This is one of those good calls, Grandpa Bob. Everything went like it's supposed to."

"A miracle," Robert whispered.

"Yes," the paramedic nodded. "Now rest. Okay? We will be at the hospital in a minute or two."

Robert's eyes were already closed. Sleep came in an instant. A dream followed right on its heels. *How could I be dreaming so quickly?* he asked himself in the moment before the dream took over. There was a wide path before him, light-colored sand bordered by narrow blocks of white limestone set on edge, like the stones lining the dirt streets in his little hometown when he was young. A warm breeze came up at his back. He stepped onto the path, allowed the air to carry him forward.

The sand was soft, giving, like walking across plush carpet. Spring grass, so green and fresh it seemed to pulse with life, grew thick outside the stones. Clutches of vividly yellow buttercups appeared close on his right, then beds of pure yellow tulips suddenly bordered along the left. Walls of forsythia joined in on the sides, a million yellow blooms, with ripe honeysuckle vines spiraling throughout. The delicious flavor-like smell of the honeysuckle lured him forward into a twisting maze of yellow roses, the roses' scent joining with the honeysuckle until the air seemed almost too sweet to breathe.

The sky took on a tawny glow, rich and comforting, as if it had all at once drawn warm color from the flowers.

He rounded another bend in the path and stopped, his progress halted by the sight a few feet ahead. A young woman stood amid the roses where the sandy path ended. Her white dress was simple, unadorned. The breeze flowed around her, pressing the thin fabric along the turns of her body. It lifted her blond hair off her shoulders, caused it to drift and sway. Her green eyes flashed emerald fire in the light, like the first time he had gazed into them. She smiled, and he smiled back in long-known recognition. Then she stepped forward, her arms opening to embrace him. Her lips parted in speech.

"Hello, my dear. I've been waiting."

Chapter 99

One Year Later

A small metal storage building covers a portion of the bare spot where Mrs. Witherspoon's garage stood. The Chrysler is gone, too, sold to a restorer for parts. Tim and Marvin come by every afternoon. They cut grass, rake leaves, carry out trash, and see to any other odd job Mrs. Witherspoon has, in compliance with the judge's sentence. In January, they started doing their homework at her house. Sometimes she helps them. The boys never leave without hugging her. Hugging was not part of their sentence.

Katie's recovery was difficult. Two weeks in the hospital, a rehab facility for a month, weeks of physical therapy at home, and finally, a month of outpatient rehab. She progressed from standing with support, to a walker, to a cane. Her pain-wracked ribs took forever to heal. There are days now—other than when taking her medications—she can almost forget the accident. Tom worries her constantly, always asking what she needs and hopping up to help whenever she rises. She likes that they hold hands a lot, though. At Clarisse's wedding in June, she intends to walk without limping.

Mary's husband, William, remains paralyzed on his left side. He has been in a nursing home since a few days after his stroke. Mary spends several hours visiting him every day, riding the bus to and from the facility. William can't speak, but Mary talks to him, telling the current news in their neighborhood and recounting every single thing she remembers about their son. Lately Tom has been coming to visit on Sunday mornings so Mary can go to church. He reads the paper to William. Sometimes, he swears when he does the funnies, he can hear the older man chuckle.

James Henry resides in the Kentucky State Reformatory in Eddyville. As if the accident and the drugs were not enough, Mr. Audie Montague came forward with additional charges. Seems James was raking off the top of his funds. James Henry does not brag anymore about his important friends. The only friend he now mentions—to keep the other cons at bay—is Big B, a large, apelike individual with a mass of back hair and a decidedly malevolent attitude. He and Mr. B, at the beast's insistence, have grown—close.

Destiny continues to take law classes, finishing at the head of her class this spring. She will complete her courses with the fall semester. Since Christmas, she and Sweetums have been engaged. Attorney Stephen Grimes recently sent her a note of apology for his caddish behavior and offered her a position once she passes the bar.

Letha Ledbetter initially refused to take blame for the fire, saying it was Odell's fault for not buying her a new curling iron. Then the seas parted. Odell shouted, "Just shut up! You don't know what you're talking about." It was the first time in their marriage he had snapped back. Shocked, Letha broke into tears. She has been markedly less hateful since—part of the time.

Charlotte Montgomery got her big break. She sent the tape of her reporting on the Shallowford water incident to a number of larger market stations, excluding the segment showing her red-eyed and shaken. A Columbus, Ohio, station hired her. Sometimes she awakens crying and cannot go back to sleep, remembering.

The cameraman, Ed Cecil, left Green Springs before Charlotte. In the fall he received an offer to work on educational documentaries. The change was welcome. He had filmed enough mayhem.

Cody and Angie broke up after the wreck. She wanted to stay together, to comfort him. Cody didn't want anything from anyone, however, and ran her off. He received five years probation and 500 hours community service, the service consisting of safe-driving talks to high school students. He would have preferred prison. Recently, he started experimenting with drugs, hoping to ease his guilt.

Emily has no memory of events at the creek. She has not asked to go to the water park since, however. Otherwise, she seems to have fully recovered. She and Miriam remain inseparable. They haven't spied a rabbit inside Brandon's head for months, though there were several reindeer sightings during the Holidays.

A retired couple moved into Grandpa Bob's house. When Emily's family stopped by in welcome, Darlene found herself asking if she could dig up their rosebush. Once she explained, the neighbors happily obliged. Frank planted the bush outside Emily's bedroom window. On their visit to Grandpa Bob's grave Sunday last, Emily placed a rosebud from it on his headstone.

Battalion Chief Pete Obermann requested a critical incident stress debriefing for all personnel at the accident scene. He attended himself, though he continued to find the going rough afterward. To have death strike in his professional family left him spinning. In his mind he knew he had something more to give. In his heart he knew the time had come. Two months after the tragedy, he submitted his retirement papers. He spends a lot of time fishing now, not caring whether he catches anything or not.

Greg had many of the same feelings. In times of solitude, he found himself dwelling on the accident. It was as if he were flipping through an album, studying each photo, trying to find what could be corrected. After a month he reluctantly allowed himself to accept the loss of his friend. He has slowly worked his way back to where he was, pre-accident, confidently leading and teaching others in the imprecise arts of lifesaving.

D. J. stayed to himself and drank a lot of whisky during the first weeks after. Though it failed to dull the pain much, he kept trying. Early one morning there was a knock on the door.

It was Tina. If he couldn't get around to asking her, then she would turn the tables and ask him. He said yes. They said their vows the same afternoon. They still act like newlyweds.

To escape his pain, Mick lost himself in studying for the engineer's exam. He finished second. A week after Labor Day he was promoted. He misses being on the nozzle with a vengeance, though the modest raise has allowed him to cut back on his off-days job and give Marge an occasional break. When he is alone with all three boys, however, and they are at their wild men best, he often wonders why they didn't stop at two kids, or maybe just one.

Caroline Jacoby's two greatest fears that terrible day were neither one realized—Ron was badly shaken, but physically okay; she did not miscarry. Now she is a proud and happy mother.

Ron yearns to be like Captain Buckman, strong and certain, unflinching in the face of danger, respected. It is one of the best ways to honor the man, he believes. The respect of his fellow firefighters is already his. Over the course of this year not one person has called him *Probie Wan*.

Virginia cried almost non-stop the day of Wayne's funeral. She doesn't remember a word the chaplain said, but she vividly recalls how her husband looked lying there in his uniform. When it came time to close the casket, she pulled away from their children and reached inside to adjust the badge on his chest like she had a thousand mornings before. Wayne's coffin—flag draped and carried in the hose bed of Engine 4— the honor guard, bagpipes playing, the folded flag on her lap all drifted by in a fog. Her tears finally ended when she collapsed into sleep late that night.

She simply refuses to feel pity for herself. There have been moments of laughter since, rare and reserved at first. These have become more frequent as the months slip by. She goes to work, visits her children, keeps the grandbabies, talks to Liz on the phone countless hours. In short, she manages to stay busy enough to ward off the demons, except late at night when a storm rages outside their bedroom window. Reaching for Wayne and finding his spot empty, she cries. She doesn't want this to change, for her grief in the dark hours is tempered by the knowledge, come daylight, there will be something to remind her of the times of joy and pride she had with him.

This day brought one such moment. The bell rang. She opened the door to find Caroline and Ron standing there. Caroline was cradling their baby in her arms.

"Your godson has been throwing a fit to see you," Caroline said with a wide smile.

"Oh, look how he's grown," Virginia cooed, reaching. "Come here to me, little Wayne."

Acknowledgements

I am indebted to the members of my writing group—Sky Writers—who worked hard to assist me throughout this project. Bobbie Falin, Noel Barton, Kimberly Bartley and John Bowers—all accomplished authors—reviewed the manuscript at every stage. Without their help and patience, I would still be wandering in the wilderness.

Greg Turner and Richard Storey, assistant fire chiefs (retired) of the Bowling Green, Kentucky, Fire Department provided valuable input and oversight regarding various technical aspects of firefighting and fire investigation, respectively, and reviewed the manuscript in its entirety.

Dixie Satterfield, attorney-at-law, helped me understand the intricacies of the legal system, as well as put human faces on those engaged in its practice.

Diane Stiffey, paramedic, reviewed medical field treatment segments for authenticity and accuracy. Jeff Treece, RN, answered my questions regarding emergency room operations.

Marilyn Turner and Liz Storey reviewed the manuscript in its entirety. Their comments and corrections were invaluable.

My sincere thanks to each of these friends.

I offer a special word of gratitude to Wordcrafts publisher, Mike Parker, for his patience and assistance.

To all the many firefighters who taught and led me as I tried to be worthy of your company, I offer my respect and appreciation. My goal has been to fairly portray your skill and courage. Any error in the attempt is mine alone.

~Jerry Harlan Brown

About the Author

Gerry Harlan Brown writes from his home in Smiths Grove, Kentucky. Stints at a factory, a farm, and painting houses have been mixed in with periods as a railroader, a volunteer community crisis counselor, and a professional fire chief. His 29 years in the fire service gave him many opportunities to meet people from all walks of life. Sometimes, this was at their best and bravest, other times, their most devastated or petty. All offered food for a writer.

Ring the Bell is his second novel.

also by
Gerry Harlan Brown

White Squirrels & Other Monsters

also available From
WordCrafts Press

Paint Me Fearless
by Hallie Lee

The Restless Earth
by Alan Cockrell

Angela's Treasures
by Marian Rizzo

End of Summer
by Michael Potts

Land That I Love
by Gail Kittleson

www.wordcrafts.net